Bone Gnawers

BILL BRIDGES & JUSTIN ACHILLI

authors:	bill bridges
	justin achilli
cover artist:	steve prescott
series editors:	eric griffin
	john h. steele
	stewart wieck
copyeditor:	james stewart
graphic designer:	pauline benney
art director:	richard thomas

More information and previews available at
white-wolf.com/clannovels

Copyright © 2002 by White Wolf, Inc.
All rights reserved.

White Wolf Publishing
735 Park North Boulevard, Suite 128
Clarkston, GA 30021
www.white-wolf.com/fiction

First Edition: January 2002

White Wolf, is a registered trademark.
ISBN: 1-56504-886-5
Printed in Canada

TRIBE NOVEL:

Bone Gnawers

BILL BRIDGES & JUSTIN ACHILLI

Prologue

Szeged, Hungary, on the banks of the Tisza River:

The doors to the JATE Klub swung open, spilling throbbing music and flashing lights into the street, along with two people who stumbled into the fresh night air. The girl laughed and shook her head vigorously, spraying the sweat she earned on the dance floor onto her male companion. Also laughing, he did his best to block the deluge with his hands, while trying not to spill his beer.

"Ah!" she cried in English. "It's hot in there!"

"Say it, don't spray it," the man said with a distinctly British accent.

She frowned at him, still smiling. "Oh, like you're not already covered in sweat anyway."

"Okay, truce. Let's get away from the noise."

"The river's down this way. I want to see it at night." She grabbed his hand and tugged him along Toldy utca toward Somogyi utca, and down to the banks of the River Tisza.

As they walked, she looked at him. She could see him better under the street lamps than in the shifting lights inside the club. About six feet tall, brown hair, slight beard from not shaving the last day or so. "So, what brings a subject of the Queen all the way to Szeged?"

"That's funny, I was going to ask you the same question, except I would have phrased it, 'what brings a hot American girl like you all the way to the southern reaches of Hungary?'"

She laughed. "I'm touring the European club scene. Looking for the next ground zero."

"What? For raves? Hasn't it moved on to Ibiza or Goa?"

"Well, yeah, but things change. You never know where the next hot scene'll appear. I think Szeged's just right for it. You got a university full of young kids, an eclectic city not far from Budapest. So, yeah, why not here? And if not, there's always someplace else to go. But you didn't answer my question, and I asked first."

"Ah, how rude of me. I'm with Amnesty International, a reporter. I came in through Budapest but I'm on my way to Serbia. I've got a lead on an as-yet-unreported mass grave. Revealing it could lead to further war crimes indictments from the Hague tribunal."

The girl grew quiet. He tried to catch her eyes, but she was watching the river now as they approached its banks. She was beautiful, with her thin chin and wide eyes. Her black hair billowed about her face in the breeze from the river.

"Oh, I've gone and done it," he said. "Brought the evening down."

"No, that's okay," she said, looking at him again, smiling more for his benefit than from genuine happiness. "It's not your fault. It's just… wow, I feel so selfish. You're here doing good for the world, while I'm out partying on my parent's credit cards."

"Hey, don't think that. The world may have troubles—serious troubles—but we've all got to keep on living, right? I was in that club for a reason. I'm not going to spend the whole of my waking hours contemplating misery. We have to celebrate life, not mourn it."

She smiled again, this time more genuine. "Yeah, I guess you're right. I shouldn't be guilty. Maybe I'll volunteer with the Red Cross or something."

"There you go. You've made a contribution all ready."

"How?"

"By brightening my world with that smile."

Her smile grew wide and completely without reserve. She leaned in toward him, and he toward her.

They both started at the nearby sound of a cough, followed by a horrible crooning in Hungarian. A man sat on the ground, leaning on a building overlooking the river, a bottle of vodka or gin in his hands. His huge black beard stretched to his waist, as did the wild mane running down his back. His long brown trench coat was stained with years of spilt food and drink, with little to no laundering. He didn't seem to notice them but continued to recite his odd verse.

The man knew enough Hungarian to recognize the words: "…with a pure heart, I'll burn and loot, and if I have to, even shoot." He recognized them— the work of Attila József, the pained poet for whom the nearby university was named. A poet who threw himself in front of a train to avoid the pain of living.

He turned back to the girl and shrugged. She smiled and grasped him by the shoulders, obviously unconcerned about their audience. He leaned in and brushed his lips against hers.

Then she screamed. Clawing at her hair, she snatched at the rustling thing that landed there and threw it into the air. It screeched and cawed, a huge black bat. As it wheeled around her, its unnaturally long tail slashed through the air, sounding like the crack of a whip.

The man stared in shock at the thing while the girl continued to scream. Instead of flying away—

like any normal bat would do following such a commotion—it spun in the air and dived straight at him. He tried to leap from its path, but the long black tail shot through the air and snatched at him, pinning his arms to his sides with preternatural strength.

The bat landed on his shoulder and let out a croak. It was like no bat he'd seen before. In place of a furry torso was a gaping jaw with huge fangs. Two clawed legs bit into his shoulder, giving the thing purchase as it began gnawing at his ear.

He screamed for help. The girl stared in shock and fear, unable to move, frozen by her terror. He struggled to knock the bat away, but the tail kept him from lifting his hands. He ran, but the bat stayed rooted to his shoulder, its claws now drawing blood.

Its jaws were tearing painfully at his ear when he felt a sudden weightlessness, a loosening of his grip on the moment, as if he were floating, not running, across the street. He halted his mad dash and stared listlessly at the river as the thing chewed through his earlobe, mesmerizing him with its deeply hypnotic gurgling. He seemed to feel it pull forth something, something like a slithering worm, a slippery, wriggling bit of ectoplasm, which it then hungrily gulped down in one swallow.

The bat let out a victorious screech and took off into the air, its tail loosening around the man and whipping off into the air after it. As it flew over the river, it disappeared from sight.

The man stumbled to the ground, clutching his ear. There was no blood or pain, just an empty feeling, a sense of vast space now opened up within his skull.

His fall brought the girl out of her shock. She ran to him, bending down to hug him. "Oh, God, you're alright!"

He flinched and looked at her as if she were a complete stranger.

"It's okay," she said. "It's gone. Whatever it was, it's gone."

He frowned at her, unsure what she was talking about. "Where am I?"

"What? You're here, in Szeged."

"Szeged? Hungary?! I can't be here! I've got a deadline in London! What the hell am I doing here?" He got to his feet, lurching for a moment before his balance returned.

"Oh God, you've got amnesia or something. You were going to Serbia, to uncover a mass grave."

He looked suspiciously at her. "Oh really? And who the hell are you? I don't have time for this! I've got to get home!" He began walking quickly back toward the city center, and then stopped and looked around. "Where am I going? Where is the airport?"

The girl sobbed and began to cry, but followed after him. "You're hurt! We've got to get you to a hospital...."

He turned up the street they had come down. She followed, trying to touch him, but he shook her off.

As they went out of sight around the corner, the drunken crooner stood up. He looked completely sober now, though very shaken. He looked out at the river and his nostrils flared wide, as if he were taking in its scent. A low, animal growl rumbled from the back of his throat, and he moved warily away from the river bank, watching it the whole time as if it might leap at him should he turn his back. When he reached the street where the couple had gone, his body melted and reformed into that of a wolf.

He turned and bounded up the street, heading away from the river and toward the Jewish Quarter.

The river flowed on, no obvious sign of turbulence or trouble except for a dead fish floating on the surface, quickly carried downstream.

Chapter One

Plane trips, Carlita decided, were vastly over-rated. Except for the fact that the plane didn't reek of urine, it was exactly like riding a city bus. No, take that back; it was worse than the bus, because at least on the bus you could move around. This was going to be seven hours—Iberia Flight 6250 to Madrid—in a tin cylinder, strapped to a seat, fed a minuscule amount of cardboardy food and subjected to the worst sort of sadism Hollywood had to offer, probably starring Mel Gibson.

Could be worse, Carlita reasoned to herself. *You could be Storm-Eye.* She spared a look over at her fellow Philodox, knowing that to be caught peeping at the Red Talon would probably be interpreted as mockery. It was obvious that Storm-Eye was uncomfortable—this was her second flight, and all of this homid rigmarole that went along with it wasn't sitting too well with "Miss Sterling," which was the name on Storm-Eye's passport. Diverting her attention just in time, Carlita afforded herself a smirk at all of those stories she had heard about wolves and coyotes gnawing off their own legs to escape traps. *Chew off whatever you want,* chica, *but it's not going to help you here.*

John North Wind's Son looked across the aisle at her, cocking his eyebrow.

"Something on your mind, Hot Air's Son?" Carlita replied before John had a chance to speak.

"Um, yeah," John answered, ignoring her taunt. "I want to know why we're stopping in Spain before we head to Serbia. Wouldn't it be easier to just go there?"

"How direct of you."

"Well, wouldn't it?"

"Sometimes running straight into the enemy's mouth—" Carlita looked around the cabin after starting her thought to make sure no one was paying any undue attention. It simply wouldn't do to talk about the specifics of what was about to go down. "—ain't the best course of action. You want to bring down a deer, you don't start by fanging up his head."

Julia was sitting next to John, and took the opportunity to become involved. "It's not just that. Once we get to Spain, we're supposed to meet with some of the Gar—some other individuals who have already dealt with this thing."

John turned to Julia, and Carlita found herself twisting in her seat to hear what the two were saying. "I've heard of the Thirteen Sorrows sept before, but I'm not sure what it is, exactly. I mean, if it's this big, important sept that's fairly renowned among our kind, why send us to handle this thing? I mean, don't get me wrong—we're obviously a capable pack—but we haven't worked together very long...."

"You mean for more than a week?" Julia interjected with a smirk.

"Exactly."

"It's because the Thirteen Sorrows is a diplomatic sept," Carlita volunteered, enthusiastic to be involved in the conversation again. "It's not really populated by adventurous types. It's sort of a way station for several of the Western European caerns, packs and septs to use as a central meeting place."

Julia cocked an eyebrow, incredulous. "Don't take this the wrong way, Carlita—"

"Hey, I told you to call me Big Sis!"

"Sorry, it just sounds so... impersonal."

"We *are* packmates now," North Wind's Son added.

Carlita sighed and shook her head. "All right, I'll let you guys get away with it. Just don't say it in front of other Garou. Big Sis is my Garou handle. All right?"

"Fine," Julia said. "As I was about to ask before, how did you know all that about the Thirteen Sorrows sept? You don't seem like the type who keeps up on the politics of the Nation."

"I read your e-mail back in New York," Carlita said. "I learned all about the Thirteen Sorrows sept that way. Oh, and I went through your browser's cache and looked over some of the Web sites you'd hit in the past couple days. Sometimes, it was pretty helpful. In other cases, I do not approve."

"You should have been a Ragabash." Julia rolled her eyes. "Anyway, how do you know stuff like that? Not that it's very complex, but it's more than most people know how to do."

"I'm just full of surprises, as you all should know by now. And I know a little bit about Web apps. They have Internet-capable computers down at the public library that anyone can come in and use."

"I'll have to remember to keep an eye on you," Julia said. "It's a good thing you can't access my PDA without angering its spirit," she said as she shut off her portable computer and put it in her pocket. "And that's that."

John looked back and forth between the two. "What just happened?"

"Nothing," they replied in unison.

Carlita turned her attention back to the Garou who shared seats in her row as the captain's voice came over the cabin speaker. Cries Havoc, sitting right next to her, had fallen asleep, his mouth agape, and Carlita hoped he didn't start snoring. That would force her to actually pay for the damn headphones and watch the movie.

The plane jerked back abruptly before beginning its smoother roll away from the gate, and Carlita heard a suppressed whine come from Storm-Eye. It was weird—just days ago, she had fought side by side with the Talon, facing down a Black Spiral Dancer in the New York subway. Now, the poor thing was afraid of a tin can that moved by itself. How strange. Then again, Carlita reasoned, maybe it wasn't so odd. She herself had felt a twinge of discomfort more than once while prowling through the scrub woods of the Pinellas Peninsula, and she'd done that a hundred times, at least.

An idea struck her, and Carlita pushed the flight attendant's call button. Within a few moments, a stewardess came up to her and smiled. "What can I do for you today?"

"My friend wants a Jack and Coke."

A few drinks later, Storm-Eye was also asleep. She was completely unused to alcohol. In coaxing her to drink enough of it to calm her down, Carlita had had a few herself. Nothing she couldn't handle, but with everybody else dozing off, she couldn't help but begin to feel sleepy herself. She fought it for a while, trying to distract herself with the movie—some piece of crap called *Pay It Forward*—and thumbing through the inflight magazines. They were full of ads for things she couldn't afford to buy. Jewelry, ferchrissake! Who buys jewelry from an airplane catalog?

The boring-ass movie finally caused her to succumb to sleep herself. Her head dropped onto her chest and she couldn't help remembering—dreaming now—of how she got here, on a plane hundreds of miles above the Atlantic Ocean, heading for a country embroiled in genocide.

* * *

Tampa, Florida, weeks ago:
"Oh, man, this stuff tastes like ass." Carlita cocked an eyebrow and tossed another cardboard Big Mac box over her shoulder.

"Then why you eat it?" asked Pillhead Pete. "That's, what, four of them? If they taste so ass, why you keep eating 'em?"

"Cause I'm hungry, jackass. When you're hungry, you eat. Even a dummy like you knows that much."

"Yeah, but I'm hungry alla time. I ain't eatin' alla time."

"That's because you're a bum, Pete. You don't have any money. If you had two nickels to rub together, you'd be down at the McDonalds, trying to convince what's-her-name behind the counter to give you some French fries for a dime."

"That's harsh, Lita. Shit, you ain't got no money and you got six hamburgers. Well, you *had* six before you started chowin' on 'em and complainin' about how bad they is. I'm just trying to get by, you know?"

"I got some hamburgers because I know how to get them without money. You just gotta be in the right place at the right time. Call it a trick of the trade."

"Shit, you know I don't have no money. Don't be tryin' to turn no trick on me."

"No, dumbass, it's a secret of the streets. If you weren't all fucked up on pills all the time, you might learn a thing or two."

"You learn plenty of tricks on pills."

"I bet you do. Hey, if you don't have no money and you don't have no food, how come you're never at a loss for that junk?"

"Priorities, baby, priorities."

"Pete, one day you're gonna die."

"We all die, Lita. We all die. It's just a question of when."

Carlita stopped stuffing her maw as Pete said this. "That's the damn truth." She shook her head and resumed eating. She kicked the last Big Mac over toward Pete. "Damn if you don't bother my ass, Pete. Now eat that hamburger and quit your bitchin'."

"Oh really? Hell yeah, I'll eat it. Lita, I owe you one."

"You owe me a lot more than one. I been feeding your ass and keeping an eye out for you about as long as we known each other."

"Yeah, but I pull my weight, and don't say I don't," Pete said, spraying a partially chewed mouthful of secret sauce and shredded lettuce in Carlita's general direction. "Any time you need to know about something going on, you know that ol' Pete heard something about it."

"Don't make yourself more important than you are. That's my advice to you."

Pete grinned. "I don't take advice from little girls."

"Oh, but you'll take a Big Mac?"

"Thass different. And you were right."

"Right about what?"

"This tastes like ass."

"You punk-ass fool! You sat there complaining for twenty minutes about not having any food and then when I give you some, you start complaining about it? Goddamn! Gimme that hamburger back. Fucking give it back!" Carlita made a big show of grabbing for the burger.

"No, no; I'm eating it! I was just kidding!" Pete tumbled backward over an upended garbage can. "It's good! One hunnert percent pure beef!"

"I should sell your ass to the McDonald's. Maybe they'd grind you up and make some Dumbass McNuggets or something."

"Hey, Lita, that ain't funny. I heard they do that."

"You get stupider every day, Pete."

"No, seriously; that's why I said a hunnert percent pure beef. The whole cow is beef. Eyes and feet and bones and shit. Long as it come from a cow, it's beef. Maybe that's why it tastes like ass. Maybe it's *cow* ass."

"Jesus, Pete, you got a lot of problems. Why you wanna think about something like that while you're eating?"

"I think about everything all the time. That's how I keep sane. Gotta keep thinking. Gotta keep a step ahead."

"Okay then, we're even. We've both given each other advice, and I don't think either of us is going to listen to a damn thing the other said."

"You got that right, you cow-brains-eating freak."

"Pete—" Something almost electric in the air cut Carlita off in mid-retort. It was a sharp smell, an animal's musk. Carla sniffed at the air—too bad Pete was here, or she could make a few "adjustments" and learn more about what was going on. Instinctively, her human hackles raised: Her shoulders tensed and she crouched forward a bit, fingers curling inward. Animal scent… and blood.

"Oh man, Pete; I hear sirens," She lied. "You got anything on you?"

"Huh? I don't hear nothin'. No I don't have anything— oh shit. Um, never mind. Lita, I'll catch you later." Pete dashed out of the alleyway, taking his Big Mac box with him.

Carlita withdrew a bit from the main street after she made sure Pete wasn't coming back. She pulled back into the shadows, hiding herself from the streetlights and the reflected glare of the strip's neon signs.

There, hidden from human eyes, Carlita willed herself to change. Her back lengthened, arms and legs drawing inward as her slight muscles redoubled themselves. She dropped to her hands and knees as her neck craned upward, her shoulders spreading to hold her growing bulk closer to the ground and support her heavying head. Any second now, she knew it would come—there!—the almost painful point in the transition where the bones of her legs loosened, tendons stretched and her knees suddenly bent backward. In mere seconds (that seemed to last forever when the change took place), Carlita was no longer a young woman. She was now a wolf. Granted, she was a rangy wolf, slighter and lankier even in her dire form than some of her fellow shifters were in their plain Lupus shapes, but she was a wolf nonetheless.

As Carlita's vision grew a bit more sensitive to motions, her senses of smell and hearing became much more acute. Her animal eyes watched as the wind picked up in the alley, whipping reeking Big

Mac boxes—she'd have to throw those away later—in a circular motion along with scraps of paper, a tattered magazine and a plastic candy wrapper. With her ears, she heard a ragged breath, a panting not unlike one of her kind might make after running a long way or very quickly. The true sense that overwhelmed her, however, was smell. She had even detected the animal scent while wearing the human's skin. Now, as a beast, she picked its many layers apart: animal, blood, the curious odor of animal exertion, something cloying… and fear. Beneath it all, it smelled a bit familiar.

Carlita loosed a furtive yip, by way of tenuous greeting, much as a man might call, "Who's there?" when he hears a foreign noise.

Rasping, whatever it was called back. It had understood—it was one of her kind as well.

The wolf Carlita called again, announcing her location. She turned sideways, just in case this was a trick, making herself look larger.

Then, from the rooftop, a heavy shape leaped down, crashing through a box and the cheap garbage can Pete had tumbled over earlier. It landed on its hind feet, but a wet sound accompanied the impact. Whatever it was, it looked like it was hurt, confused by pain. Strange… the shapeshifting Garou usually healed their wounds at a prodigious rate. Only those enemies of the werewolf race could leave telling wounds on them for any length of time. For something to hurt a Garou and leave the wound open and bleeding….

After regaining its senses, the Garou held itself up, slowly changing form as Carlita had just done.

Its change was different, however. When it had fallen from the rooftop, it was in its "halfway" form, the Crinos, a combination of the wolf and man forms. Now, after the change, it had shifted to its Lupus form. To Carlita, this meant one of two things. First, it may have shifted back to the form of its birth, being more comfortable in that form and better able to escape should Carlita prove to be the treacherous one. Second, it realized that Carlita was in her Hispo form—it might well have taken the Lupus form to show deference to her, to put itself in a submissive position to let Carlita know it needed help.

The Garou spoke to Carlita in the quirky patois of the animals. "It is you, Carlita. I need help."

Carlita realized now that she knew this Garou: It was Brittle Leaf, one of Mother Eldridge's septmates from the Sept of the Wounded Bay. Carlita trusted Mother Eldridge intimately—the elder woman had helped the young girl come to grips with what she had become shortly after her First Change. She had significantly less trust for Brittle Leaf, who wasn't even of her tribe. He was Uktena. The Garou was always skulking around, and Carlita suspected that he was only part of Mother Eldridge's sept only because of the benefits it gave him.

Her own tribe—the Bone Gnawers—was fairly prominent in Tampa, and being part of the Sept of the Wounded Bay carried with it a certain amount of prestige. Of course, the Bone Gnawers weren't of particularly noble birth, which meant that many of the Garou didn't want to be associated with them. They were gutter trash to other werewolves, mutts and half-breeds who had lost the wolf by tying themselves so closely to the cities. It was all bullshit, of course, but the tribal society the Garou had established for themselves since time immemorial... well, it carried certain prejudices. Most of the Garou bought into those prejudices, and since Brittle Leaf didn't, well, that made him suspect by way of being outstanding.

Then again, Carlita wasn't without prejudices of her own. Brittle Leaf was a metis, the product of the forbidden union between Garou. His name reflected his condition—Brittle Leaf's bones were weak and prone to breaking. If she had been around to name him, Carlita had joked in the past, she would have called him Plate Glass instead of Brittle Leaf. It was a crippling weakness among werewolf society, this deformity. Because the Garou were a brutal race, many of their policies were set by the one among them whose might made right. Someone who couldn't excel at combat had to resort to other tactics. Many Garou regarded those other tactics as weak or duplicitous. In addition to being scorned for his metis heritage, Brittle Leaf was also scorned for his inability to keep up with the rest of the Garou when it came to fighting. Being a Bone Gnawer, Carlita should have been above such petty bigotry, having suffered plenty herself, but when the oppressed have the chance to exact their revenge... what was it that Silicon Tears had said? It didn't matter now....

"Call me Big Sis. You know that. I am Big Sis. You may not call me Carlita."

"I make apologies, Big Sis. I am wounded. I need help."

"I see that. What happened? Did you fall down stairs?"

Brittle Leaf smiled, a curious thing to see on the face of a wolf. "That is funny. More funny if you knew my history, but I don't blame you. But enough time for joking. The threats are here."

"Threats? What threatens?"

"Men."

Carlita cocked her head. "Many men? Why not stand and fight? Men will flee."

"These men will not flee. These men know us." Brittle Leaf licked at his haunch. Carlita could see that his weeping wound was there. It was a pattern of torn flesh that looked not unlike a buckshot wound. But buckshot would heal quickly, within a matter of moments. "Silver shots. Hunters of Garou."

Carlita recoiled a bit. "Hunters? Skilled hunters? And many? Why not escape to the spirit world?"

It was Brittle Leaf's turn to be taken aback. "Run? From men?"

Carlita pressed her muzzle forward. "More glory to be killed by men?" It was the Garou's classic debate, the matter of men. Some werewolves advocated war on humankind and their cities, which left scars on the face of Gaia, the mother spirit the Garou were born to protect. Such had indeed happened far in the past of the Garou. It even resonated deep within the souls of humans in modern times. Those who saw the Garou in their monstrous Crinos forms suffered the Delirium, a form of madness that caused the individual to panic and have trouble remembering details about the Garou later. The Impergium, the war on man, had been roundly decried as a debacle among Garou.

Brittle Leaf, Carlita knew, was a Ragabash, a sort of trickster or comedian among the Garou. As low as they got at times, even they wouldn't accept running from a man as excusable. Carlita, a Philodox, was more even-purposed, more rational—a judge. To her, it wasn't even a question. To die tonight or to fight tomorrow—what was the issue here?

"Winter Moon is very proud. He will not flee."

So *that* was the problem. Winter Moon was an Ahroun—a warrior—and a young one at that. Saying he was very proud was an understatement. Carlita had heard through her friends in the Hidden Eye Pack about a youngling who had just had his First Change several weeks ago. Winter Moon was still delirious with the power being a Garou had given him. In fact, knowing this, she was surprised Brittle Leaf had even had time to make it here to ask her for help. It would have been more of Winter Moon's style to take on one of the hunters and die in the swarm of silver buckshot. She had to give the cub credit. That he wasn't dead already attested to the fact that somebody's lessons were making it through to him. Granted the Garou were tough, and certainly more than a match for any one man, but a team of experienced hunters was almost certainly more than a whelp could handle, at least in sum.

"Enough talk. I will see these men."

* * *

It wasn't far, or so Brittle Leaf said, and the two traveled in their Lupus forms to the storage lot on the outside of Tampa, camouflaged by the cover of night. With any luck, Carlita hoped, Winter Moon hadn't done anything too stupid and she could still get there in time to help him out. Not that she liked him—Winter Moon had just graduated high school last year, and like the few comfortable suburban kids she knew, he was immature and a grade-A dick. Add his Ahroun nature to the inherent invincibility teenagers feel, and the kid was as bullheaded as... well, a bull, to be frank. Carlita was three or four years younger than Winter Moon and was already a good deal more sensible, understanding the fineries of Garou life, such as respect for achievement and the wisdom to understand that getting in a fistfight with a cop over being caught drinking underage didn't count as achievement. Still, in these days, Garou were rare, a dying breed, and even the stubborn, stupid ones usually had something to redeem them when it counted. Winter Moon just needed to find out what his something was.

Carlita could sense something amiss from the moment they neared the lot. She smelled something familiar in the air, but couldn't figure out what it was. Apparently, Winter Moon had been fooling around at the lot on some business or other (Brittle Leaf didn't quite know, though he said one of the elders had sent the whelp out to search for something), only to be ambushed by the hunters who must have followed him or seen him change form. On the crest of a hill above the lot, Brittle Leaf laid out the land: Winter Moon was inside the lot, which was surrounded by hurricane fence. Any Garou worth the pelt on his hide could get through that without difficulty. On the outside, however, a perimeter of a dozen or so shotgun-wielding good ol' boys took aim now and again, threatening the young wolf, who at least had the sense to zigzag while running between a corrugated shed on the lot and three parked heavy-duty pickup trucks.

Carlita and Brittle Leaf assumed their human forms—Carlita a lanky, swarthy-skinned Hispanic teen and Brittle Leaf a dusky but winnowed man, perhaps in his mid-twenties, with red hair and a wispy beard. They crouched at the top of the hill, overlooking the scene.

"These hunters are good, Big Sis. They've fought Garou before—look how they keep him moving around, hoping to tire Winter Moon. There's more of them, so each of them has to move less, but Winter Moon always has to keep on the move."

"I bet the poor kid's going out of his mind down there. Maybe it'll wise him up. He probably hasn't faced anything he couldn't overcome by pounding on it."

"I know." Brittle Leaf suppressed a smile. "Well, it's good that he's learning it all now, before he undergoes his rites of passage and ends up failing because of some foolish vanity."

"Says you, weak-bones. I say let the cliath learn the hard way. How's that wound?"

"It's a little better. I'll probably be sore for the next few days."

"Yeah, well, that's not really what I meant. You see, that's sarcastic for 'If the hunters came after Winter Moon, how did you end up being shot?'"

"Oh, sorry. Don't have much use for sarcasm. For the weak and all that."

"Look, Brittle Leaf, don't jerk me off. I don't care about some high-minded quote that you probably just read off the side of a bus anyway, and don't forget who the big wolf is here."

"Pulling rank are you? Fine, fine. And it was John Knowles."

"Quit changing the fucking subject or you'll end up like the chicken wings your frail ass reminds me of."

"Right. The hunters shot me. I heard Winter Moon howl while I was passing through, on my way to the Follow North Sept. I crept up and I guess one of them must have seen me. I recognized Winter Moon before I got shot, but I couldn't do anything to help him, so I went looking for someone who could. I just ran across you first—I smelled your nasty 'dinner' about a half mile away and just followed the trail of flies." Brittle Leaf smiled.

"You know, for someone who was wise enough to go looking for help, you're not smart enough to speak respectfully to your elders."

"I'm *your* elder. You're just more renowned."

"Well, whatever. Just watch it. I'm here because of my own free will, not because it's Sticky Fingers Pack's responsibility to baby-sit this brat."

"That's fine, but look at those hunters again. They must have paid for their shot themselves, because they're being real stingy with it."

Brittle Leaf was right, Carlita realized. She thought before that they might have been trying not to draw attention to themselves with gunshots, but they were far enough out of the city proper that anyone who heard a shot or two would probably just believe that the locals were chasing alligators or coyotes. No, these guys were remarkably economical with their weapons. That meant they were on a limited budget, or that they were caught unaware and had only the silver shot they carried with them.

"Yeah, now that you mention it. And look at them. They look like yokels. They're not those black suits from the government's Operation: Teen Wolf or whatever. That probably means that unless Pentex is working on some *Deliverance* project, these mullets aren't part of some larger organization."

"Well, they're not driving government cars. It's all Pontiacs and pickup trucks."

"So we know they're inbred and stupid?"

"No, I was going to suggest that they're freelancers."

"I know, but give me a break. I was just making a joke, Leaf. It's how I cope with stress."

"That was pretty insightful."

"Oh, fuck off. I heard it on Dr. Laura."

"Well, then, to get back to the issue at hand, what do we do?"

"If they're being so frugal with their shotguns, that probably means they don't have much ammo. If we can distract them and get them to waste a few shots, we'd be in a better position to take it to them, if that's what it comes down to."

"Why don't we just call the cops, Big Sis?"

"No, that wouldn't work. Assuming the rednecks don't own the property, they'd get dragged away, but the police would have Animal Control out here to deal with Moontard, and either they'd get mauled or his dumb ass would just end up in a zoo."

"We can howl to him to change form. When the cops come, they'd find these guys surrounding some poor suburban boy. Who knows; maybe it's legit. Maybe he tried to get a little action from the farmer's daughter, and the farmer doesn't like werewolves."

"No, there's too many of them. Even if the cops wrote the whole thing off as a dozen hillbillies hallucinating on moonshine, somebody somewhere would hear about it and know what was going on. Then we'd be up to our armpits in hunters who have all their teeth and don't grope their sisters."

"There you have it, Big Sis. Now you know why I went to find somebody else."

"Good work, boy wonder. Now let Batgirl think for a minute." Carlita sat up and grabbed a stick, tracing rough lines in the dirt and grass. "As much as I think the kid's a dimwit, I want to get him out of there with as much dignity as I can. He's already going to have his ass kicked once he goes back to the Sept of the Wounded Bay."

Brittle Leaf shrugged, sitting back on his rear end and looking over the situation below.

"I'm going in," Carlita announced suddenly.

"I knew you were going to say that, Big Sis. So here's the arguments against it I thought out in advance. First, they'll see you. Then they'll shoot you. Second, all that'll accomplish is to have two Garou trapped in there instead of one. And then they'll shoot both of you. Third, there's nothing in there that'll help you—what you see is what you get. Unless you're planning on hotwiring one of those trucks and running the hunters down—in which case, they'd shoot you before you had a chance—it's a waste of time. Fourth, maybe it's the cynic in me, but I can't help but think that dashing in there is going to upset the balance of the situation in some way that I haven't explained yet."

"Tell me when you're done, Brittle Teeth." Stupid Ragabash.

"That's pretty much all I have."

"Okay. Then just stay here and shut up. Hey, make yourself useful. Draw their fire."

"You're kidding, right?"

"A little." With a feisty smile, Carlita walked down the slope.

As she descended toward the storage lot, she invoked the chameleon-spirits. "Hide my presence, hide my passage; protect me from sight and sound," she whispered beneath her breath. With no more than her own will and the blessings of those spirits, she vanished from the hunters' collective senses before she had even appeared there. Invisibly and inaudibly, she crawled beneath the rolling gate, striding confidently toward one of the trucks, where Winter Moon had just taken cover. She climbed underneath the truck, invisible to the Garou as well as the hunters and tapped him on the haunch.

"Boo, shithead!" Winter Moon, in his Lupus form, practically jumped out of his skin, bashing his head and hindquarters on the underside of the truck's chassis. "Follow me." Without giving him a chance to reply, she climbed back out from under the truck and jogged toward the metal shed, where she opened the window and climbed in.

Peeking out the window, she heard a shotgun go off and felt a brief pang of nervousness in her gut, but that subsided as the hulking form of Winter Moon crashed through the too-small window. A bit of blood spattered on the ground, but before he had fully assumed the Homid shape, Winter Moon had healed.

"Big Sis, you crazy bitch, what the fuck are you trying to do?"

"Whoah, slow down, Stalks-the-Cheap-Beer. That doesn't sound like gratitude."

"Gratitude? Hell no, it's not gratitude. You're fucking it all up!"

"What? I'm here to *help* you, stupid."

"You can't help me on my rite of passage, you fucking spic. It's not allowed."

God.

Damn.

Brittle.

Leaf.

"Your rite of passage? That's what this is?"

"Yep. And I was doing pretty well until your fool self walked in here and wrecked the whole thing. Claws-of-Vengeance is up on the hill watching."

Carlita gave Winter Moon—fuck it, she gave *Jeremy Bleddsoe*—a hard look and sighed. "Well… crap. I'm just going to walk back out and if Claws-of-Vengeance says anything, I'll, uh, tell him that I didn't know and that it doesn't matter anyway because I didn't help you anyway."

"Yeah, good idea, Big Sis. See if he'll bring you a pizza while you're at it."

"Don't push me. I'm out of here now, but I still don't like you."

"Does that mean you won't be my prom date?" Jeremy sneered.

"Count yourself lucky if I don't kill your prom date as a joke." And with that last, weak bon mot, Carlita crawled back out the window. She knew she would still be invisible to the hunters—whoever they were— but unless Claws-of-Vengeance had missed her talking with Brittle Leaf, he'd probably be waiting at the fence for her. And somehow, she doubted that Claws-of-Vengeance hadn't seen her, or else why would Brittle Leaf have fooled her into coming over here?

Sure enough, the tall black man waited at the gate. A few of the hunters were gone, but a fair-sized group of them were huddled around their cars and trucks, looking bemused.

Brittle Leaf was nowhere to be seen.

Chapter Two

Somewhere over the Atlantic Ocean, now:

Carlita blearily opened her eyes and saw that the cabin was dark. The lights had gone out so that people could watch the in-flight movie. She stared at the figures on the screen but didn't make any connections about who they were or what they were doing—she was still half asleep, thinking back to Brittle Leaf and that crap he'd pulled on her.

She closed her eyes and groaned slightly, suppressing a growl. Within moments, she was asleep again, remembering the outcome of Brittle Leaf's prank....

* * *

Tampa, a few weeks ago:

Big Sis grimaced, as much from the taste of the boneless barbecued chicken wings she had found in the dumpster behind the strip-mall restaurant as from the repudiation she was now receiving in her own apartment from Mother Eldridge. The whole thing had obviously been Brittle Leaf's plan to begin with, but because Brittle Leaf was part of Mother Eldridge's sept and Big Sis was technically a member of a pack whose sept no longer existed, Mother's sympathies had to go with her septmate rather than her fellow tribe member. Well, they didn't, but familial obligation was a weird thing among Garou.

"Brittle Leaf says he tried to convince you not to go in there. He says he gave you—" Here Mother Eldridge broke into a wet, hacking cough. Nobody knew what it was from, and the running joke was that she had smoked so many cigarettes before her First Change that lung cancer had set in before the old Garou hardiness had a chance to kick it out. Unlikely, to be sure, but the cough defined much of her speech pattern, and it was certainly less terrifying to consider it the result of a known evil than the work of some hellish toxin that worked on the hale Garou and refused to be expelled. "Gave you four reasons, only one of which was, 'Just don't do it because you don't know what's going on in there.'"

"He's a goddamn liar, Mother. He's a liar and you know it. He's lied to you before."

"But he's not the one who ruined another sept's rites of passage for one of its newest members. That's you."

"I can't believe you're taking his side in this. And what kind of rite of passage was that anyway? He was locked in somebody's backyard and all he had to do was get out? Jesus! Why didn't they just have him fight his way out of a wet paper bag or collect some Coke cans or something? Maybe turn a light switch on and off...."

"Don't call Claws-of-Vengeance's motives as sept leader into this. I'm not taking sides. You did what you did and you can't argue."

"But Brittle Leaf tricked me!"

"Only because you let him. Admit it, Carlita. You went off halfcocked—" *hack hack hack* "—because you wanted to show him up. If you had questioned him a little more, he probably would have exposed the flaws in his story and you would have been able to make a better judgment."

"See? See? You *are* taking his side. You *know* he led me into it, and now you're defending him."

"Carlita, that's his purpose. As a child of the new moon, his duty is to warn the Garou so that we do not become complacent and headstrong. It seems that you were the latter in this situation. I do not have to point out to you—" *hack hack hack* "—that you are of higher rank than he. Yet he brought you low; he exposed your flaw. Be noble, accept what you have done and learn from the mistake."

"I'd do a lot more learning—you want one of these chicken wings? I think they're all made from beaks and feet—I'd do a lot more learning if I didn't think his sorry ass was laughing all the way back to whatever sewer pipe he calls home."

Mother Eldridge waved away the dubious wings, taking a swig from her can of warm Pabst Blue Ribbon instead. "That's not your concern. By being stubborn, you're only adding to the recognition he's going to reap from this escapade."

"Recognition? That piece of shit is earning renown for this? Jesus Christ! I didn't know being an asshole got you a merit badge these days. Get someone else to wreck a rite of passage and you're king for the day!"

"Oh, he's not being commended for ruining the rite of passage. He's not the one who did it. All he did was point out your error. Stop blaming him, Carlita. You are a Philodox—you should have been the first to know what you had done wrong. Instead, you're quick to blame others. That is not the habit of a wise Garou."

Carlita grunted. She knew she was wrong. Still, she didn't think she should be getting the third degree. Brittle Leaf went a long way to make his story believable. He had scored his skin with a silver blade so that he looked wounded and he had chosen his words *very* carefully, never indicating that he knew Winter Moon was undergoing a rite of passage but never denying it—because he had led her not to ask. "I know, Mother—"

Hack hack hack. "And that's why you're going to have to accept a quest of penance to restore your good name."

"Hey, what?"

"You heard me."

"I was about to say I was sorry."

"Sometimes, my dear, sorry isn't enough. If you ask Winter Moon or Claws-of-Vengeance, I'm sure both of them would reply that if you were sorry, you wouldn't have done it in the first place. Be calm; that doesn't make them right. However, they are in the position of having been wronged, so some hostility is to be expected of them."

"Well good then. Now I'm not sorry."

"Don't be petulant. Your rashness has ruined more than just a simple rite of passage. And you're right, it was a bullshit rite of passage, but that's not the point. You know the hunters surrounding the storage lot? Those were Bone Gnawer Kinfolk, brought down from southern Georgia and from the Alabama border. Claws-of-Vengeance doesn't have any nearby Kinfolk of his own, and most of the American South is Bone Gnawer and Fianna stock. I offered to allow the Follow North Sept to call upon our Kinfolk's aid."

"Um… why do I get the feeling that what you're about to tell me is really going to suck?"

"Because—" *hack hack hack* "—because it's really going to suck. Because Claws-of-Vengeance asked for my aid in procuring the Kinfolk's help. Not only did you spoil the rite of passage, not only did you ruin the efforts of the Kinfolk, you cancelled that favor for which Claws-of-Vengeance had indebted himself to me."

"Is it too late go back and take back the time I took back saying I'm sorry?"

"Don't interrupt me. I'm not done." Mother Eldridge's eyes were positively glowing, but whether out of anger or discomfort with the coughing fits, Carlita couldn't tell. She wasn't a tall woman, and age had hunched her a bit, but she made Big Sis feel very small, especially in this pique of discipline. "You also made me look like a fool. Claws-of-Vengeance knows you're a Bone Gnawer, and the fact that I've given you some advice and spoken out for you in the past didn't help your case yesterday. Add to that the fact that you're not a bumbling whelp—that you're an esteemed Bone Gnawer," Mother almost broke her train of thought suppressing a cackle at the thought, "and you've made Bone Gnawers across the state look like buffoons. You're ranked above both the cub whose rite of passage you invalidated and the trickster who convinced you to make an ass of yourself. What kind of light do you think that casts the rest of us in? When our accomplished Garou practically break their legs trying to put their own feet in their mouths?"

"Oh, that's a load of shit, Mother, and you know it. Being a fucking Garou isn't like being Catholic. You don't inherit the sins of the father or the sins of the mother or even the sins of the Big Sis. I'm the one who looks like a clown here, and I'll fix the mess I've made."

"It's not that simple, Carlita. You know that Tampa Bay Buccaneers cap you have on your head? When Trent Dilfer throws an incomplete pass, does Trent Dilfer lose the game? No, the Bucs lose the game."

"Trent Dilfer doesn't even play for the Bucs anymore. You're thinking of Shaun King. Or Brad Johnson this year, but that's probably not who you're talking about. Dilfer played for Baltimore for a while, but not anymore."

"That's not the point. Well, actually, it proves my point. On the Ravens, what's that football player who was mixed up with that killing in Atlanta? The guy who got off scot-free?"

"O.J. Simpson?"

"Stop being cute. Ray Lewis. Ray Lewis fled the scene of the murder, but the Baltimore Ravens still won the Super Bowl. Despite the actions of one of their members, the team is still known for its collective effort."

"Yeah, except for the fact that the Ravens *won* the Super Bowl."

"Exactly. So tell me, Ray Lewis, what have you won for the Bone Gnawers?"

Carlita had nothing to say.

Amid a cloud of wet hacks, Mother Eldridge roused her old form from the rude couch that Carlita had salvaged and brought back to her efficiency apartment. "I want you to come by the club in two days. Then, I'll tell you what you're going to do to make this up to everyone you've disappointed. Shaking her head at the poster of Tupac Shakur stuck to the wall with strips of electrical tape, Mother Eldridge showed herself out of the apartment.

Dropping herself, defeated, to the couch, fingers sticky with honey-barbecue sauce, Carlita just pursed her lips. What an awful two days, and no doubt it was only going to get worse. It was a whirlwind of bad karma—she should have known that the antics of a mutant Ragabash would end with something like a family of discombobulated Georgia hillbillies, football metaphors and nigh religious guilt. Carlita took Mother Eldridge's can of PBR off the table and drank deeply.

All backwash.

* * *

Mother Eldridge looked up at Carlita's window, a little regretful that she'd been so forceful. While Big Sis was certainly responsible for her own actions, she was still just a girl. Fifteen, maybe 16—Mother Eldridge didn't know. A fit of coughing interrupted her thoughts. But she had come a long way in that short time. She was so young when she had her First Change. Age 12! She remembered talking with Gloria, the girl's mother. The woman was traumatized. They hadn't had a Garou born to the line in generations, and none of the modern Gutierrezes had really put much stock in the old family tales of shapeshifters in the family. And that's assuming that Gloria was the one from the Kinfolk family. With much of the Bone Gnawer lineage, nobody knew any more. Carlita's body had rebelled against itself for a while after the change. She was sick every morning, sick after eating, sick at school; any time there was movement or thinking involved, really, the poor thing gave it up until all she had left to puke was bile. Gloria thought she was pregnant. Javier hadn't been home in a few weeks, as he was working a long haul on Highway 95. No one, really, for Carlita to turn to.

Those first few months were the worst, but Carlita came through it all right. She constantly needed new clothes, puking on or sweating through the ones the Wounded Bay Garou found for her. But she passed her rite of passage with flying colors, stealing a tooth from the Wyrm-beast the pack of younglings had encountered and convincing the Master of the Rite to consecrate it as a fang dagger. The girl had skill, sense and charisma.

Not that you'd be able to guess from this little episode, Mother Eldridge worried to herself. Puberty wasn't being so nice to Big Sis, and the only people who had any sympathy for her were the street perverts who didn't know what she was and wanted desperately to go up in... well, anything, young girls included. It still seemed as if Carlita's body was at war with itself, her skin breaking out in adolescent acne and her Garou vigor healing zits almost as fast as they formed. The kid ate constantly, no doubt to keep that furnace of a metabolism from digesting the body that held it. She must suck down twice the food a normal kid her age eats, and even those normal kids are bottomless pits.

"I'm sorry, Carlita," Mother Eldridge coughed aloud to no one in particular. "It's going to get worse before it gets better."

Chapter Three

Over the Atlantic Ocean, approaching Spain:

Carlita grimaced and looked through slitted eyes at Cries Havoc, who had nudged her shoulder, startling her awake. "What?" she said, tired and angry.

"Uh," Cries Havoc said apologetically. "I gotta go to the restroom. I have to get past you."

Carlita rolled her eyes and stood up into the aisle as Cries Havoc slipped past her, heading to the rear of the plane. Carlita sat back down but this time took Cries Havoc's seat in the middle, next to Storm-Eye, who still slept soundly. She looked over at John and Julia. John was asleep but Julia was watching the movie. Carlita shook her head and glanced at the screen. Some kid was weeping. She didn't know how anybody could stand watching such junk and closed her eyes, trying to fall back asleep. She still couldn't forget Brittle Leaf.

God. Damn. Brittle. Leaf.

* * *

Tampa, weeks ago:

Prowling around the bawn, Carlita watched as Brittle Leaf, in Lupus form, made his way out of the caern. It wasn't a glamorous place, just a copse of scrubby trees on Pinellas Peninsula, but it did the trick. The Sept of the Wounded Bay was surprisingly multitribal. It had the expected dominance of Bone Gnawers and Glass Walkers, being a fairly urban caern, but it was also attended by a few of the Native American tribes, particularly of the Tocobago heritage, now little more than a historical footnote.

But of all the Garou, it was with Brittle Leaf that Carlita had an issue. Tomorrow, she'd find out just what Brittle Leaf's ruse had earned her by way of penance, but today, she wanted to find out why. For hours, she had hidden herself among the pines just outside the caern's perimeter, waiting for the treacherous little scumbag to creep out. She hadn't wanted to cross the bawn—no doubt the Master of the Rite would know she was there (if he didn't already, owing to the spirits who flitted in and out of the place, the little chatterboxes).

When Brittle Leaf came loping out, Carlita changed to her own scrawny and drawn Lupus form, taking great care to remain downwind from him so that she could follow him by his scent if she lost sight of him.

Carlita tracked Brittle Leaf for perhaps half an hour, until she was sure she was far enough from the caern to "discuss" things with the metis in her own way. He seemed to be slowing down a bit, so she moved closer, closing in behind him so that he wouldn't see her on her final approach.

With a burst of speed, Carlita broke into a full run toward Brittle Leaf, launching herself into the air and transforming into her Crinos form. From its place at her waist, she drew the dedicated fang dagger. Too late, Brittle Leaf heard her rushing through the air, springing somewhat to the side and spreading his paws, lowering himself, hoping to outmaneuver whatever it was that had tracked him.

Carlita landed hard on the surprised Garou, hearing a satisfying *crack* that must have come from a hind leg. Instinctively, Brittle Leaf assumed his own Crinos form, a wiry, red-furred form. By the time he had adopted the battle-form, however, Carlita already had a great set of claws around his throat and her fang dagger perched just below his eye.

"Move and you are more feeble than before."

"Big Sis, I—"

"My turn to talk. I ask, you answer."

Brittle Leaf changed forms again, this time to Homid, so that he could speak more eloquently and demonstrate his submission. Following his lead, Carlita shifted to Glabro, maintaining a strength and size advantage (actually closer to a balance, but Carlita figured Brittle Leaf's broken leg would keep him deferential, at least until it healed in a minute or so). She kept her dagger close to his cheekbone.

"Now, whelp, you're going to tell me all of your motives for the stunt you pulled," Carlita rasped, her Glabro lips and tongue straining to form words, "or I'm going to put out your eye and cauterize it with maggots inside."

"It was to find a volunteer! They needed a volunteer! All I did was give them someone to do what they wanted. They needed someone to help."

"Who? And what is the volunteer for?"

"I heard Mother Eldridge and Claws-of-Vengeance talking about it. Something about a Red Talon and a Stargazer—some prophecy and a third pack. They needed someone for the third pack."

"The third pack of what?"

"I don't know."

"Then why the hell did you volunteer me, fucker?"

"I didn't. You did. I just gave you the opportunity."

Carla was growing angrier by the second. Her lips pulled back into a snarl, and she pressed the side of her dagger against Brittle Leaf's eye. "You don't know what this is for, but you want me to do it? You don't know what's going on, but you need me to handle it? You're not making any sense. Give me more to go on. You'll regret it if you don't."

"I didn't think you'd listen."

Carlita released her grasp around Brittle Leaf's throat, but she kept him pinned to the ground with her knees on his shoulders and her dagger at his eye.

"I saw it in a dream. A fish-spirit came to me and told me that 'In the third pack, the balance will be upheld by the young.'"

"Don't fuck with me. *Something* came to *you* in a dream?"

"Yes! I swear—and then when I heard Mother Eldridge and Claws-of-Vengeance talking about this Stargazer and Red Talon and their third pack, I knew that it was more than just a dream. It was a real prophecy. The fish-spirits—they're servants of Uktena. Uktena itself is the patron of this third pack!"

"You're walking dangerously close to blasphemy, Soon-to-be-One-Eye."

"It's true. I'm of Uktena's tribe. I know what I'm talking about."

"So how does it involve me?"

"The balance will be upheld by the young. You're the youngest Garou I know, and you're a Philodox. You're the young and the balance in the fish-spirit's message. It's not like I could just tell you 'I had a dream and a fish told me that you need to volunteer for something coming up soon.'"

"You got that right."

"See? I had to get you to volunteer. I had to make sure the others saw the best choice for the job."

"And what is this job?"

"I don't know that."

"You son of a bitch! You set me up for whatever this is and you don't even know what it's going to be?"

"I don't question the spirits. If it's not supposed to be you, someone else will step forward."

"Goddammit. This is why I didn't trust you to begin with, Brittle Leaf. A little honesty would have gone a long way."

"Luna didn't pick me out for my honesty. You're saying that only because you're a Philodox. And if you had the chance to volunteer, you could have backed out. This way, you have to do it."

Her lip curling in anger, Carlita raked the sharp edge of her dagger across the top of Brittle Leaf's cheekbone. "You will let me make my own decisions, cliath. Fish-dream or not, I can take care of myself."

"I know you can," Brittle Leaf replied as blood welled up in the cut and rolled down his face. It would leave a scar. No doubt that was what Big Sis had intended, but he had to admit, if he wasn't so enamored with his own brilliance at concocting the ruse, he would probably be more than a little upset if it had happened to him. "In fact, I'm hoping for it. It'll be the only thing that gets you back alive."

"If you're trying to flatter me, you're just pissing me off."

"No, Big Sis, I'm serious. I know we don't get along, but that's not the point here. I respect you. I respect your station and I respect that you know far more about certain things than I ever will. Why can't you do me the courtesy of respecting what I know?"

Big Sis leaned back, rolling her knees off Brittle Leaf's shoulders. "You know what, Glass-Bones?

That sounded like something I'd say. Except I'd only say it when I haven't just been screwed into accepting some bullshit vision quest that I haven't even had the courtesy of seeing the vision for." She stood and extended a hand to Brittle Leaf, shifting back to Homid as she did so.

"Think about this, too, Big Sis. You fucked up Winter Moon's rite of passage, too. Now he's going to have to undertake it again, and maybe this time Claws-of-Vengeance will think of something real to challenge him with. It'd serve him right, the little turd." Brittle Leaf brushed off the leaves and dirt clinging to him.

"There is that. But do me a favor."

"What's that?"

"Don't do me any more favors."

With that, Carlita walked into the pine woods. Tomorrow, she had this moon-calf's prophecy to determine her role in.

* * *

It wasn't a club so much as it was a pool hall. The thing seemed like it was never closed, despite the fact that liquor licenses would have kept its taps dry for at least six hours a day. Then again, maybe that was the secret: Maybe Eldridge's Social Club didn't have a liquor license. Stranger things could have come to pass. With the nonstop stream of scabrous villains and more civilized slummers who made their way through the dancehall, to the pool tables and out the back door, anything was possible.

Carlita had been a fixture here for a while. She wasn't a very good shot, but she was on good terms with Oliver, the pool counter's manager, and if she was at Eldridge's and not talking with Mother, she was eating three baskets of crinkle fries (don't ask what oil they're fried in) and shooting the shit with Oliver.

Carlita waved to him—"Hi, Sis," in return—and made her way to the back. A few of the pool-shooting *caballeros* turned a lurid eye to her, but she stared them down, exuding as much bravado as any of them could have mustered. After passing the last table in the room (occupied by a half dozen white boys who were spending more time arguing than shooting pool), Carlita moved through a pair of saloon-style doors to the bar lounge. Mother was there at the table with her "boyfriend" of a thousand years, Earl. The two were playing poker.

"Hey, Mother. Hey, Earl." She sidled right up to the table next to them, waving down the waitress and holding up her usual three fingers.

"Hey, Lita," Earl said, not bothering to look up from the five queens he held in his hand. "Wanna buy in?"

"Not with the hand you're holding. Mother, he's cheating like a son of a bitch."

"You can say that again. And he's not playing a fair game of cards either." Her laugh turned into a fit of coughing.

"I thought that shit only happened in the cartoons and movies, Earl."

"Nothing ventured, nothing gained. I would say we were playin' Mexican Sweat, but I'm afraid I'd offend."

"Nah. I'm Puerto Rican." Earl was like a slow-witted uncle, Carlita reasoned. He was nice enough, but he really cared only about himself. Why Mother let him be her… well, whatever he was, she couldn't guess.

"Don't get too comfortable, Carlita. We have somewhere to go."

"Well, can I at least wait for my fries?"

"Get them to go."

* * *

Mother Eldridge drove a battered old Chevy van, which Carlita had nicknamed the Molester Mobile. The thing looked awful. It was all white, with a teardrop-shaped Plexiglas window in the back on both sides. Mother had bought it for a song, and with her keen Bone Gnawer gifts, the former meth lab on wheels had never needed a day of maintenance since. That was an appreciable feat, given that she had bought it maybe 15 years ago, never changed the oil or transmission fluid or brake fluid and had refilled the gas tank exactly once, during an uncomfortably hot summer day in 1993 when she was terribly drunk on some Kinfolk's horrid joke disguised as strawberry wine.

"You should have Doria make tater tots instead of French fries," Carlita posited absently, looking out the window for the police cars that would pull over a Chevy van the moment they saw it if they had a brain in their heads. "These crinkle fries taste like crap."

"You say that about everything."

"I mean it about everything."

Mother hadn't said where they were going, but it soon became clear. After half an hour or so, most of which was occupied by her relentless cough, she pulled the battered old van into the short term parking deck of the airport. She and Mother got out of the van, Carlita fighting the urge to finger "wash me, bitch" in the grime on her side of the Chevy behemoth.

Mother opened the rear doors and pulled out a small carry-on bag. It looked like it had been bought for a nickel at a thrift store. The zipper was broken and it was held together by string, but Carlita could see a change of cloths stuffed inside it. Mother headed toward the terminal.

"Okay, I get it," Carlita said, following beside her. "I'm going someplace. Where to?"

Mother pulled a plane ticket out of a worn and greasy purse, probably another thrift store purchase. She handed it to Carlita almost hesitantly, as if she had second thoughts. But as soon as the girl took it, she sighed and seemed resolved; her part was done.

"It's a ticket to New York," Mother said as she began coughing up a storm. "The Big Apple itself. That's sort of like Mecca for Bone Gnawers."

"This ain't no vacation, Mother," Carlita said. "Where am I going and who am I meeting?"

"Don't worry. It's all taken care of. 'Little Al' Henry will meet you at the airport. You'll know him 'cause he smells like fish and trash. He's a bargeman up there, hauling away New York's garbage across the river. He'll tell you where you need to go."

When they reached the terminal, Mother stopped and hacked into a trash can full of cigarette butts. She then looked Carlita in the eyes. "You be strong girl. You always have been."

"Can you tell me anything about what this's about?" Carlita asked. She suspected now that what Brittle Leaf had said was right. This was something big, involving more than just a Tampa sept. New York City, ferchrissakes!

"I wish this turned out otherwise," Mother said. "If you weren't between packs and all, maybe somebody else would have been chosen. But, no, that's not how things are. I wish I could tell you, but I don't know. They don't tell me anything anymore. All I know is there's some Wyrm thing called 'Jo' that's stirring up trouble, and there's prophecies involved. Normally, a Bone Gnawer knows to go into hiding whenever Garou prophecies are spouted, but this one caught us all by surprise. Carlita, just be safe. Be smart."

She patted Carlita on the arm and turned to go, coughing all the way back to the van.

Before she got there, Carlita cried out, "You take yourself, Mother! And get that cough looked at!"

Mother smiled and laughed, leaning against the van to steady herself as the laugh turned once more into a cough. She winked at Carlita and climbed into the driver's seat.

Carlita swallowed. Whatever this was, it was big.

God.

Damn.

Brittle.

Leaf.

Chapter Four

Madrid, Spain, now:

Carlita's eyes sprang open and a growl escaped her throat before she caught herself and relaxed back into the seat. The impact of the plane's landing wheels on Barajas Airport's runway in Madrid had rudely awakened her, and now the rushing of the plane and the braking of the wheels gave her stomach a lurch.

Cries Havoc stirred, yawned wide, and reminded everyone that they were supposed to meet their liaison from the local sept when they deplaned. They gathered their carry-on bags and walked down the runway.

At the gate, the pack saw a shortish, dark-complected man in priest's garb holding a sign that read "Julia Spencer." He wore glasses and had dark hair parted severely on the right. He obviously knew the pack for what it was, having that incomprehensible revelation of recognition that strangers sometimes have, and his face broadened into a smile.

"I hope no one is offended," the man announced. "But with your names being as they are, I thought Miss Spencer's was the least likely to arouse suspicion. I am Father Hernando Cisneros, your contact from the Church of the Thirteen Sorrows."

A few members of the pack looked at each other with mild surprise in their eyes.

"You speak English like someone who learned it from books," Carlita commented, holding out a handful of little Runts candies in case anyone in the immediate vicinity was interested.

"I do not have much cause for practice. Our church is a diplomatic one, and much speech is done in French or in a more native tongue."

"Yeah, well, let's stick to Spanish," Carlita replied in that language, to which the good Father grinned. "What? What's funny?"

"You say I sound like I learned English from books. You sound like you learned Spanish from the streets."

Carlita prepared to make a smart remark, but Storm-Eye cut them both off. "Continue this later. I'm tired."

After gathering the rest of their luggage, they made their way to the curb outside, where a pair of C-Class Mercedes sedans waited for them. "I'm sorry to split the group, but the ride is short," Father Cisneros informed them. "And we have plenty of space at the church."

"Wait—make sure that Big Sis isn't in the same car as the Father, here," Cries Havoc said.

"What's that about?" Carlita asked, not yet knowing whether to be upset or not.

"It is because you speak Spanish," the priest offered. "In case we become separated, someone in both cars will be able to converse in the local language."

"You say that like it's bound to happen," Julia replied.

"I know that you do not have to worry about such things here. Both of the drivers are part of our family," Cisneros pointed a thumb toward the cars. "But I also wouldn't want to question a guest's desires."

"Thanks for indulging me," Cries Havoc said without a hint of embarrassment. "Maybe it's past experience raising old hackles, but I know that when things can go wrong, they often do."

"Like in New York," Storm-Eye offered.

Father Cisneros shrugged, "As I said, the guest's wishes come first." He entered the car with a nonplussed John North Wind's Son and a sheepish Julia Spencer.

* * *

After helping John and Julia load their bags into the trunk, Father Cisneros settled into the front seat. He introduced them to Miguel, the cab driver and Kinfolk, and he asked them if they had any questions. Before Julia even had a chance to reply, John asked about the Thirteen Sorrows sept.

"So, it's a church?"

"Correct," Cisneros answered. "Actually, it's a monastery. It's been standing since the late sixteenth century and became a sept shortly after it was dedicated as a home for men of God."

"And all these men of God were Garou?" John asked, a note of disbelief in his voice.

"Of course not. Some were, but only a rare few. After the church was dedicated and became a sept, it naturally drew Garou from the surrounding area. Some of the men were Kinfolk, others were Garou and still others were just simple human men, who came to the monastery with secrets of their own and gladly hid the nature of the place in exchange for not being asked too many questions about their own past."

"Pardon me, Father, but that all seems very strange," Julia interjected. "I've never heard of a sept that worked so closely with humankind."

"It is the difference between your New World and the one the Americanized Garou left behind. In fact, it's probably unique to America and Canada, at least as far as the Western world goes. You might find similar situations even down in Mexico, where the Old World's ways are still practiced."

"No, no. I'm not saying it doesn't happen. I'm just wondering how it happens." John nodded his head in agreement at this. "In the United States, septs are very personal, secret things. In fact, many of the American Garou are so reactionary as to kill first when a human even accidentally stumbles across the bawn."

"The difference is cultural. In America, you have wide-open spaces. You can have the luxury of claiming a tiny portion of it for yourselves. Here in Europe, the people are different and the space is far more limited. Look around when we get further into the city. Notice how much we take advantage of all three dimensions. The population is denser here—it always has been—and even conservative Garou understand that we must share the limited space that exists."

"Well," John commented, "that brings us back to my question. Why a church? I mean, doesn't a church have to meet certain… requirements to still be considered a church?"

"Ah yes, that is complicated, and leads to the inevitable question: How can we serve both God and Gaia? Let me tell you simply: There is no conflict.

For those who follow the spirit, all paths lead to one. We are humble, after all. One of the founders of the sept was a Bone Gnawer. The other was a Fianna."

"This story gets stranger as it goes. A Fianna?"

"Why is that strange?"

"Well, aren't the Fianna part of the Irish culture? I mean, one might have come over here of course. Maybe during the dark ages, when the Irish monasteries were part of the stronghold of European civilization."

"Pardon me if this sounds rude, but I do not think you know as much as you think you know."

John shrugged as Julia looked sideways at him, tilting her head toward the priest.

Cisneros resumed. "The Celtic tribes hailed from these lands—and all of Gaul, besides—before they moved over to England and Ireland. The Fianna have been a part of Spain longer than they have been a part of Ireland. The Bone Gnawers as well. While Spain is more culturally diverse today, at least with regard to Garou heritage if nothing else, that is largely a result of modern travel conveniences. Traditionally, the Fianna and Bone Gnawers were part of Celtic and later Basque ethnic groups. The Black Furies were part of the Greek culture that was at least partially subsumed by the Roman Empire during its heyday, in whose footsteps the Children of Gaia and Warders of Men also followed. For such a small land, at least relative to how you Americans must see it, the Garou culture of Spain is as diverse as any that can be found on the face of the Mother."

John sat back, a look of respect in his eyes. He liked Cisneros—the priest readily shared his knowledge without so much of the bluster that some Garou back home used to season their arguments.

The father was a humble person, but obviously a man of much thought and understanding. Moreover, John understood some of the ways perspectives among the Garou differed. While he had thought of himself as "American" before, he never really considered himself as closely tied to the Americanized Garou. And that was Cisneros' point, John North Wind's Son realized. It was all a matter of perspective. For such a studied individual, Cisneros didn't want to *know*; he simply wanted to understand enough to figure out what he *believed*.

Chapter Five

And here's the Ahroun, Big Sis thought to herself. The strapping Spanish brute had taken no chances with the arrival of this new pack, regardless of whatever Father Cisneros might have told him prior. He was obviously the Guardian of the Sept, or at least training underneath one. Cisneros introduced the hulking Glabro as Runs-to-the-Sun.

Unsurprisingly, John North Wind's Son had risen to the challenge posed by Runs-to-the-Sun and had himself assumed the Glabro shape. John stood turned to the Spaniard, either in preparation to launch some Ahroun attack or out of a canine desire to make himself seem larger. Carlita had seen common cats and dogs doing this before, playing this sort of optical illusion on potential threats. She called the trick "getting big," and it amused her a little bit to see these warriors of Gaia, these creatures of supposed higher evolution, resorting to the same techniques that animals used when fighting over territory or scraps of food from a trash can.

"Can it, you guys," Big Sis said, first in English and then again in Spanish, looking pissed. "Look; we're only here as long as it takes for us to learn about the situation. Then, I promise, Runs-to-the-Sun, we'll untangle ourselves from your fur."

Storm-Eye stood on all fours next to Carlita, her own fur bristling as she took deep breaths, broadening—"getting big"—herself, putting another obstacle between the two full-moon warriors. She had a much simpler message than Big Sis, simply, "stop," growled in the undeniable lupine cant of the

Garou. Storm-Eye had made a big show of assuming her Lupus form once she exited the taxi at the Thirteen Sorrows sept. Cries Havoc had carried her bags, and Storm-Eye presumably had taken the wolf's form to let her fellows know that she was more interested in the business at hand than the words spoken to get there. Carlita also suspected she wanted to scare the hell out of the handful of human monks and attendants. Surely they were no strangers to the wolves who walked as men, but that didn't mean they were comfortable with them.

Even Cries Havoc himself, burdened with bags, had assumed a defensive position, not wanting things to escalate, but ready to leap to John's aid should it become necessary. It was surprising that this pack, which had spent no more than a few days in each other's company, was already taking up their second-nature roles of protection and defense, Carlita thought to herself. Sure, she and Storm-Eye had interposed themselves between John and Runs-to-the-Sun, but had the confrontation come to blows, there was little question as to whose side they would have rallied.

Julia and Cisneros peeled off from each other's sides, Julia interrupting her packmates' posturing.

"They are our guests, Runs-to-the-Sun," Cisneros pleaded in Spanish. "They have asked for our help in combating a common enemy."

"They do not show proper deference," Runs-to-the-Sun countered. "If they want help, they should ask for it graciously."

"What's he saying?" Cries Havoc asked, as Carlita stepped around Julia to reply.

"He's pissed that we haven't made a more formal introduction or commented on the fine decoration of their caern," Carlita spat over her shoulder. To Runs-to-the-Sun, she objected, "Look, we just got here. You knew we were coming, and we just got off the plane and took an hour's cab ride. Maybe we're a little cranky from the trip, but what's *your* problem?"

"Please, Big Sis, don't frustrate him any more," Cisneros objected.

"This is Big Sis?" Runs-to-the-Sun asked incredulously, stepping back a bit.

"That's me. I see my reputation precedes me." Big Sis put her hands at her hips, casually pushing back the flaps of her oversized jacket to reveal the fang dagger hanging from her belt.

"Mother Eldridge described you differently," Runs-to-the-Sun replied, shifting from Glabro to, presumably, his native Homid form.

"You know Mother Eldridge?"

"She sent a spirit telling me to watch for your arrival. We are of the same tribe."

"You're a Bone Gnawer? Damn!" Carlita asked. "Pardon my French, or Spanish, or whatever, but you don't look like one." She noted Runs-to-the-Sun's good looks and sense of style, which a more traveled person would probably describe as continental. Now that he had shifted back to his human shape, Carlita noticed that Runs-to-the-Sun wore an oxford shirt and leather pants, in the sincere way that only a European man can, whereas an American wearing the same thing would look hopelessly cheesy. "I mean, where's the grease? Where are the mismatched socks? Why do I feel so damn underdressed?"

Runs-to-the-Sun laughed. "Things are different here. These aren't even really my clothes. I found them in town. I mean, someone gave them to me. I mean—oh never mind. Father, I'll give them back once the guests have been shown to their rooms." Cisneros shook his head and clucked his tongue. "But it is an honor to meet you, Big Sis. I was just expecting someone... bigger."

"Well, sorry to disappoint, but it's not the size that counts," Carlita grinned.

Father Cisneros took the conversation as an opportunity to apologize to the pack. "You must excuse Runs-to-the-Sun. He is training beneath the Guardian of the Sept, and we have so many visiting Garou here that his patience is sorely taxed."

"What just happened?" John called to Carlita.

"Shut up, would you, stupid? I just charmed him with my feminine wiles, that's all," Big Sis hollered back.

"That girl is trouble with a capital 'T,'" Cries Havoc mumbled to no one in particular.

* * *

The church itself was a subtle affair, laid out in quadrants, with the chapel occupying one quadrant, other functional buildings in another, the third occupied by a large garden and the fourth dominated by two dormitories. One dormitory was obviously far older than the other, and Father Cisneros revealed that the second dormitory had been built two centuries after the monastery itself. According to the history of the place, the second dormitory was built under circumstances not unlike the ones these particular

Garou faced right now: A moot was being held to discuss the best course of action against an unspecified enemy, and Garou visited from all over the continent and required housing. Since then, the monastery's new dormitory had become far more traditional in its purpose, housing the ranks of the monks who had come to devote their lives to God. Briefly, during the late eighteenth century, the monastery had become coed, with an abbot and abbess presiding over the brothers and sisters, respectively. Charges of witchcraft and heresy arose soon after that, however, and in order to preserve the Garou's secret, the monastery was forced to disband its membership, subsisting quietly, forgotten on the Church's rosters.

The spirits seemed to like the place, however, or if they didn't, they were abundant for some other reason. Julia suspected that it was because of the aura of reverence and respect the caern had. This was not a place of war, even if it was a place where the courses of struggles were planned. This was a caern with a history among Galliards and Philodox, a place where the Garou sang of their victories, reveled in their achievements, planned their next successes and negotiated for heroism. While the Thirteen Sorrows sept was not without its past treacheries—its name reputedly came from one great betrayal of a member of each tribe—but those were largely anomalies in the otherwise esteemed if quiet history.

Tonight was a somber night for the sept, however, as the Garou who had convened here faced a desperate threat that had already laid two packs low. Tensions ran high among the assembled werewolves, and the non-Lupine monks—Kinfolk and otherwise—sagely kept out of their guests' way or received sometimes painful reminders of the Garou's temper and power. Two monks had to be carried to the apothecary for being in Anthius Morningkill's way, and John North Wind's Son, frustrated by the aspersions cast on his young pack's ability to perform, raised his hand to strike a brother who had followed too closely. Only Storm-Eye's growl of disapproval stopped him. He thought it strange, that a lupus-bred Garou of the hostile Red Talons would speak up to defend a human, but he remembered the Talon's disapproval of attacking a lesser foe. Admonished and embarrassed by his own anger, John apologized to the monk, who fled before the Wendigo's final words were uttered.

Carlita had never seen such a small place so busy. While the monks' normal tenancy of the monastery ran only to maybe a third of its capacity, entourages of werewolves had overrun the place. No doubt, that was part of what had everyone on edge—20 Garou packed with 20 or so humans and Kinfolk, all in just a few thousand square feet, was more than even a Bone Gnawer could handle with grace. It didn't help that so many Garou luminaries were rumored to be present. Galliards from all over the world had attended as well, which lent credence to Cries Havoc's half-joking assessment that it was more like a rock concert than a moot.

"Tell me again why this is such a big moot?" Carlita asked Runs-to-the-Sun.

"The Wyrm-beast your pack is trying to stop—Jo'cllath'mattric—has defeated other packs before. The survivors of those packs are here to tell everyone what they know about it. The Galliards have gathered from all over to recall legends of the Garou that might give some more insight."

That was grave. This was a Grand Concolation in all but name. Well, maybe not that big, but with elders of the tribes in attendance and a collection of Galliards for the purpose of trying to recall the ancestral memories of the Garou... Carlita shuddered in spite of herself. It would certainly be an event to remember.

Despite the various moods of the assembled Galliards, all of the Garou felt a pall hanging over the moot, and either sulked in it or denied it as their own tastes dictated. Carlita was usually the type who would laugh at the end of the world, denying the pain with forced good spirits, but she found herself unable to do so this time. The rest of her pack noticed this and left her to herself, though Julia made sure to come by and ask if everything was all right as Carlita sat cross-legged on her dormitory bunk.

Carlita had remained silent, nodding in acknowledgement until the last time Julia had asked, just a few hours before the moot was supposed to begin.

"Why us, Julia?"

"I know what you're feeling. Believe me, I feel it, too. It almost seems like we're being set up to fail."

"Yeah. I mean, if packs of *elders* haven't been able to handle this thing, why the hell do they think we can?"

"It's not always a question of capability. It's a question, sometimes, of destiny. Do you remember being a little girl?"

"Of course. I'm not old like you."

Julia smiled at Carlita's defensive attempt at levity. "Well, then you remember seeing your mother leave for the store, or maybe your father coming back from work?"

"It wasn't all *Leave It to Beaver* like that in my house. I do remember seeing my Papa not drunk once, if that's what you mean."

"No, I'm talking about things they did to help— whoever earned the money to pay the rent, or someone cooking dinner. Something like that."

"Sure, I know what you're talking about. Papa wasn't around much, but Mama always figured out how to pay the bills somehow."

"That's what I'm talking about. Didn't you see them as heroes of a sort? Or someone who could do things that you couldn't?"

"I guess so."

"Well, look at you now. You can do things they'd never even dream of being able to do. It's all in your perspective."

"But it's different, Julia. Everybody grows up to be an adult. Not everybody grows up to be a Garou. The Garou who have gone before us are literally legends, and—no offense—we're just whelps."

"I suppose it wouldn't help to bring up the story about the mouse who pulled the thorn out of the lion's paw?"

"That's just a kid's story."

"I understand. I have the same fears you do, Big Sis. But sometimes you just have to accept what you have to do and face it, and trust that by the will of Gaia, things will end up as they're supposed to."

"That's what's got me worried. What if we're supposed to die at the end of it? I'm not scared of doing what I have to do, but I don't want to die yet."

"That's pessimism."

"It's realism."

"No, it's not, necessarily. You don't *know* you're going to die. You're just more afraid of death than you are secure in life."

"No shit. I live in an efficiency apartment in Tampa Fucking Florida. When I'm not running around Spain and putting my ass on the line, it's not exactly like I'm living in the lap of luxury."

"Now you're just being resentful."

"I'm sorry, Julia, but I'm really overwhelmed here. On one hand, I feel that I'm too young and inexperienced—we're all too inexperienced—to come through for everybody who's counting on us. But on the other hand, I feel like there's something I don't know about myself yet that's going to make a big difference here. And I'm scared as hell because people who were *way* more… who were better than I am had their chance and weren't able to do it. I mean, what right do I have to think I'm any better than the Garou who came before us?"

Julia put her hand on Carlita's shoulder as she rose from the bed to leave. "It's not a question of being better. It's a question of being the one for the job."

Chapter Six

As had always seemed to be the case with such things, the moot began in a tumultuous fashion. The esteemed Galliards who had traveled from far and wide to attend had different opinions on how to begin the matter. Some were raucous and enthused, used to moots that at least began as wild parties and somewhere during the course of the revelry settled down to the business at hand. Other Galliards were far more austere, seeing their verbal Garou tradition as one of preserving lore, not debauchery. Still others stood tensely by, waiting for an official commencement that never seemed to come.

For those unfamiliar with Garou culture, it would have been a surreal or even unsettling scene. Stoic wolves sat erect next to knot-browed men; languid wolves sprawled by massive wolf-headed women; twisted metis leaned on walking sticks next to veritable gods, who crossed their heavy arms over their barrel chests. Although only 25 or so Garou were in attendance, 25 or so of Gaia's warrior race are a fearsome sight, indeed, and all cross-sections of the Garou Nation were represented.

The tone of the moot took an abrupt shift to the formal, as the sept leader, Marino Laguia, stepped before the gathered Garou in the church nave and assumed the wolf-shape. Laguia was a burly homid, and an equally bulky wolf with fur as black as a starless night. A long, low rumble rolled from his mouth and built to a sonorous Wail of Foreboding. Others among the crowd took the wolf-shape themselves, or joined the sept leader in his howl from their powerful Crinos forms. Their accumulated voices reverberated through the church, sounding like a bestial choir that no churchgoer would ever have thought to gather in a house of God.

Carlita followed suit, assuming her own rangy Crinos shape and joining in the solemn wail. She did so nervously, however, looking about her while many of the other Garou had closed their eyes and howled to the skies.

The wail went on for several minutes, and it was no doubt Laguia's intent to not only honor the fallen Garou who had fought against the Wyrm-beast but also to mourn the creature's very existence. As the howl wound down, even the Garou who had been the most irreverent before the howl began hung their heads.

"Among men, I am known as Marino Laguia," the sept master began, after assuming his human shape. "But among the revered family of Gaia, I am Swallower-of-Fire. I have fought the Wyrm a thousand times and felt its hellish sting more than even Luna might remember. I am the master of the Thirteen Sorrows sept, and while it does my heart good to see so many strong and quick fellows, it is another sting from the Wyrm that we must gather to discuss. I ask that all Garou enter their war-forms, that we may better understand each other and that we may show the Great Defiler that when it rises, we shall sharpen our claws against its evil bulk."

Carlita scanned the crowd again, seeing Father Cisneros, who looked at her and gave her a nod that somehow strengthened her resolve.

"What did he say?" John North Wind's Son asked.

"He revered Gaia and acknowledged Luna and said everyone should go Crinos," Carlita whispered to her gathered pack. "So everybody can understand each other and look tough and all."

One by one, the attending Garou entered their Crinos forms, a savage transformation performed in uncharacteristic quiet.

"Our time is short. The beast rises and a pack must again bare its fangs in hopes of bringing it down." As Swallower-of-Fire spoke these words, Carlita exchanged a grave look with Julia. "This is the prophecy of Antonine Teardrop; this third pack must succeed where the others have failed. Winter's Breath, step forward."

A white-furred Garou appeared from the first row, one marked across his entire body with battle scars. His adornments appeared to be Nordic, and Carlita assumed he was a Get of Fenris. He spoke.

"I am Winter's Breath, from the sept of the Anvil-Klaiven. I tell now a story that is not my own, but was told to me by its witness, the Galliard Mephi Faster-than-Death."

The Get of Fenris Galliard related the tale of Mephi's pack's own conflict with Black Spiral Dancers, and of the horrors that befell his packmates. The Galliard proudly told of a victory wrenched from them by the Wyrm tribe. Mephi had escaped, however, carrying hints of some terrible creature that would soon cast its tainted shadow over them.

The Galliard also spoke of the River Tisza, which, as Mephi noted while he and his pack fought the Black Spiral Dancers in the spirit world, had deviated from the course its physical counterpart followed. Something had diverted the river—but what and to what purpose?

He also told the fate of the second pack and their valiant deaths fighting the strange new creatures of the Wyrm. Among them was Mari Cabrah, who was now lost in a coma none at the Anvil-Klaiven could cure. Enemies had come for her, but Mephi Faster-Than-Death had run with her, escaping by moon bridge to none knew where.

The Galliard fell silent and then began a low whine from deep in the back of his throat, one that grew and soon became a howl, the Dirge for the Fallen, honoring the fallen packs that had died opposing Jo'cllath'mattric. From this howl, Winter's Breath began a series of rhyming cantos that made much of the fact that Antonine Teardrop's prophecy had rung true not once but twice… and the verses ended with Antonine's suggestion that a third pack would be needed.

When the Galliard finished, Swallower-of-Fire spoke again. "It has now come to pass that the third pack must take its place in Antonine's prophecy. Members of the third pack, come before me."

What was this? No one had told Carlita to be ready for such a thing! Her eyes went wide, but she had no choice, as John North Wind's Son, the dumb brute, was making his way out there. Julia didn't even look at Carlita, probably so as not to offer a compassionate way out. Storm-Eye padded after her.

Awkwardly, with an adolescent self-consciousness more appropriate to Carlita's teenaged girl aspect than her Lupine blood, she also moved to the center of the nave. She gulped for air, but hoped she was comporting herself with enough dignity to… oh, for fuck's sake, she could hear her blood pounding in her ears.

"This is the third pack?" A voice from the back of the moot intoned, obviously incredulous. "These whelps will surely die," came another voice. "Prophecy must come cheap," followed a sarcastic third.

Swallower-of-Fire drowned out the detractors' comments with his own booming voice as Carlita wished she were not wearing her Crinos form. She had to fight to control the anger that leaped all too easily to the fore in that form.

"Of the assembled Galliards, do any recall earlier tales of Jo'cllath'mattric? Its name is familiar to us, but the story of its ultimate defeat is not."

Yeah, Carlita thought to herself, *so shut the fuck up about how we're going to fail if you can't fulfill your own obligations.*

"No one can remember the tale?" Swallower-of-Fire roared. "The story-tellers and song-singers cannot remember the words to their verses?"

One Garou came forward, a curious look on her face. Carlita had seen this one around the church before; she was one of the fulltime caern residents. Her name was Luna's Song, and she was the fledgling Talesinger, having only recently taken up that position in the sept after the death of the previous, aged Talesinger who spent his last days looking for the very stories Swallower-of-Fire demanded.

"If I may speak, sept leader?" Swallower-of-Fire nodded. "Before my mentor Rovio passed on, he told me many of the stories surrounding this caern, which his mentor told him and on down the generations, before any of us had been born. We all know now, because we are here, that the Thirteen Sorrows sept has always been a place where Garou come to speak, to discuss their differences and to bury their grievances. In these modern times, it is easy to simply take a car or a plane, but such was not the way hundreds of years ago. When the Garou needed to travel long distances then, they turned first to the Umbra."

Muttering and whines went through the crowd. Carlita had an inkling of where this was headed, but she wasn't yet quite sure.

"What are you saying, Luna's Song?" Swallower-of-Fire asked, and Carlita thought she could detect a slight hint of pride in the sept leader's voice.

"It is not news to us that several moon bridges converge here on this caern. Some are still open, some have fallen into disuse, and some have been forgotten completely. However, I believe that one of the disused ones goes near the den of Jo'cllath'mattric—I know it goes east, and I can hear water trickling from it when I listen at the convergence point. If the old legends are true, it rests near the Tisza River."

"And to what caern does this path lead?" Swallower-of-Fire asked.

"I cannot be sure, for its path is long disused," Luna's Song responded, "but if the songs of old hold true, it is a truly ancient caern, one once held by the Shadow Lords of old and known to their famed kin, the Hun who was called Attila."

A shocked murmur went through the assembled crowd, and Carlita groaned. What the hell kind of B movie was this? Attila the Hun?

"What's more," said Luna's Song, "it is said to be the legendary site where his treasure was hoarded, guarded all these long years by spirits bound into duty to hide its secrets from all who were not of the caern's sept. Even those Shadow Lords living today remember little of it, and are unsure if the tales be true."

"Why haven't they investigated?" someone cried out. "Do they know it's all a lie?"

Others grumbled and muttered about the whole thing being a wild fancy unsupported by fact, but Swallower-of-Fire glared them all into silence and then nodded to Luna's Song to continue.

"We can open a moon bridge to the caern's old center, although I am unsure if its spirits will welcome those who enter."

"So be it," said Swallower-of-Fire. "There is where the third pack must go, for there is the River Tisza, which leads to Jo'cllath'mattric."

Carlita felt sick. She didn't feel at all up to the pressure a whole room of esteemed Garou had just put on her shoulders. She looked at her packmates and saw that Julia shared her consternation, but North Wind's Son was smiling, as if he were looking forward to a glorious death. Storm-Eye's expression was unreadable in her Lupus form.

Cries Havoc placed his hand on Carlita's shoulder. "Remember Uktena's lesson. Don't fight the current, but guide yourself through it, wherever it leads."

"Yeah?" Carlita said. "But how do I keep from drowning?"

Chapter Seven

After the moot ended, everyone filed out of the church, back to their rooms or to congregate in small groups whispering among themselves. Except for Carlita. She broke off from her pack and wandered into the gardens. She needed air and space, time alone to figure out how to deal with everything going down.

Her first reaction had been dread, but now she was growing accustomed to it all. With new surprises waiting around every bend, the past few weeks sort of blurred together. It had been tough to get her bearings—first being sent to New York, and then here, to Spain—but the moot was the final straw. She could take anything after that. Nothing worse could possibly happen.

Tomorrow night they would depart for the Tisza, and for the domain of Jo'cllath'mattric. How do you top that in the "oh shit" department? *You don't,* she thought, a bit of a smile creeping onto her face. *Bring it on! I'll chew it up and eat it for breakfast, lunch, dinner and a midnight snack afterwards.*

With that thought, she realized how hungry she was. The monks would be at complin or in bed, and the kitchen would be all but deserted. Though the monks were a little simple with their foods, she was sure to find something in their pantry a damn sight better than a Whopper.

She headed toward the kitchen, retracing her steps through the garden—and almost ran head-on into Runs-to-the-Sun. Startled, she moved into a defensive posture and was ready to smack his head with a swinging kick before she realized who he was.

Runs-to-the-Sun raised his eyebrows, a sort of *Well, are you going to do anything?* look. Carlita gave him a light punch in the shoulder.

"Shouldn't sneak up on a girl," she said. "Never know what she'll do."

"I wasn't trying to be quiet," he said. "You were too busy thinking, not watching where you were going."

"Yeah, well, sorry 'bout that. Catch ya later." Carlita moved past him as fast as she could, but stopped when she felt his hand on her shoulder.

"Hey, I came looking for you," he said. " I want to apologize for earlier, at the gate. I didn't know it was you."

"Yeah, you said that already. Okay, fine, apology accepted. That all?"

He looked hurt but didn't remove his hand. "No. There's something else. I… I just wanted to tell you that you're a very brave girl to be doing this." He took his hand away and raised it in a truce sign as he saw her frown. "I don't mean you can't handle it. But you're very young. You can't deny that. This threat… it's too big for the young. I don't know why they're sending you guys, but they seem to have their reasons. Who am I to question?"

Carlita gave him a playful punch again. "Yeah, they know best, right? Tomorrow we'll save the world and be back in time for desert."

Runs-to-the-Sun smiled. "You have quite the sense of humor in the face of all this. I respect that. I didn't just come to compliment you, but to give some advice. Our tribe is different all over the world. I may not be what you expected, but you will not be what others expect. Eastern Europe views the world in outdated ways, some of them quite prejudiced—especially among the Garou. If there are any Bone Gnawers there in Serbia, treat them well, but be wary. They have made many sacrifices to survive, some of them unwise."

"So you're telling me to watch out for our own kind?" Carlita sat down on a nearby bench, watching Runs-to-the-Sun with a mixture of curiosity and disbelief.

"No, just to be ready for… differences," he said, sitting down next to her. "In truth, I suspect you'll need to be wary of everyone *but* Bone Gnawers. There is honesty in poverty, unlike the guile others will use to protect what is theirs."

Carlita nodded. "Yeah, I suppose that's true. But not all the time."

"Most Bone Gnawers here are from old peasant stock. They tend to be raised with strong beliefs about right and wrong."

"That ain't so different from America. Puerto Ricans know the score, too."

"You are Puerto Rican?"

"No, I'm American. But my mom was Puerto Rican. I grew up in a Puerto Rican neighborhood."

"I grew up in the country, Andalusia. My grandfather was an anarchist during the civil war. He fought for equality among all classes."

"Guess we all got to fight our own doomed battles."

Run-so-the-Sun smiled, but it was a painful smile. "Yes. Reckless idealism, perhaps. Utopianism. But I think my grandfather was right. I believe that Gaia sees no social classes when she looks on her children, regardless of what the Silver Fangs and Shadow Lords say."

"Was your grandfather a Garou?"

"No, Kinfolk. I don't think he even knew it. It was a family secret handed down only to those of direct blood. The Garou blood is on my mother's side."

"That's irony."

Runs-to-the-Sun looked at her quizzically. "How so?"

"The differences between Garou and humans—that's a form of class divide, right?"

Runs-to-the-Sun looked down at the soil. "I had not thought of it that way before. I saw us as equal under Gaia."

"Is a panther equal to a rabbit? There's this thing they call the food chain that keeps someone on top all the time."

"If you look at these things from the material world, yes. But not from the spirit world. Each has its gifts to give, realms in which each is king. It is only here that they must share an unequal portion now and then."

"And why's that?" Carlita said. "What's more, what's to be done about it? How do you eliminate class struggle when the basic fact of the material world is limited resources and the fight to hoard them. Yeah, I've read Marx. Sure, there's endless plenty in Gaia's bosom, but she ain't sharing it here."

"Through no fault of Hers! The Wyrm is what causes shortages and envy, greed and a hunger to devour more than we need. Our natural state is one of bounteous plenty."

"Yeah, but it always comes back to the same question: How do you fix it?"

Runs-to-the-Sun was silent for a while, and then he looked into Carlita's eyes, staring deeply as if he wished to burn the moment into his memory forever. "You fix it by killing Jo'cllath'mattric."

Carlita looked away from him. It was too intense. It was almost getting mushy. If things weren't so damned important and significant, she would have snickered at her fellow Bone Gnawer's earnestness. He was indeed an idealist, with a passion she had never mustered for anything, except maybe getting a free lunch. It made her feel small by comparison. But then, he wasn't the one going to Serbia.

"Yeah," Carlita said. "Or die trying."

* * *

The center of the caern was in the midst of the four church quadrants, in a small courtyard. Moon bridges opened and closed in a space before a small fount, where water trickled up from deep springs below the flagstones.

Upon moonrise on the night after the moot, the pack gathered to travel to only-Gaia-knew-where-exactly. Carlita looked at the few other Garou who had gathered into the small courtyard to see them off. Others watched from windows in all the quadrants or from the trees in the garden that some onlookers had climbed to get a good vantage point. Carlita felt like the pack was all on camera, watched by the entire Garou Nation. In a sense, they were. The Galliards would surely take back tales of what they'd seen, so if she were caught chewing gum or picking her nose now, everybody would soon know about it.

She stood up straight and tried to adopt a careless pose, something that said yeah-who-cares-let's-just-get-on-with-this. John North Wind's Son also seemed aware that they were posing for posterity, and he hammed it up for all it was worth, frowning intently and nodding as the Gatekeeper went through the rites to awaken the spirits.

Julia was intent on checking her bags, to make sure she had everything: batteries for her PDA, a charger that worked on European standards, notepads and pens just in case the power went out anyway, and Michelin maps of Serbia.

Storm-Eye sat still, in Lupus form, waiting patiently, uncaring that eyes were upon her. Next to her, Cries Havoc peered sheepishly up at the windows and the faces looking back at him. He knew what it was like to garner attention from strangers—powerful ones at that—at the Anvil-Klaiven concolation, where he was almost sacrificed to the Get's anger. He didn't seem to relish such notice.

Carlita's survey of her packmates was cut short by the sudden shimmering of moonlight in the square as a moon bridge spun into being, opening a hole into a protected path through the Umbral skies. The Gatekeeper nodded at Storm-Eye, and before any farewells could be said, the wolf walked resolutely through the silvery opening. Cries Havoc followed quickly after, followed by John North Wind's Son. Julia looked at Carlita, who gestured for her to go first. The Glass Walker went through, and Carlita began to follow, but she stopped at the edge, looking back at all the eyes intently watching. She nodded at them and raised her hand with a "peace up" sign, as if she were simply getting onto the subway rather than going to her certain doom.

She then disappeared as the hole in the air closed behind her.

* * *

It was a long walk from Madrid to the banks of the Tisza. The moon bridge cut the distance remarkably, but not entirely. They felt like they'd been walking for three or four hours before the distant shimmering of an exit could be seen. They picked up their pace, each eager to be at their destination, regardless of what awaited them there. The walking was just too damn monotonous—bring on the Wyrm-beasts.

Storm-Eye hesitated at the shimmering hole, sniffing, but Cries Havoc didn't seem to care. He went through. His cry was cut off by a splashing sound, as if something big hit water. Before anyone could react, the bridge began to fade, and everyone felt themselves drawn down by gravity's pull.

"Shit!" was all Carlita could say before hitting the water herself and plunging into its cool depths. They all struggled to stay afloat in the midst of a large, rushing river. North Wind's Son was handling it best; he had shifted to Lupus form and was making his way to the nearest shore. The others followed suit when they realized wolf forms were best. Even in her native wolf form, however, Storm-Eye did not have an easy time of it. She was the last to reach the shore, finally dragging herself up with the four other wet wolves onto the sandy banks.

Coughing and sputtering—and shaking off sprays of water—they gulped for breath and tried to get their bearings.

They were in a park or beach of some sort. They could see buildings nearby, and larger ones across the bank, where lights glowed on many streets and from a number of buildings—a city of some sort, very

European by the look of the architecture. The buildings nearby were dark, and looked like hotels. The city was on the other side of a large bridge that spanned the distance not too far from the spot they had clambered onto.

"Aargh," Cries Havoc groaned, shifting into Homid form. "I'll never be dry again."

"Tell me about it," Carlita said, wriggling her finger in her now-human ear, trying to work out some moisture. "Where the hell are we? Belgrade?"

"I don't know," Cries Havoc said. "There's a sign over by the bridge."

"Can you read Serbian?" North Wind's Son said.

"No, but if it's Belgrade, it should at least say so in Roman letters."

North Wind's Son nodded and wrung out his jacket.

Storm-Eye had shifted into human form. She spoke, a note of concern in her voice: "Julia?"

They all looked at Julia, who sat on the ground in human form, shivering, clutching her shoulders.

"Yo, girl," Carlita said, stepping over to her. "You all right?"

Julia nodded. "Yes. I'll be fine. It's just… I saw into the Penumbra as we fell. Thank Gaia we landed in the material world. I don't think we would have survived the Umbral Tisza."

"What did you see?" North Wind's Son asked.

"It's a raging torrent, like the worst storm imaginable. It's practically flooding the banks. Oh, sweet Gaia, the bodies. Hundreds of spirit corpses and toxins— boiling, green and purple oil slicks. All heading downriver as if drawn to the world's biggest open drain."

"Holy shit," Carlita said. "How do we fight that?"

No one answered. Storm-Eye headed toward the bridge, saying, "Follow."

They did. When they reached the road, they could see a sign: Belvarosi, obviously the name of the bridge. Another word: Szeged.

Julia pulled out her PDA and turned it on. "At least my fetish is waterproof." She pulled up her geography index and wrote out Szeged with her stylus. It brought up an entry: Hungary.

"Well, it's not Serbia," she said. "But we're awfully close. Serbia's not far south of here."

"Let's keep going," Cries Havoc said. "There's got to be some clue as to why we were dropped in the river instead of at the caern. Who's running the caern, anyway?"

"Didn't you listen?" Carlita said. "Maybe nobody. It could be abandoned."

"Then why is it still capable of receiving a moon bridge?" North Wind's Son said.

"I don't know," Julia said. "Maybe it was left open before its owners left. Or maybe someone is still at the helm."

"Then why dunk us?" Cries Havoc said.

"Let's look for them and find out," Julia said, placing her PDA back in her pocket and ambling onto the bridge. The others followed.

As they reached the center of the bridge, Cries Havoc stopped and looked around, perplexed. The others stopped and looked back at him.

"I heard something call my name," Cries Havoc said. "But I don't see anything."

Julia cocked her head. "I hear something, too, but it doesn't sound like a name. It's coming... from the Umbra. Something's crying loud enough for us to hear it in the material world."

"Then we need to step sideways and see it," North Wind's Son said.

"Oh, no," Julia said. "You didn't see the river over there!"

"We are Garou! We must be prepared to handle whatever is here. Something called for Cries Havoc. We must see what it is."

"Yes," Storm-Eye said, staring resolutely at Julia.

Julia nodded. "Okay. I'll guide us in." She withdrew her PDA again and turned it on. She did something to the screen and its plastic surface became a silver mirror. The others gathered around her, each holding onto an arm, shoulder or part of her suit jacket. She stared into the mirror, into the reflection of her own eyes, as if searching for something. "All right… hold on… I see it…."

The world grew pale around them as Julia stepped sideways, drawing herself and her pack into the spirit world.

A crash of thunderous river spray drenched them. The river tumultuously leaped from its course to crash over the bridge, drenching the pack in its sickly, oily water. They clutched the railing to keep from getting knocked over the side and into the raging flow.

They could all see the horror that Julia had described before. The river was thick with corpses, bloated animal carcasses and acid-eaten fish. Green and purple oil swirled into its eddies like paint pouring from some unseen sky.

They all heard clearly now a deep, resonate voice begin to speak. As it did, another great wave struck the bridge, deafening the pack with its roar. As the water sloshed away, a screech broke through the stagnant air.

"Look!" Cries Havoc cried as loudly as he could, pointing into the sky. A flock of bats circled above them. They each bore a long, whipping, barbed tail, creating a net of slashing blades as they circled down in unison.

"I know these things!" Cries Havoc cried. "They were mentioned in a tale I heard once by the Dawntreader's side..."

Before he could finish his message, one of the bats broke from the flock and darted down straight at him like a missile. Before the Child of Gaia could react, the bat's tail whipped about him, trapping his arms at his side. Cries Havoc fell to the ground.

The pack leaped forward to help their fallen, but the other bats now descended, barbed tails whipping through the air, seeking out the running Garou. Storm-Eye howled as two tails slashed into her. She tried to shift to Lupus to escape them, but they were too quick, ensnaring even her wolf form, their barbs cutting deeply and painfully into her fur.

North Wind's Son tried to sever the tails with his claws, but a new tail, borne by another bat, snatched him and almost lifted him from the bridge. Only his struggling kept him on the ground.

Carlita and Julia evaded a wall of whipping tails and reached Cries Havoc just as the bat's jaws tore at Cries Havoc's ear. Julia reached to swat it, but a tail appeared out of nowhere and grabbed her arm, pulling it up and away. She struggled to reach Cries Havoc with her other arm, but the tail tugged her whole body back.

The bat began pulling a glowing, liquid taffy from Cries Havoc's ear. Carlita, dodging another group of tails, wanted to wretch just watching it, but she slashed at the bat with her claws. It tumbled back, screeching, half of the taffy disappearing down its gullet, the other half slipping back into Cries Havoc's ear.

The bat jumped forward again, and Carlita reached for her fang dagger, but the tails won the bout. Her leg was snatched from under her and her chin smacked the pavement. Dazed and dragged backwards, she saw the bat once more root into Cries Havoc's ear.

A heavy shape leaped over her and onto the bat. The bat squawked as the new shape struggled with it, its hairy claws digging into its feathers. Purple, sickly blood sprayed across the bridge as the two struggled.

Carlita blinked and came out of her daze. The figure grasping the bat was a Crinos form Garou, large and black, its fur flecked with gray.

The bat slipped from the Garou's hands and into the air. It screeched and dove for the safety of the river. Its mates cried out and followed it, their tails loosening from the others, but not without leaving raking trails of blood as their barbs tore free. They soon disappeared from sight in the darkness over the Tisza.

The Garou, purple blood covering his hands, shifted into human form. He wore a stained, brown coat and looked as if he hadn't shaved in years. His black beard reached practically to his waist, as did his hair. He looked at the pack in bewilderment, as if unsure what to do next. "Americans?" he said in accented English.

"Yeah," Carlita said, standing up and heading over to Cries Havoc. "Who're you?"

"I am Halászlé. Welcome to Szeged."

"I heard them speak," Storm-Eye said, picking herself up from the ground. "The bats, I mean. I know what they said—'Secrets! These ones hold secrets! A feast of secrets!'"

"What does that mean?" Julia said, examining the tears that the tails had made in her business suit, now stained with her own blood. "What secrets?"

"I don't know," Carlita said, kneeling over Cries Havoc's body, "but I can't wake Cries Havoc up. That thing took a bite out of him somehow. Maybe he's poisoned." The fallen Garou was completely still, as if deep in sleep.

"My mother," said the strange Garou who had called himself Halászlé (it sounded like *hal*-aas-lay), "she is a *boszorkány*. She may be able to help him. Please, if you carry him, I can guide you to her. But we must leave the Umbra!"

Julia quickly stood beside Cries Havoc. The others touched her, including Halászlé, who looked around them worried that something else would leap from the river before they could be gone. Within seconds, however, Julia pulled them back into the material world, the glow from her PDA's screen lighting up her face.

Here, the river was calm and the night silent. No distant roar or bat screech could be heard. At this hour, no cars passed by.

North Wind's Son and Carlita bent down together to lift Cries Havoc. His human form wasn't heavy, but they both shifted into Glabro forms for the extra strength. Halászlé led them to the far side of the bridge, into the city center of Szeged. He guided them through the old streets down Hid utca, toward the Jewish Quarter. A mixture of classical and baroque buildings gave the city a grand aesthetic.

Storm-Eye, still in wolf form, sniffed the air and looked about suspiciously. She then looked back to them and continued on. "It is nothing. I thought I smelled the river, but it was just the breeze."

"It travels far here," Halászlé said. He led them on.

"So what the hell were those bats? And where did you come from?" Carlita said.

"I don't know what they were," Halászlé said. "I have seen them before, and I was very afraid. They come from downriver, where evil now lives. As for me, I heard something call my name from the spirit world. I resisted, but curiosity overcame me. I meant to only peek, but then I saw you and those things."

"Cries Havoc heard something too," Carlita said. "That's why we went over. Some chump Wyrm thing must have been messing with our heads."

"Evil is very strong here, these days," Halászlé said.

"I'm sorry we haven't said it before," Julia said, "but thank you for your help. Are you a member of the caern here?"

Halászlé frowned as if he did not understand the question. "Caern, you say? There is no caern here. Only a few of us Garou, living however we can."

"But we just came by moon bridge. We were dropped into the river."

Halászlé eyes widened. "Oh, that caern. I begin to understand. I didn't think it still worked. But since you are here, I suppose it must."

"Hold on," North Wind's Son said. "You mean you know there's a caern here but you don't use it?"

"That is true. We dare not risk it. The pathstone, you see, it is buried somewhere in the river. The river, it is tainted now. Cyanide poisoning from far upstream. We don't dare go into it to search for the pathstone. So, we leave it be. It is a cursed caern anyway."

"How is that?" Julia asked. "Is it Wyrm-tainted?"

"Oh, no. Not yet, at least. Perhaps soon. For now, it resists. But the Shadow Lords, they who built it long ago—" he stopped to look them each over, as if wondering what their tribal allegiances were, "—cursed it before losing it to the Silver Fangs. It brought many a flood to the Tisza until the Fangs gave it up after the Great Flood last century. Since then, no Garou has claimed it."

"Excuse me," Julia said. "I don't mean to be rude, but we need to know this, I suppose: What tribe are you?"

"Me? Oh, I… uh, I am what you call a Bone Gnawer." He seemed ashamed to say it.

"No kidding?!" Carlita said. "So am I! I didn't know there were any of us here."

Halászlé looked at her in surprise, his eyes scanning up and down over her tough body. "You? You seem… confidant. We are not like that here. How is that you are not cowed among the other tribes?"

"Cowed? Me? That'll be the day. How is it that you *are*? You let them push you around?"

"Well, it is hard to stand up to the Shadow Lords."

"They giving you trouble? Your fight is my fight, brother."

"No! No, they are not here," he said, waving his hands as if to indicate the city around them. "They are in Budapest. That is where I originally come from. They did not like me there, so I came here, with others of my kind. Mother Sárköz, she took us in."

"So this isn't your actual mother you're taking us to?" Julia said.

"No, she is our leader. She is eldest Bone Gnawer among us."

"Huh," Carlita said. "We call our elders 'mother' also. Or 'father.'"

Halászlé smiled at that and was silent for a while. They passed a city park, a regal place of trees towering over monuments and statues.

"Széchenyi tér," he said. "We sleep there sometimes, when the weather is good. Botond, the restaurant there," he pointed to a place on the corner with outdoor seating, closed now at the late hour, "it is where a Glass Walker named Nagy Pénz can often be found."

He took them across the street to their left and then back up a new street in the same direction they had been traveling. He pointed to a square with two large synagogues, one in an older classical style, the other built in amazing Art Nouveau style. "It is not far. Just down the street from here."

"By the way," Carlita said. "I'm Big Sis. You got an interesting name, Halászlé. Does it mean anything?"

"Ah, yes. My name means Fish Soup."

North Wind's Son could not suppress a chuckle. Carlita frowned at him, but Halászlé seemed pleased that he had brought humor to the group.

"Are you not going to ask why we are here?" Storm-Eye said.

"I am curious, yes, but that is Mother's question to ask."

He brought them to a row house in a shabbier district than they had come from, but it still looked sturdy and well kept. He rapped on the door with a quick series of short and long knocks performed so fast that no one in the pack was sure he or she could repeat it.

A small window in the middle of the door slid open. Two eyes peered out, buried in ancient skin cracked with wrinkles. They seemed to nod, and the window slid shut. The pack heard the sound of a lock being undone, and the door swung open. A large Hungarian woman stood in the tight hallway. "Come, come." She motioned them in with an impatient gesture.

As soon as they entered, she shut the door and locked it again. She pointed them down the hall to a sitting room adjoining a kitchen. They carefully carried Cries Havoc down the narrow hall and into the room, placing him on a couch.

Halászlé spoke to the old lady in Hungarian. They seemed to have a short argument, but it ended with Halászlé smiling and mother disappearing into the kitchen. "She is getting her herbs. She will help your friend."

The old woman soon came out of the kitchen with a tray of steaming tea and an old leather bag. The tea she placed on the table, speaking to Halászlé, who then scrambled to pour it into teacups. The bag she took over the Cries Havoc. She leaned over him, lifting one of his eyelids and peering within. She muttered something that sounded like an expletive and fished through the bag for a wad of herbs. She set them on his chest. She pulled out another handful, a different herb this time, and dropped it straight into the oil lamp on a stand by the couch. The herbs immediately began burning, filling the room with a stench.

"Ugh!" Julia said. "It smells awful."

Mother spoke as she sat down in a chair by the table, accepting a cup of tea from Halászlé.

"Mother says it is good for him," Halászlé said, handing cups of tea all around. "She has seen his sickness before, and says there is no cure, but herbs will calm his soul."

"No cure?" North Wind's Son said. "Is she sure? There's got to be something we can do."

Halászlé translated, and then Mother spoke, in broken English. "No cure. I never see a cure. But this is new. Who knows? I only see humans suffer it, not Garou. Maybe he will heal."

"Thank you for trying," Julia said. "We greatly appreciate it."

Mother waved her hand dismissively. "Trying? I could do nothing. Do not thank me."

She looked around the room at them, seeming to size them up one by one. "Are you hungry? I have pot of *halpaprikás* on stove."

Halászlé whined, looking almost like he was salivating. "It is my favorite. Fish soup with paprika!"

"Then I'll have some," Carlita said. "We all will."

Mother got no resistance from the others. A few minutes later, they were sitting or standing around the room, each nursing a bowl of fish soup and loving it. It had been hours since they last eaten, and this spicy concoction tasted wonderful. When asked about it, Mother said only: "Is special recipe. Taught by paprika spirits." She was then lost in a fit of laughing.

"Mother is only kidding," Halászlé said. "Every-one knows paprika spirits are stingy and do not share their secrets easily."

None of them could tell whether Halászlé was joking.

"Halászlé," Mother said. "You are rude. Show me your friends."

"Ah," Halászlé said. "Of course. My friends, this is Mother Sárköz. Please, introduce yourselves."

Carlita realized that, except for her, they hadn't told Halászlé their names yet. He had placed a lot of trust in them without even know-ing their names or tribal affiliations. She introduced herself first, emphasizing that she was a fellow Bone Gnawer, which seemed to impress Mother. Then the others introduced themselves, each telling their name and tribe.

Mother seemed most interested in John North Wind's Son. "Wendigo? I have never seen Wendigo before. Never in Hungary is there Wendigo. Welcome."

North Wind's Son bowed. "Thank you. If all here are as hospitable and generous, I will consider Hungary a great nation among the Garou."

Mother smiled, but it was an uneasy smile. "You flatter. But you do not know Shadow Lords here well. You will."

Storm-Eye shifted into human form and began to speak: "We are on an important mission for the Grand Concolation overseen by the Margrave Yuri Konietzko." Mother's eyes narrowed as she said this, but she did not interrupt. "A great evil is awaken-ing in Serbia, and it is powered by the tainted Tisza River. It is called 'Jo.' We have come to stop it."

Mother let out a hiss at the mention of the name. "It is good you do not know its full name! We are too close to it. Even hearing its name spoken gives it strength."

"So you know about it?" Julia said. "Can you tell us where to find it?"

Mother looked at Julia as if she were a mad woman who had somehow come into her home. "Why would you do this? You are cub! Why is Konietzko not here?"

"He has other troubles to handle," North Wind's Son said. "Besides, we are part of a prophecy, a third pack that will succeed where two others failed. Uktena has bonded us to this purpose."

Mother shook her head, obviously impatient with them. "Cubs. You do not know what this is. Uktena? I hear of Uktena, mighty river spirit. But he is far and the Tisza is near. He has no children here. How can he help the Tisza? With prophecy? No prophecy knows what this is. It is ancient thing. Even ancestors forget this thing. I know only because I talk to creatures that flee from its waking place. Rats, birds, bugs—they know better. They run from it."

"You don't understand," Julia said. "We don't have a choice. This is the duty we've been given by the Garou Nation."

Mother began speaking in Hungarian, a long stream of words spat angrily forth. She ended by turning away from the pack and staring into the flickering light of the oil lamp, as if remembering something from long ago.

Halászlé nervously spoke as if he didn't want to disturb the scene any further. "Uh, she says that the Garou Nation is full of fools and always has been. She mentioned specific names, but I don't think I need to translate those. Mainly local Garou, anyway. However, she says she will help you, although she has seen too many cubs sent to their deaths to enjoy doing so."

"Thanks, Mother," Carlita said. "You aren't the first Bone Gnawer elder to reluctantly help a bunch of cubs who want to get themselves killed. My own elder didn't want to send me here, but she didn't really have much choice. That isn't what it's all about, anyway. There aren't any choices for any of us here. Not you, not us. Not as Garou."

Mother nodded and seemed resolved to the matter. "I will summon others. All in the area. A moot. There you can ask about the beast and where to find it."

"Um," Julia said, sheepishly. "Can I ask you about the caern we came in at? The one that seems abandoned. The Garou who sent us here seemed to think it was associated with Attila the Hun and some old treasure of the Shadow Lords."

Halászlé rolled his eyes. "Treasure! If there were such a thing, it would have been found long ago. Do you know how many Shadow Lords have combed this area since the Silver Fangs left, searching for it?"

"It was taken away," Mother said. "Before the Silver Fangs came. Removed to Serbia, and hidden there with other secrets. Beware secret things—if left unwatched, they fester and become poison."

"Great," Carlita said. "Maybe it's buried wherever Jo—uh, you know, that Wyrm thing—is buried."

"It doesn't concern us," North Wind's Son said. "We are here for one thing only: to destroy the evil that has awakened."

No one had anything further to add. They each fell silent, thinking about what to do next. Cries Havoc could be dying, for all they knew, and they had no way to help him. If Mother's medicine didn't do the trick, what could?

"Sleep," Mother said. "You need sleep. I have extra bed upstairs. And blankets for the floor."

Storm-Eye was already back in her wolf form, and she curled up before the couch, as if guarding Cries Havoc. Before she put her head down, she looked at her packmates.

"Downriver," she said. "Soon."

They all knew what that meant. They had to travel on foot to Serbia, to the heart of the Wyrm-beast itself. And they would have to do so without Cries Havoc.

* * *

There was a knock at the door. Mother was just then climbing the stairs after making sure the pack had all the blankets it needed. Carlita could see that she wasn't happy to hear someone at the door. The old Bone Gnawer hesitated, as if considering whether to answer it, but she then came back down the stairs and peered out the tiny window. She looked puzzled, but unlocked the door and opened it.

She spoke in Hungarian, something that sounded like a question, and then opened the door wider and stepped halfway onto the landing, looking around puzzled. She shrugged and closed the door, locking it again.

Halászlé, watching her from the floor on the kitchen, asked her something. She responded with another shrug and then headed for the stairs. She stopped before getting there, looking down at the floor and grimacing.

"What's going on?" Carlita said. "Who was at the door?"

"Nobody," Halászlé said. "Whoever knocked ran away."

Mother was looking at her shoe and glaring angrily at the floor. Carlita stood up and moved into the hallway. There was a wide puddle of water covering the front of the hall. Mother stood in its midst, obviously unhappy.

"Where'd that water come from?" Carlita said.

"Water?" Halászlé said, getting up from the kitchen floor and coming into the hall. He saw the puddle and stared at it for a moment, as if he had never seen water before. Then his eyes widened and he yelled something at Mother. Startled, the old Bone Gnawer leaped onto the stairway, out of the water.

As she did, the puddle moved. It sloshed under Carlita and Halászlé, flowing into the sitting room. Carlita spun around and saw the water rise up toward the ceiling, taking shape and form like something from a cheap *Terminator* remake.

Its shape wasn't human. It looked like a cross between a spiked and finned fish and a Crinos-form Garou. Its bulbous eyes stared at the pack and its mouth gasped for air, but it somehow didn't appear to be asphyxiating. Then, in an instant, quick as lightning, it leaped toward the couch and onto Cries Havoc.

Storm-Eye was on it in a flash, her jaws clamping onto its neck. The thing was clearly not strong enough to resist the violent throating the wolf delivered, but instead of falling or even bleeding, it melted back into a wide puddle, sloshing across the floor of the room.

North Wind's Son, now in Crinos form—almost too tall for the ceiling—slashed the water with his claws, but they simply passed through without affecting the liquid in any obvious way.

Julia leaped onto a chair and yelled: "Everybody out of the water! I've got an idea!"

Carlita backed down the hallway, tugging Halászlé with her, until they were by the stairway, their feet no longer touching the wetness. North Wind's Son shifted to wolf form and joined Storm-Eye on the couch.

As soon as North Wind's Son was out of the water, Julia reached into her pocket and pulled out a black plastic rectangular item with two metal nubs on one end—an electric stun gun. She dipped it in the water and pulled a trigger. Sudden arcs of electricity shot through the room, conducted throughout the entire puddle in an instant.

The water dried up, becoming vapor. The mist dissipated around the room. Everyone could hear a fading scream from somewhere far away, as something died in the spirit world and cried out in its final agony loud enough to be heard in the material world.

Mother, standing on the stairs, waved a fist at its remains, her thumb held up between her first and middle fingers.

"It came from the Tisza," Halászlé said, leaning against the wall and reaching into his coat for a cigarette, his hands shaky. "I have seen one before. I call it a Flood Bane. For it to come here, so far from the river, things are much worse than even *I* thought." He swallowed and tried to spark his lighter, which seemed to be out of fluid. Nonetheless, a flame soon welled up, and he took a long drag on his cigarette.

"We were driven from Budapest," he said, now more in control after a hit of nicotine. "We will not be driven from Szeged. Here we stand. I will help you hunt the source of this thing, and kill it so that the river may flow peacefully again."

Chapter Nine

The Garou of Szeged came together in a class-room on the Attila Jószef Science University campus. It seemed that a Garou—a Fianna, if it could be believed—was a professor there, teaching poetry. Mihaly Long-Ear was one of the rare members of the Celtic tribe whose ancestors stilled lived in Hungary and occasionally produced a Garou offspring. An expert in Hungarian folkways, he was an old friend of Mother Sárköz and readily arranged for an empty classroom for those few times she called moots.

He greeted the pack when they arrived, making a show of his interest in each one of them, seemingly fascinated to host Americans. Julia went out of her way to make it clear she was British.

"I have a fetish here that will prove most useful for you," he said in very good English as he produced a stick painted with some sort of faded ochre coloring and tied with a few bird feathers on top and bottom. "This will allow you to understand the others when they speak Hungarian. All you need to do is hold it, and anything they say, you will understand, and anything you say, they will understand."

"What a great idea," Julia said. "I hadn't even considered the language barrier for the moot. But why not just speak the Garou tongue?"

"There are other classes going on here today. We don't wish to disturb them with growling noises."

"So why have the moot here? Why not somewhere less crowded?"

"In Szeged? There is the country, yes, but we all prefer to stay in the city. Besides," he said, looking around to be sure none of the guests had arrived before he spoke further, "in such a crowded place, few will risk initiating dangerous challenges. Mother can more easily control arguments that way."

"I hadn't thought about it. That's subtle planning for such an old lady."

"You don't get to be old without gaining some wisdom. Ah, here is gracious Nagy Pénz, right on time!"

Mihaly broke away to greet a conspicuously tall and well-groomed man. Halászlé, standing with the pack, whispered to them about the newcomer. This was Nagy Pénz—"Big Money"—a Glass Walker from Budapest who preferred the eclectic charm of Szeged over what he believed was the overcrowded metropolis of Hungary. He was an art financier, helping to stock the local museum with rare pieces. He was also one of the best-dressed Garou anyone in the pack had ever seen. He was decked out in the height of European style: expensive, custom-cut suit and shining leather shoes. Rather than greet the pack, Pénz chose to take a seat, just as the rest of the group arrived.

Mareen Scents-Evil was a Get of Fenris from Kiskunság National Park to the west. She was a radical Green Party environmentalist who had come from Germany a number of years ago to try to kickstart Hungary's own environmental conscience. She was dressed in the functional local style of farmers and outdoorsmen.

Also here were two Shadow Lords, István and János, both come all the way from Hortobágy National Park in the north. They were *gulyások*—cowboys. They were devoted to protecting wildlife on the vast range of the steppe *puszta*. Otherwise, they resembled typical Shadow Lords—sullen and withdrawn, watching all the others in the room as if they were sizing them up as potential rivals.

Halászlé whispered that the two Shadow Lords were renegades of sorts from their own tribe. They refused to deal with the Sept of the Night Sky, disagreeing with its supposedly lax policy on protecting Hungary's environment. They instead agreed to aid Mother Sárköz in return for her aid whenever they asked it, which they had never yet done.

Halászlé had accompanied the pack and Mother from the small house, but only after the arrival of Szabó and Ferenc, his two Bone Gnawers friends in the city. They had come with him from Budapest and enjoyed their new home much better. Szabó was a street busker, singing Hungarian folk songs on sidewalks for money, while Ferenc was a taxi driver. They swore to guard Cries Havoc with their lives while the others went to the moot. In case more Flood Banes tried to enter the house, Julia had given them her stun gun. Nonetheless, they were fully prepared to flee with Cries Havoc in Ferenc's taxicab if it became necessary.

"Please, Mother," Nagy Pénz said, glancing at his pocket watch, "can we start this meeting? I do have other matters to attend."

"Nothing is more important," Mother said. "Our fate is to be decided here."

The others sat straighter in their chairs at this, all of them looking from one to the other, and then all staring at the strange new pack. *If Cries Havoc were here*, Carlita thought, *he'd be squirming now*. She realized that Mother spoke a lot better now;

her vocabulary was greater. Carlita wondered what the trick was until she remembered that she—along with the rest of the pack—was clutching the stick fetish that allowed her to understand Hungarian.

"This is the Pack that Runs in the Silver River," Mother said, addressing the whole room. "They come from America, but they are sent by the concolation at the Anvil-Klaiven. They come with the knowledge and blessing of Margrave Konietzko."

The two Shadow Lords nodded gravely, obviously taking the matter much more seriously now that Konietzko's name had been invoked. Mareen, the Get of Fenris, also looked more concerned at the mention of the Anvil-Klaiven sept. Even Nagy Pénz looked impressed.

"We all know the taint that has infected the Tisza in the last few years. The cyanide poisoning from Romania is only the most obvious sign in the physical world. The spirit world is worse. There, river spirits are devoured by the river itself, which flows like a storm-driven flood to the south, to Serbia, to a beast that awakens and calls to it.

"It is not the river spirit that responds, but the Banes that infect it, possessing its flow for their own corrupt uses. For too long, we have ignored this, too sure of our own smallness to act. What can we do? How can we stop it? These are questions with no easy answers, and so we have stopped asking them.

"No longer. Last night, this pack arrived from Spain by moon bridge."

A murmur went through the room.

"What bridge?" Nagy Pénz demanded. "How did they open a bridge to Szeged, that has no caern?"

"It does have a caern," Mother said. "One we thought long lost and forsaken. They arrived above the Tisza River, through a bridge to the Korös caern."

"Impossible!" István yelled, rising from his seat. "If it were still functioning, the Shadow Lords would know!"

"Not true!" Mother yelled, staring him down. "Your own ancestors bound spirits there to keep the Magyars and Kavars from finding it, and then their ancestors used the same spirits to foil the Angevin Silver Fangs. The caern knows how to keep its secrets, even from its own kind."

István sputtered, but had no response. János tugged István's pants leg, bidding him to sit down. He stared at the pack but his expression was unreadable.

"If this is true," Nagy Pénz said, "we must work now to reclaim it."

The room fell silent. Everyone seemed to contemplate this statement.

"What did he say that's so meaningful?" Julia whispered to Halászlé.

"Everyone knows his meaning: We must take the caern before Konietzko hears of it."

The pack members looked at each other, obvious guilt on their faces. They brought more than word of Jo'cllath'mattric to Szeged—political turmoil came with them.

"We cannot," Mother simply said, after giving everyone enough time to figure the issue out for themselves. "The river is corrupt, and the pathstone lies within it, impossible to reach without risking our lives. Is a caern worth that?"

"Yes," Mareen said. "Easily. We are fleeting, a caern is everlasting—as this pack has shown us."

"Um… Mother?" Carlita said, tired of being a passive observer.

Mother looked at her, obviously waiting for her to continue her question.

"I appreciate the decisions you have to make and all, but we have a mission here. We can't wait much longer."

Mother nodded. "I am aware. How could I forget? Yes, it is time to tell the others of it."

All eyes were on the pack again. Nagy Pénz and the two Shadow Lords' gazes were suspicious, while Mareen and Mihaly's seemed expectant.

"The pack has come to seek the source of the corruption," Mother said. "They hunt a beast I fear to name, but I must say it so you will know: Jo'cllath'mattric."

The response was confusion rather than fear, except for Mihaly's sharp intake of breath. Obviously, the name wasn't well known here to anyone but the folkways professor and Mother. "It is something very old that now awakens," Mother said. "I can say little else, for so much has been forgotten. Should it become free… it will be terrible for us all. Perhaps it is the Apocalypse itself."

"I have heard Konietzko speak of it," Janós said. "He has known for some time of its awakening and has tried to destroy the Wyrm's servitors before they, too, became aware. What has transpired that a pack of cubs now comes to fight it?"

"We were chosen," Storm-Eye said, in her human form, holding the stick like the others. "A prophecy told by Antonine Teardrop at the Anvil-Klaiven concolation foretold the need for our pack, and Uktena has bonded us. We come not because we are fools, but because it is our duty."

János nodded, seeming to have gained somewhat more respect for the pack. He leaned back in his seat and said no more.

"Tomorrow, the Silver River Pack must travel down the Tisza seeking the source of its taint," Mother said, "to the Hellhole that sends power to the beast in Serbia. We must help them however we can."

"I have already pledged to go with them," Halászlé said. "I will not be driven from this place."

"This is very brave," István said. "For a Bone Gnawer. I mean no disrespect, but you have little to lose. Szeged is not our home. We have spent much time defending the *puszta* from the Tisza's blight. We cannot risk leaving now to chase something that even Konietzko will not fight himself. Who will then defend the *puszta*?"

"Your beloved steppe will fall like the rest of the world," Mareen said, standing up angrily, "if the threat is not stopped before it rises." She looked at the pack. "I honor you for your courage, but I must say this—if you are fated to do this by prophecy, then you will either succeed or not. I do not see how more warriors will aid what is already an undermanned mission. Are we to all die throwing ourselves down this thing's gullet? Why not join Konietzko's army instead and stand before it with a true chance of winning?"

Nobody answered. Even the pack could not respond. They knew their mission had the thinnest of chances. What right did they have to ask others to risk themselves for a prophecy that concerned only the pack?

Mother spoke: "You must decide however you will. I cannot—I will not—sway your choice. I only say that Gaia watches us all at this moment, and sees how her children choose. I tell you my role in this—I will stay in Szeged, for I am too old to travel far, and do what I can to keep the Tisza from drowning us all."

The others were lost in thought, each deciding how to react to the momentous choice.

"I will stay in Szeged," Nagy Pénz said. "I have nothing to contribute in Serbia. I must defend this city, especially if there is still a caern here."

"I doubt I would prove any use to you," Mihaly said to the pack, looking guilty. "I fear my days of long travel on foot are behind me. I will do what I can to help you prepare for the journey."

"Again, I honor your courage," Mareen said, stepping to the pack to meet each of their eyes. "But I will not aid you. If fate has chosen you for the role, what role is there for me? I am not sworn to Uktena, but to Fenris. I shall join Konietzko's forces and prepare to combat what may follow from your mission—praying to Gaia that it succeeds."

István and János sat thinking a while longer before finally shaking their heads. "We shall not go. Our duty is in the north. Whatever you do in Serbia shall surely rile the Tisza spirit and send trouble upriver all the way to us. We shall make our stand there and fight it. If you, by some chance, do succeed, know that your names will resound with glory in our howls."

They stood up and headed for the door. János stopped and looked at Storm-Eye. "Regardless of what happens next, know that you stand high in my regard." The two then left.

Mareen also exited, looking guilty but also sad, as if she pitied the pack and wished she could take their place.

Nagy Pénz stood and straightened his suit. "Thank you, Mother, for calling us here. We do not gather often enough. If there is anything you need from me, do not hesitate to call. I will prepare what defense I can for the spirits of this city, so long beleaguered by the river, both blessed and angry." He nodded to the pack and left the room.

Mother sighed and shrugged. "I expected no different. We are too few here. If there were more young, they would clamber to join the crusade. Alas, we are all so old here." She sat down in a chair and closed her eyes.

Halászlé tapped Carlita's shoulder and motioned to the rest of the pack. "Come, let us go outside, into the air. I will show you the city on the one day we have left of it."

The pack placed their stick on a desk, thanked the professor, and followed Halászlé from the room.

* * *

After the sound of their footsteps was gone, Mihaly turned to Mother. "What will you do now?"

"What I hoped I would not have to do, but fear that I now have no choice but to do. I will contact Konietzko and tell him of the Korös caern."

"That will only cause him to send Shadow Lords down here to claim it."

Mother sighed. "I know. But who else could possibly rescue it from the Tisza now? Poor Nagy Pénz lusts for the caern, but his city spirits are not powerful enough to resist the Tisza and deliver the pathstone. No, only Konietzko's sept is so strong."

"Remember what they did to Halászlé? They will force him to move again."

"We shall see. We shall see."

Chapter Ten

As Halászlé showed the pack around Szeged, the daytime light afforded them a good look at the people of the city. Near the university, it was mainly the young, dressed the way late teens and young adults do in most European cities these days—which is to say, much like Americans. As they moved away from the university, they saw more of the working locals—well-dressed businessmen and women, and more functionally dressed delivery drivers and laborers. And, of course, tourists from all over Europe and even America.

Not far from the university was the Dóm tér, a huge square flanked by gothic churches, columns, busts and statues. It was noon, and they could hear a wonderful chiming nearby. Halászlé laughed. "Just in time for the music clock. See?" He pointed across the square to a water fountain with moving figures, the source of the music. Tourists flocked about it as it chimed its midday notice. Halászlé seemed disappointed when this only evoked faint smiles from the pack. "Let's go this way, to the museum." They followed without comment, each seemingly lost in his or her own troubled thoughts.

As they left the square, Carlita watched a group of American tourists with children, laughing at the clock's moving figures. She envied their ignorance of the war going on around them in the spirit world but also hated it. If they knew about the Wyrm, they wouldn't do things to keep feeding it.

Halászlé led them up a large thoroughfare crowded on both sides with classical and baroque buildings, mainly shops and banks. The museum itself sat in an area of greenery on the banks of the river, almost directly across from the shore they had all dragged themselves onto the previous night.

Julia stopped and looked around at the parkland. "Hey, Halászlé? Can we just wander around out here for a while? I don't feel like being inside a musty museum today."

"Okay, sure," Halászlé said, shrugging. "I just want to show you around. I thought you might like the museum. Most Americans come to it."

"Well, we're not your normal tourists," Carlita said. "But thanks anyway."

"Let's go up to Széchenyi tér," Halászlé said. "It's my favorite place. We passed it the other night, but you can see it better in the day."

They all nodded and followed him the few blocks to the large inner city park, stretching for a number of blocks away from their corner. Halászlé led them to a bench under the chestnut trees, in view of the beautiful, bright yellow town hall. He pointed to two fountains. "The River Tisza—the 'Blessed and the Angry.' She gives and she takes away. Many of these statues commemorate those *kubikosok* who worked to keep her blessed."

"I kinda get the idea it floods a lot, right?" Carlita said.

"Oh, yes," Halászlé said. "It used to. Not in many years, though. I cannot say what will happen if it is not healed soon. I fear to look at it from the Umbra."

"That Flood Bane thing that attacked us," Carlita said. "You said you'd seen one before. What're they all about?"

"I do not know. Not really. I think they represent the river's attempt to flood, to travel beyond its banks. But it cannot. Human technology—the work of these *kubikosok* engineers," he waved his hands at the statues, "keeps the physical river in its place. But in the spirit world, it writhes at the summons from Serbia. It resists, but even its resistance is tainted."

"Maybe it was trying to warn us," Julia said. "Maybe it wasn't trying to hurt Cries Havoc but help him—or even alert us to the Tisza's plight."

Halászlé shook his head. "I doubt that. Maybe once, when its spirits were uncorrupted, but not now. The Tisza is now angry, and wants to drown any who touch it."

"Then we must strive not to touch it tomorrow," John North Wind's Son said. "We have a long journey down its banks, one which we cannot make in the physical world alone. The danger will be great."

"What do you mean?" Carlita said, frowning. "Why can't we just go where we need to go in the material world?"

"How will we know our destination?" North Wind's Son said. "We have to track it down ourselves, by whatever clue it gives us. That won't be in this world, but in the Umbra."

"Oh, shit," Carlita muttered. "But Julia said it was a Hellhole on the other side!"

"I did," Julia said. "But John is right. Maybe downriver, it won't be so bad."

"It can only get worse," North Wind's Son said. "The only way we'll know the source of its corruption is to find it, and that won't be pretty."

Storm-Eye, who had silently and sullenly followed them in human form all the while, spoke: "Why do you talk, talk, talk? We will see it soon enough. Talk will not defeat it any sooner."

That shut them up. They sat uncomfortably on the bench, watching the slight breeze sway the chestnut trees.

"So," Halászlé said, finally breaking the silence. "Who's hungry?"

* * *

The rest of the afternoon and evening were uneventful. They checked back at Mother's to make sure Cries Havoc was okay and saw no change in his condition. Halászlé introduced them to a variety of Hungarian cuisines—*pörkölt* goulash and *gulyásleves* beef soup—and helped them gather packs and provisions for the long walk. Mother gave each of them a tiny leather bag with herbs and claimed the herb's smell would keep their legs from tiring.

And then they curled up in their blankets on the floor of Mother's small house and tried to sleep.

Storm-Eye had no trouble dozing off immediately. There were advantages to being wolf-born, one of them being a decided lack of anxiety about the future. She knew she would need rest for the work to come, and so she got it.

John North Wind's Son likewise had little trouble sleeping. He knew he needed strength, and so prayed to his spirit ancestors and Gaia to bring him refreshing rest. Under such solace, he was soon quietly sleeping, without the slightest snore.

Julia and Carlita had a harder time of it. Each was trying to figure out the best game plan for the next day, but the lack of knowledge made forethought next to impossible. What's more, worry over Cries Havoc and whether he would ever come out of his coma—or even live through it—kept both of them tossing and turning. It was only after Julia realized that the source of a cure for Cries Havoc required confronting the cause—which waited downriver—that she could finally put her worries to rest and sleep.

Carlita was the last to drop off, and even then, her sleep was full of half-nightmares, causing her to start awake many times in the night. Before she could examine the dreams for any spiritual clues, they'd vanish from memory, leaving her to struggle her way back to sleep again.

* * *

They left the next morning. Mother cooked them *palacsinta*—pancakes—and urged them not to worry about Cries Havoc. She would guard him with the help of Szabó and Ferenc, and she swore that she would let any attacker kill her before they harmed a hair on Cries Havoc's body. "I will show them that this old woman still has much fight in her, if they dare to come."

She grasped Halászlé by the shoulders and kissed him on the cheek, saying something to him in Hungarian that had him smiling. She then ushered them out of the house and closed the door behind them— their cue to get a move on.

Halászlé led them down the Semmelweis utca for a ways and then pointed them closer to the river, to follow it along its course southward through the countryside.

It was only a few kilometers to the Serbian border. Halászlé admitted that he had never been there and had no idea whether someone would be guarding the border along the countryside, away from the roads.

"I'm not sure we should risk it," Julia said. "The UN forces, they might actually be watching who goes in and out. I think that'll be our cue to step sideways."

"What?!" Carlita said. "Are you nuts? You remember what happened the last time? We'll be fighting every step of the way."

"No better time to find out than the present," Julia said. "We might as well do it now. It's only going to get worse the deeper we go down the stream. This way, we at least find out what we're up against. C'mon, I'll guide us."

The pack hesitantly gathered around her as she activated her PDA and turned its screen into a mirror. She stared at it as if daydreaming, looking away onto far horizons. The world grew pale around them and faded, matter giving way to the features of the spirit world. They took defensive stances, ready to repel any Bane that had been following them or noticed them from the river.

Nothing.

Although the Tisza roared with a howl as loud as a waterfall crashing right next to them, no creatures were in sight. The river flung itself forward within its banks, wilder and frothier than in the physical world, but certainly calmer than it had been on the night of their arrival. They peered at it, try-ing to discern the things floating on its surface, and then looked away in disgust as they recognized again what they were: spirit corpses, ethereal animal bones whose personalities had been scoured off but were prevented from dissipating to reform elsewhere in the Umbra. Each was a living crypt of sorts, unable to move or act, but nonetheless aware of its own tortured, paralyzed state.

"It's monstrous," Julia cried, shutting her eyes, shouting to be heard over the river roar. "Something that would do that to a spirit is... beyond redemption."

Storm-Eye growled low, desperate to howl her anger and sorrow but afraid of what such a gesture would attract. They had to walk carefully here, lest they too became bones.

North Wind's Son stood still but trembled with anger. He fought to shackle his rage. He controlled it only by promising himself that, as soon as he found what had done this thing, he would let all his anger loose to wreak havoc upon it.

Carlita was more sad than angry. She wanted to help the spirits, but they were carried too quickly down the river, and there were far too many of them. She was no stranger to helplessness in the face of terrible crimes. Her entire tribe knew such frustra-tions intimately.

"Come," Halászlé said. "We should move on. Before anything awakens."

"You think the Banes are sleeping?" Carlita said, following Halászlé along the bank. The others turned their attention away from the Tisza and concentrated on walking.

"Yes. The moon agitates them. They get more furious at night."

Walking the spirit world in the daytime was not usually wise, when the moon was in hiding, allowing all manner of Banes to roam freely, but what Halászlé said made sense. The only reprieve the Banes got from the moon was during the day, and they used the time to replenish their lost energies.

"It's obvious now," Julia said. "Something's pulling at the river, causing it to flow faster than it wants to."

They walked onward, each unnerved by the thunderous sound of the chaotic river, but thankful that nothing leaped from it.

At one point, Storm-Eye stopped and cocked her ear away from the river, as if listening for something. "Do you hear that?"

Everyone stopped and strained to hear any sound besides the river's rushing torrent, but could make out nothing.

"What is it?" Julia said.

Storm-Eye shook her head. "I don't hear it now...."

"Wait!" North Wind's Son said. "Something... there, far off... calling my name."

"Yes," Storm-Eye said. "I thought I heard my name...."

"Oh, shit," Carlita said. "That's what happened the last time, when Cries Havoc got hit by those bats!" She scanned the dark sky for any sign of movement.

"It's gone," North Wind's Son said. "I don't hear it anymore."

"Did the river just get louder?" Carlita said.

No one could be sure. They all stayed there for a while, trying to hear their names again, but the sound of the river drowned out anything else.

"Look," Carlita said. "This is just eerie. Whatever's out there's calling our names, I don't want to answer it."

"You're probably right," Julia said. "Let's just move on."

The rest of them nodded and resumed their march, but even more warily than before. Now, they took turns watching on all sides, in case whatever it was that called them came from a direction other than the river.

After an hour of walking, Carlita urged them to stop again, motioning them closer so she could speak without yelling. "We must be in Serbia now. Is the river bending up ahead?"

"Yeah," Julia said. "I noticed."

"It's heading more westward," North Wind's Son said.

"I don't think it does that in the material world," Halászlé said. "It does bend to the west at some point, but surely not this close to the border."

"It is more than just a bend," Storm-Eye said, staring in the direction of the river. "Something is diverting it on purpose."

They all looked, but could not see so far ahead in the dark. North Wind's Son shifted into Lupus form and stared at the spot Storm-Eye seemed to be watching.

"Yes," he said. "There's something there. Something white."

"Screw this," Carlita said. "I'm not going to be left behind." She shifted into Lupus form herself, and with the keen eyesight of that form, she saw something pale in the distance, something the river was clearly battering itself against.

Julia and Halászlé also shifted into wolf forms, and the pack moved cautiously closer, everyone now on all fours.

As they drew nearer the paleness, it appeared to be a dam of some sort. The Tisza battered against it but couldn't rise above it, and so twisted to its left—westward—and flowed down a new path, different from its physical counterpart. The division of spirit and matter, however, was not accomplished without harm. Where the new river flowed, the water grew black and oily, more like a moving oil slick than a river.

As they approached the dam, they could see that the pale whiteness of it came from the mass of bleached bones piled high and wide across the river's original flow. Thousands of bones, dead animal spirits—fish, birds, even dogs and cats—were placed in a tight foundation that blocked all the Tisza's attempts to smash it.

Still-living spirit fish were flung from the flowing river onto the dam, flopping in pain and agony as they asphyxiated away from the river's wetness.

The pack froze as they watched a shape rise from some hole in the far side of the dam. A misshapen meld between fish and wolf—a Flood Bane—scuttled across the top of the dam to snatch at the stranded fish. It was more substantial here in the spirit world, not simply a shape of sculpted water, but a thing of flesh, fin and scale. As the pack watched, it swallowed the spirit fish whole, gurgling as it slipped into its gullet. It then peered about, seeking more. When no fresh spirits were flung forth from the river, it crept back out of sight into it hole.

Once it was gone, Carlita let out the breath she had been holding. As she did, she caught a whiff of its scent, strong enough to travel across a raging river. It was so rank and rotten that she wanted to stick her nose into the river to wash it off. She knew better than to do that.

John North Wind's Son was the first to speak: "We have to break that dam."

"It's killing the river," Julia says. "It's helping it travel to Jo'cllath'mattric. If we can bust it down, maybe the river will flow right again, and not feed the Wyrm-beast so much power."

"How do we do that without having to fight those things?" Carlita said.

"We can't," Storm-Eye said. "Be prepared to fight. And die, if we must."

"But you saw what happened last time we fought one—we don't all have tasers!"

"This the Umbra," Julia said. "Our claws should be good enough here. Did you notice how this one was more substantial? I could even smell it!"

"There must be a better way," Halászlé whined. "Can't we sneak around the dam and see if there's a weak point? Maybe we can batter it down—or even better, remove part of it so that the rest comes down?"

"It's worth at least looking into," Carlita said. "Before we plan on getting any battle scars, we should at least scout that thing out. We got no idea how many of those things are in that dam."

"I agree," Julia said. "Let's sneak up to it and see what's on the other side before we plan on attacking anything."

Storm-Eye and North Wind's Son nodded. The pack moved off together in a long arc around it, approaching it again from behind. As they got closer, they could see no substantial differences on the back. It was a massive construction of piled bones, with no other features except a dark blotch toward the top that was clearly the hole the Bane had crawled from. It was a fairly large opening, certainly big enough to fit a Crinos-form Garou.

"I say we go in the hole," North Wind's Son said. "There's got to be some weakness within it. It's too thick from this side to simply bust through."

"Hold on there," Carlita said. "Let's think this through. Julia, is it possible to maybe break up some of those bones, cause the spirits to dissipate? Maybe that could cause a chain reaction."

Julia thought about it for a moment. "We could try it, but it might draw attention, and since I don't even know what's causing them to stay in their dead forms, I can't begin to speculate on how to break them—except by claw, perhaps."

"If it fails," Storm-Eye said, "Banes would come and we would never get inside. I say go now, before they know us."

Carlita couldn't see any other option. She'd hoped something else would present itself, but it looked like they had no choice.

Halászlé shivered and hid his face in his hands, shaking his head back and forth, muttering something in Hungarian.

"Hey, calm down," Carlita said, putting her hand on his shoulder. "If we get through this and bust that dam, there'll be lots of fish soup in your future."

"Hah," Halászlé said, peering at her from his hands. "*If* is a pretty big word right now. And after seeing this, I'm thinking maybe I'll change my name...."

"Go," Storm-Eye said. "Now!"

The wolf leaped forward, heading for the dark hole. North Wind's Son was immediately behind her.

Carlita hesitated for only a second, long enough to grab Halászlé's collar and tug him along after the rest of the pack while shifting into Crinos form and reaching for her fang dagger with her other hand.

"C'mon, homeboy! Let's get these dogs some bones!"

Chapter Eleven

Storm-Eye paused only a moment outside the hole to sniff it, and then plunged in. North Wind's Son had no such hesitation, leaping in feet first, wearing his bulky Crinos form. Carlita didn't like being last, but the rest had all leaped forward before her. Julia slipped through the opening in Lupus form just as Carlita reached it, with Halászlé right behind her. He, like Carlita, was also in Crinos form.

As she slipped through the hole and landed in a tunnel below, the others had already formed a defensive wall around the opening. Storm-Eye peered in both directions—right and left—sniffing for clues as to which way they should take.

The floor was covered in puddles, but they seemed full of normal water, not the unformed spirit flesh of a Flood Bane. Halászlé stuck a single claw into one and swished it around, just to be sure. There was no reaction beyond the expected swirl of disturbed liquid.

Storm-Eye moved off to the right, followed by North Wind's Son. Carlita was next, since Julia had fanned out to guard their left flank upon entering the tunnel. She now turned and urged Halászlé on before her, but walked warily, constantly aware of the tunnel behind them.

The roar of the river was more distant now, as if blocked by the mass of bones. Julia risked whispering a message to them over the background thrum and dripping water that seeped through the walls: "I think we're in a sub-realm. This place could be bigger on the inside than out."

The passage sloped downward and ended at an intersection, with new passages going to the right and left. Again, Storm-Eye sniffed the air, seeking scent of the Flood Banes. She then quickly backed up into the original passage and shifted into the dire wolf Hispo form, her hackles rising. The others knew what that meant and prepared to attack whatever came around the corner.

Moments later, a Flood Bane entered their tunnel, its finned feet slapping loudly through the puddles. It stopped when it saw them, its eyes huge and unblinking, its hand waving about in surprise and fear.

Storm-Eye was instantly upon it, her huge dire wolf jaws clamping onto its neck. Her immense weight brought it down to the floor with barely a struggle. A snapping noise echoed through the tunnel and its gesticulating hands stopped moving. Storm-Eye released its neck, which now hung backward at an impossible angle, clearly broken. Its spirit flesh began to vaporize, hanging in the stagnant air for a moment before thinning out into nothingness.

North Wind's Son moved past Storm-Eye and took the lead. He turned left—the direction from which the thing had come—and motioned for them to follow. They crept through the next tunnel, cramped and wet, until it likewise branched, these two new passages both leading downward in opposite directions.

With no apparent clue as to the best route, North Wind's Son went left again, figuring it was easier to retrace their route if they chose a consistent direction. It was pitch black now, and they each relied on their senses to guide them and inform them about one another's location.

"I can't do this anymore," Julia said. "I'm not as well trained at moving in the dark as you Grizzly Adams types." She pulled out her PDA and turned it on. The faint glow from the screen brightened the corridor, providing enough light for them to see one another.

"Keep it in middle," Storm-Eye said in her gruff Hispo-throated voice. "We block it with our bodies."

They moved on, North Wind's Son and Storm-Eye's bulks keeping most of the light from traveling too far ahead of them so that any Banes would not be alerted by the alien intrusion of light.

"I don't see any weakness in these walls," Carlita whispered. "They're just getting stronger. If this is a sub-realm, we may not be able to break it up."

"But we may find out what's keeping the spirits bound to their bones," Julia said.

North Wind's Son halted and motioned with his arm for them to stop. He stood still, sniffing the air, as did Storm-Eye. He then crept forward into what Carlita could now see was a larger room, a circular cave with no passages leading from it—a dead end.

Instead of just bones, however, there were odd, milky white balloons scattered across the floor, piled into groups.

"Ugh," Halászlé said as he entered. "Fish eggs."

Carlita slowly approached one, trying to get a better look. Past the opaque skin of the egg, something squirmed. Something with fins and scales. "The Flood Banes. This is where they hatch."

Storm-Eye could not suppress a growl as she looked at the others and then back at the eggs. They all got her meaning. On cue, when Storm-Eye lunged forward, they each leaped at a separate pod and sliced at it with their claws.

The Banes squirmed and struggled but quickly died, too weak to withstand the onslaught. A momentary pang of guilt swept over Carlita as she sliced through another wriggling fish-thing, but she reminded herself that these weren't babies—they were monsters. Birthed not by Gaia but by the poisons flowing through the river. They had probably been real spirit fish eggs once but had since become anointed in toxic sludge, warping them into Banes.

It took only a few minutes to kill them all, and Storm-Eye marched resolutely from the room, paying the splattered eggs no more heed. The others followed, assuming the same order they had first taken.

When they reached the intersection again, they went forward, which would have been a right turn from their original direction. The grade was steeper here; they seemed to be traveling deeper under the river, maybe to the riverbed itself.

Soon they saw a wavering light on the tunnel walls ahead, reflected as if through water from a large room ahead and to the left. They slowed their pace and crept forward. At the entrance to the room, Storm-Eye cautiously peeked in and swiftly drew her head back. She motioned for them to back up a ways down the corridor and then whispered to them.

"Ten Flood Banes. Eating spirits. Window into river. They watch new spirits come, dragged against will."

"What's the window made out of?" Carlita asked.

Storm-Eye cocked her head quizzically and shrugged.

Figures, Carlita thought. *What would a lupus know about building materials?* "If it's glass," she said to the others, "we may be able to break it and let the river in. That kind of force is sure to flood the dam and bust it up."

"It's the only plan I've heard so far," Julia said. The others nodded.

"You break window," Storm-Eye said to Carlita. "We kill Banes."

She lead them back down to the entrance and, after looking over her shoulder to make sure they were all ready, she burst into the room.

The Banes were scattered about, tearing with their sharp teeth into bloated animal carcasses—spirit victims of the floods. They seemed completely surprised by the sudden assault.

Storm-Eye knocked a large one over, her jaws gnawing at its throat. North Wind's Son lunged forward at one, driving his clawed fist completely through its stomach and out its back, severing its spine in one blow. Julia used the shock caused by his sudden attack to slip in behind another one, who had turned to witness his fellow fall before the Wendigo warrior. She raked her claws from its head to its tailbone, flaying sections of flesh as a fisherman cleans a catch.

Halászlé hesitated at the door, unsure which one to attack. He was obviously scared out of his wits and unused to such raw combat. He seemed to gain courage from North Wind's Son's startling blow, so he bounded into the room and latched his jaws around one of the Bane's arms, trying to wrench it from its socket.

The Bane didn't seem to feel pain. Ignoring Halászlé's struggles, it drew back a clawed hand and slashed him across the snout. He whimpered but did not let go, tugging even more fiercely. Then came a popping sound as the thing's arm dislocated from its shoulder, but the muscles still bound it to the torso. The Bane opened its maw and bit down on Halászlé, who released the arm and tried to dodge at the last minute. The teeth caught his ear and ripped it off as he jumped aside.

The Bane swallowed the ear and made an odd gurgling noise of satisfaction, as it stumbled forward to get another bite off the fleeing Garou.

Carlita ran past all this to the window set at a crooked angle in the wall. It looked like a car windshield—perhaps salvaged from some riverbed wreck—set firmly now amid the bones.

She drew back her leg and kicked it with all her Crinos-form might. Her foot bounded off it. Nothing. She realized that the force of the river on the other side was working against her. No way could she kick the window out with all that water coming at her—it was too strong. She had to find some way to pull it in.

She shoved her fang dagger into the edge of the window, scraping into the bones, trying to pry the thick glass loose. While her fetish knife whittled through some of the bones, she couldn't get enough leverage to reach the edge, buried deeper in the bones than she had thought.

She turned to look at the others—and gasped.

The remaining Banes—at least seven of them—were melting together, forming themselves into a giant wave of water. Just as Carlita realized what was happening, the wave rose up and then crashed down on her packmates, submerging them. The water rushed toward her now, expanding as it came, engulfing the entire room. She sucked in a deep breath and braced herself for the blow.

The wave slammed into her and knocked her back against the far wall. Once submerged in its wake, she opened her eyes. In the distance, she could make out her packmates, struggling to slash at the water but seeming to do no harm to it. Halászlé tried to swim out of the room, but he seemed caught in some sort of vortex, spinning about frantically.

Storm-Eye went limp, her snout open. Carlita could see a small whirlpool forming at her mouth, forcing itself down her throat. North Wind's Son had his hand clamped over his own snout, as if trying to keep it closed against some unseen force attempting to open it. Julia was nowhere in sight.

Shit! Carlita thought. *Shit! Shit! Shit!*

Suddenly, she couldn't move. The water froze around her, and she was trapped in ice. She tensed her muscles and slashed out with her dagger, shattering the block around her. A gust of air rushed in and she gratefully filled her lungs with it—only to shiver as the ice-cold air nearly froze her lungs.

She heard a howl of rage and looked for its source. North Wind's Son stood amid chunks of ice, slashing away at it, chipping it to pieces, howling into the frigid air, consumed by rage. *So that's it!* Carlita thought. *He called the north wind and it froze this shit! All right! I may get pneumonia out of this, but at least we got a fighting chance.*

She crawled from her own block of ice and began furiously chipping away at it with the fang dagger. The chunks that tore loose dissipated into whisps of frost, then nothingness.

But the icy ground began to melt. It sucked at her, as if trying to pull her down. She slashed at it with her toe claws and leaped onto a taller block of ice. "This shit's melting!" she yelled to the others.

"I know! I know!" Julia yelled. Carlita could see her now. She was trying to slash as much of the ice as she could before it turned back into water, but wasn't getting as far as Carlita or North Wind's Son. Storm-Eye lay on the ground, vomiting up water, looking weak and miserable, barely able to keep her eyes open. Halászlé tried to stand but kept slipping on the ice. He gave up and started chipping away at it with his claws, but was even less effectual than Julia.

Carlita suddenly realized that, with the room turned to ice, maybe the window had been weakened. It might shatter more easily. She shifted into Hispo form, her fang dagger in her mouth, and bounded across the slick ice sheet to the window, her four legs getting her there faster than two. Only half of the window could be seen above the ice level.

She shifted back into Crinos form and slashed the window with all her might. The point of her blade impacted and bit into the thick glass. Cracks instantly spread out in a wild spider-web pattern, but the window still held.

She drew her hand back for another blow but then fell into the frigid water as the ice collapsed, replaced once more by a lake of Bane liquid.

She had no time to gulp in any air and knew she couldn't hold out for long. She kicked at the window and saw the cracks deepen, but it still held against the force of the river on the other side. *It can't end like this! There was a prophecy, damn it!* She felt the last of her air giving out. *God. Damn. Brittle. Leaf.*

Almost as soon as she cursed the Uktena Ragabash, something called her name.

She heard it clearly, as if from across a calm sea on a bright day. She listened again.

Carlita... my chosen child... open yourself to me. Heed my call. Heed the one you made your pact with....

She realized who it was, the thing that had been calling their names before, but whose voice was drowned by the tainted river. She heeded it, relaxing and giving herself over to it fully with complete trust.

She could suddenly breathe. No air coursed through her lungs, but it was as if she didn't need it. With mouth still closed, she had no need to breath, for all around her was spirit, sustenance enough just by its touch. She didn't need to follow the laws of the material world here.

Outside the window, something moved upriver. A dark shape growing in size as it approached, moving like a torpedo through the already speeding waters. Within seconds, its features became clear: the head and arms of a cougar stroked the water, propelled faster by the undulating tail of a snake. Its visage was terrible to watch, anger and rage streaming from its eyes. It was the one whose call Carlita had heeded.

Carlita turned and swam as fast as she could toward the door, away from the window. As soon as she got out of the way, the window shattered inward with the force of the great bulk that rammed against it. Cold, pure water jetted into the room with it, overpowering the Bane water, mixing with it, cleansing it in a tide of crystal-clear purity.

A snapping sound reverberated through the rushing lake, followed by a massive cracking as of a thousand trees falling at once. Against the force of the pure river, the bones could not hold, and they cracked and splintered, blowing outward, opening a channel for the water.

The resulting maelstrom thrust Carlita through the new opening and past, downriver amid the rejuvenated bones that were growing once more into fleshy spirits, freed of their unholy bondage.

She felt once more the desperate need for air and struggled to right herself and reach the surface. She broke the water and gulped in a deep breath of fresh, cool air. The river carried her on, and she could see the bodies of her packmates floating on the surface around her.

She swam to the closest, North Wind's Son, and pulled him with her toward the shore. As she did, she saw another figure moving, pulling Julia to the bank—Halászlé, worn and tired but whole. As soon as she had the Wendigo on land, she dove back in and headed for Storm-Eye, who seemed caught in an eddy. As soon as she grasped the Red Talon, the eddy dissolved, as if it had appeared only for the purpose of holding her packmate in place.

She crawled onto the riverbank to help Halászlé pump water from her packmates' lungs. In moments, they were all up and coughing, spitting out remnants of the Bane water, each looking around wide-eyed and wondering why they were still alive.

As if in answer, a great bulk rose up from the water, unmoved by the mighty torrent spilling around it.

Uktena looked at his children, but then a darkness came over his eyes and he glared into the distance, toward the horizon where the diverted river had flowed before the dam had burst and restored its natural course.

A deafening cry rang out from his throat, an echoing cougar howl that chilled their blood even in the face of what their totem had done for them.

Then, as if in response, an earthshaking roar was heard from far off. It did more than chill their blood— they felt frozen before it, gripped in terror so primal that they had no conscious memory of its source. They finally had an inkling of what it was like for a human to witness them in their Crinos forms, to succumb to the blessed forgetfulness of the Delirium. But they could not forget that terrible roar and knew it would haunt their nights for years to come.

The river sloshed and ran faster, ignoring Uktena now, rushing once more to the bidding of its distant master. Its course was restored, but its flow still delivered it to Jo'cllath'mattric.

Uktena hung its head in defeat. It looked at its children, wet and exhausted in the river, and spoke: "I could not enter the Tisza without awakening Jo'cllath'mattric. But if you could carry a small piece of me here, to this realm, through your bond with me, I could enter the waters without alerting the beast. And so it was done. But too late. Jo'cllath'mattric's power is now too great. Even without the river, it will break its bonds and rise. The Tisza flowed for too long toward it, strengthening it. The prophecy of the Third Pack was true, but it was delivered too late."

"No!" Carlita yelled, trying to stand but too weak for the moment. "We'll keep going. We'll get to it and stop it!"

Uktena looked down upon her, its terrible eyes almost tender for a moment. "This is no longer a task for cubs. Return to your elders and tell them that you have both succeeded and failed." It then sunk beneath the water and was gone, its presence now absent from the realm.

Carlita practically sobbed. "Succeeded? Where the fuck did we succeed? We failed, goddamn it!" She struck the ground with her fist in anger and frustration.

"No…" Storm-Eye said, still spitting out water, weakly rising to her four feet. "We broke dam. We brought Uktena here. You… you called him to window…"

Carlita looked at her bedraggled and worn packmate. She couldn't bring a smile—her sorrow was too strong for that—but she nodded at the lupus. "And you led us. As you had to. As Uktena had you do."

The pack sat on the shore, watching the river flow past. It was no longer oily and black, but it still frothed too quickly to be natural. There were still too many poisons in it that called to Jo'cllath'mattric.

Carlita stood up, still dripping wet. She tried to think of something to say, to bring some sort of victory out of their defeat. All that came out was "Shit."

Chapter Twelve

The pack made their weary way back to Szeged along the road, in the relative safety of the material world. They had been too tired to speak, but the questions were just too persistent. Finally, Carlita broke the silence.

"I don't understand it," Carlita said. "If we were just here to provide a stepping stone for Uktena's entry into the realm, why didn't he choose a more accomplished pack?"

"He couldn't," Julia said. "Most packs of any but the beginning rank have already made their totem bonds."

"Then why not use one of his bonded packs?"

Julia didn't seem to have an answer.

"Do not question him," North Wind's Son said. "He is Uktena. There is no totem that holds more secrets than he. I once distrusted Older Brother, but I do not doubt that he has reasons for what he did. He needed stealth for his mission. Higher-ranking Garou would surely have attracted more attention than cubs."

Halászlé spoke. "I have seen a mighty thing tonight. Uktena risked much to travel here, far from his home, to restore the Tisza. He failed to destroy Jo'cllath'mattric, but the river flows cleaner now, if not more gently. For that, I will always honor him. As should you! A mighty honor he paid you, choosing you to be his limbs."

Storm-Eye let out a short bark, a sort of statement of approval and end of discussion cue.

The moon was ascendant by the time they reached the outskirts of Szeged, and they all felt safer under its lambent glow. Halászlé led them through the city streets back to Mother's and knocked on the door. This time, his secret knock was slower; he didn't have the strength to rap more quickly.

The little window slid open and Szabó looked out, his eyes widening when he saw who it was. He quickly turned the lock and opened the door, throwing his arms around Halászlé and hugging him tight. "Oh, my friend! You have returned!"

Halászlé smiled and slipped from the embrace. "Yes, we are back. Is there food?"

Szabó looked nervously into the house. "Uh, yes, of course. Come in." He stepped aside so they could enter and closed the door behind them, locking it.

The pack stumbled into the sitting room. Two strangers—a dark-haired man and a woman—stood there, on either side of the couch where Cries Havoc slept. They stared at the pack with curiosity but no sign of friendliness.

Storm-Eye, shifting into her natural wolf form, began to growl at the two strangers hovering so close to her packmate.

"Calm down," Mother said, coming from the kitchen. "There is no cause for trouble here. It is good to see you safe and whole." She hugged Halászlé tightly. The Bone Gnawer didn't try to slip out of this one.

"Greetings, Silver River Pack," the strange male said. He was dressed in black leather pants, boots and jacket, like something out of a spy novel. "Do you have news of victory for us?"

"Who're you?" Carlita said, sitting down. "And what's it to you?"

"Ah," the man said, looking at his female companion, dressed similarly. "I apologize. You could not have known of our arrival."

The female stepped forward. "I am Ilanya Silverfoot and this is Bela Storms-the-Heights. We are from the Sept of the Night Sky."

Halászlé seemed dismayed and slunk into the kitchen. Mother moved to stand between him and the guests, smiling at him protectively.

"Konietzko's people?" Julia said. "What are you doing here?"

"We have come to claim the caern, which our septmates have already accomplished in your absence."

"Huh?" Carlita said. "You rededicated the caern while we were gone? How the hell did you do that? The pathstone was hidden."

Bela Storms-the-Heights shrugged. "We found it. With Mother's help, of course."

The pack turned to Mother, looking for confirmation. She shrugged. "It is true. I invited them after the moot. I had no choice. The caern could not become tainted. That would have doomed us all."

Halászlé whined. "But Mother, if they come to Szeged… what will become of me?"

"Hush," Mother said. "Worry not. The Margrave made an oath to me, and his people would not dare break it for risk of angering him."

"This is true," Ilanya Silverfoot said. "We care not about your transgressions, Halászlé. Those are in the past. Margrave Yuri Konietzko is a fair man. He has absolved you of your crime, in return for the favor Mother has given him."

"Wait," Carlita said. "You said you've already found the pathstone and rededicated the caern? That doesn't seem possible."

"The pathstone is in our hands," Bela said. "We will remove it to a safe place and perform the rite to awaken it tomorrow night. You are, of course, invited. But please, tell us of your trials and victory."

The pack shared glances, each wondering who would do the talking. It seemed that Carlita was elected. She summed it up as best she could, trying not to emphasize how easily they got their asses kicked. If it weren't for Uktena, they would have never made it out alive.

The two Shadow Lords nodded as they listened and seemed both impressed at Uktena's intervention and dismayed at his failure to destroy Jo'cllath'mattric.

"It does explain one thing," Bela said to Ilanya. "Just as we prepared to fight an army of Banes to win the pathstone, they were sucked downriver, as if a great force suddenly pulled them. This must have been when you—Uktena, that is—breached the dam." He stood up. "Good then, we know what happened. I do not like to bring the dire news of Jo'cllath'mattric to the Margrave, but he must be informed. Mother will bring you to the rite tomorrow night. I invite you to share in our joy at recovering a caern for Gaia."

He said this with such perfunctory joylessness that Carlita almost sneered, but she held back her opinion as the two Shadow Lords headed for the door. Szabó let them out and locked the door behind them. Mother sighed and sat down, obviously as weary as the pack.

"I only pray things will come out right."

Halászlé placed his hands on her shoulders. "You did what you thought good for the city, Mother. Our own lives are secondary to that."

She put her hand on his and rubbed it. "A city you will always be a part of, Halászlé. Always, even after I am gone. So the Margrave has sworn."

Carlita had a burning desire to know just what it was that Halászlé had done to piss off the Shadow Lords, but since it wasn't being volunteered, she felt it would be rude, especially now, to ask about it.

Mother got up and yelled at Szabó and Ferenc, who appeared from upstairs. They rushed about to gather blankets and put them out for the pack, while Halászlé brought out bowls of soup. The pack ate gratefully and collapsed into their blankets without another word exchanged between them. Tomorrow would surely bring enough words, not all of them good.

* * *

The pack, bearing Cries Havoc with them in Ferenc's taxicab, followed Mother and Halászlé to an incredible house not far from the Tisza's banks, north of Szeged, built in intricate Art Nouveau style. It was owned, apparently, by a distant Kinfolk of the Shadow Lords, a banker. The tribe had just now moved in, helping their Kinfolk to relocate while he deeded the place to Ilanya and Bela.

The pathstone was now placed in the house's guarded basement, and the newly rededicated caern would be centered here. The old caern was strong enough to extend its bawn around all Szeged; hopefully, the new one would do the same.

The local Garou from the previous moot arrived, each looking rather unhappy to be sharing a caern with Shadow Lords from the north, but Nagy Pénz was hiding his disappointment well, doing his best to ingratiate himself to the new neighbors.

When Ilanya and Bela saw the pack, they approached them. Bela spoke: "I have had word from the Margrave. We are to open a moon bridge immediately to the Anvil-Klaiven and send you there to report to the Jarlsdottir. I am sorry you will not be able to stay for the rite."

"I don't get it," Carlita said. "How can you open a bridge before rededicating the caern?"

"Because the old caern still exists," Ilanya said. "It can still open moon bridges, as well as receive them—as you discovered upon coming here. With the help of the Anvil-Klaiven's Gatekeeper, we can open a bridge to that caern. He will wait for our signal and work from his side to forge a path."

"So that's it?" Julia said. "Run along and tell your story? What about Cries Havoc? We still haven't found the Banes that did this to him! We can't leave until we cure him!"

"I am sorry," Bela said. "This comes straight from the Margrave. If anyone can help your friend, they are surely gathered at the Anvil-Klaiven right now."

"I don't like this one bit," Carlita said. "And I don't trust you to keep your word about Halászlé when we're gone!"

Bela looked offended. "If you knew what he did, you would respect even more that we honor the Margrave's oath to Mother."

Carlita looked at Halászlé, who stared at the floor in shame. "I've seen Halászlé in action. He self-lessly chose to come with us and almost died. Nothing he did could be that bad."

"Then ask him," Bela said, walking away. "I will prepare the gate."

Carlita and the rest of the pack looked at Halászlé. Mother stood nearby, looking at neither of them, leaving the matter up to them and Halászlé to resolve.

"I don't want to know," Carlita said. "It's that simple. People make mistakes. Especially Bone Gnawers. And Shadow Lords tend to hold grudges longer than most. So, it doesn't matter. Don't tell us."

"I feel I must," Halászlé said.

"I don't want to hear it!" Carlita said. "So shut your mouth!"

"Please, I do not want you to leave doubting me the rest of your lives. I must say this."

Carlita fumed, but was silent.

"I… uh… I slept with another Garou. It is forbidden. No child resulted, but… it was an unwise choice."

"Is that all?" Carlita said. "That isn't good, but hell, there's a whole lot worse a Garou can do."

"Yes, but this was with the Caern Warder's daughter. He was not pleased."

Carlita smiled. "You got it on with a Shadow Lord's *chica?* Ooh, yeah, not bad for a Bone Gnawer."

Halászlé grimaced. "She did not know I was a Bone Gnawer. I was young, bohemian, an artist. I did not have the beard you now see. I was a handsome man."

"She didn't know you were Garou?"

"No. I… did not bother to tell her."

"That wasn't fair. No wonder the Shadow Lords don't like you. Hell, even I can't get behind that."

"But it was for love! I really loved her. At least, I thought I did."

Carlita looked at the poor Gnawer chewing his beard in shame. "I forgive you. Who the hell am I to judge others? We're all just trying to survive, right?"

Halászlé smiled and nodded. He didn't say anything else and the pack dropped the matter. Szabó and Ferenc came in, bearing Cries Havoc on a hospital stretcher. They lowered it to the floor, and Storm-Eye went over and licked Cries Havoc's face but got no response.

Ilanya came from the nearby room and motioned to them. As they followed, Mother blocked their way.

"Do I not get a hug?"

They all piled around and each wrapped arms over her. Halászlé joined them. Carlita and North Wind's Son then lifted Cries Havoc's stretcher, and the pack followed the Shadow Lord into the other room.

A shimmering moon bridge was already open. Bela stepped aside to allow them admittance. "The path is clear. My spirits have contacted theirs. Nothing will impede you. Go with Gaia."

They nodded in return and stepped up to the glowing portal in the air. Carlita turned to look through the doorway they had come from and saw Halászlé standing there. He waved to her.

She raised her fingers in a peace sign and followed her pack through the gate into the skies of the spirit world.

About the Authors

Bill Bridges was the original developer for White Wolf's **Werewolf: The Apocalypse** storytelling game line. He has numerous writing credits on most of White Wolf's World of Darkness line, including the Werewolf novel **The Silver Crown**, which first introduced the conflict between King Albrecht and Lord Arkady. He is presently developer and cocreator of *Fading Suns* for Holistic Design Inc. His current projects can be seen at www.fadingsuns.com.

Justin Achilli is the developer of White Wolf's **Vampire: The Masquerade** and the author of numerous products for that and other lines of storytelling games. He is the author of **Clan Novel: Giovanni**.

TRIBE NOVEL:

SCARGAZERS

BILL BRIDGES

author:	bill bridges
cover artist:	steve prescott
series editors:	eric griffin
	john h. steele
	stewart wieck
copyeditor:	jeanée ledoux
graphic designer:	pauline benney
art director:	richard thomas

More information and previews available at
white–wolf.com/clannovels

White Wolf Publishing
735 Park North Boulevard, Suite 128
Clarkston, GA 30021
www.white-wolf.com/fiction

First Edition: January 2002

White Wolf, is a registered trademark.
ISBN: 1-56504-886-5
Printed in Canada

Dedicated to Gary Snyder, who inspired a generation of Zen wilderness ramblers and still inspires a practice of the wild today.

SCARGAZERS

BILL BRIDGES

Prologue

Purest Resolve Monastery, Western China, 1962:

Master Chien faced east in the moonlight, perfectly balanced on his right leg, his left leg tucked in as if he were sitting lotus style on the air. His broad shoulders barely moved as he breathed deeply, floating in place, waiting for his chi to settle. He then spun rightward—still on one leg—nearly tracing a full circle, until he faced north. He stamped his left foot down and unfurled his arms like scrolls or silk drapery. Drawing his feet together, he circled both arms over his head, bringing the palms together, and then slowly lowered them down past his front energy centers, pausing at each one: third eye, throat, heart, triple warmer and finally the lower dantian in his belly. He placed his left palm just below his belly and his right palm over it, sealing the energy, eyes still closed.

He then turned and walked over to the young Westerner sitting uncomfortably with his legs drawn up under him. The young man—hardly more than 17 years old—nobly tried to hide his discomfort and concentrate on the lesson.

"That is how you walk the Pole Star Path in human form," Master Chien said. "Once you master it, I will show you how a wolf may do it."

Antonine Teardrop bowed deeply to the revered Stargazer master. He had watched every one of the Theurge's 108 forms with careful concentration, attempting to memorize them all. He knew he had failed and would be able to execute only the first third from memory, but he hoped that if he performed that part well, Master Chien would be lenient and repeat the lesson.

Chien grunted and walked away, passing through the courtyard gate and down the long, winding stone stairway that hugged the side of the steep mountain. Mists clung to the walls and eaves of the yard, part of a perpetual cloud that served to hide the mountaintop monastery from the outside world. The lower temple complex was a forgotten Taoist monastery still populated by several dozen human priests, Stargazer tribe Kinfolk smuggled here from other monasteries across China, fleeing Mao's persecutions. The upper levels were reserved for the Stargazers and their unique forms of practice, similar on the surface to those known by humans yet vastly different in content and efficacy. Taoists and Buddhists believed that humans had to spend a lifetime cultivating enough virtue to unlock the mystical arts; Stargazers were born to them, although they, too, like humans, had to struggle to realize enlightenment.

Antonine stood and limbered up, loosely shaking his body to get out the kinks and muscle tension. He still hadn't fully adjusted to the strange postures the tribe required him to assume during his meditations and lessons. Raised in America, he was used to sitting in chairs with his feet on the floor. Now, he most often sat with his legs tucked under his butt—guaranteed to cut blood flow and put his legs to sleep—or curled up in a lotus stance, the soles of his feet facing upward. He was getting better at it, no doubt, but it was still uncomfortable.

Once he felt his blood flowing again and his muscles relaxed, he began the sequence of forms, taking it slow and easy, not allowing his mind to wander and forget the image of his master walking the steps. He had to try to put as much of his mind's memories into his body memory as he could before it was gone. What the body remembers, it never forgets.

As he stepped from one foot to another, shifting weight and spinning now and then, accompanying the footwork with mudras, he tried to imagine the constellation of stars he was supposed to be walking over. It was no pattern discernable in the night sky, for it existed only in the Aetherial Realm of the Umbra, the night sky of the spirit world. While some stars were the same, others had either never existed in the material world or were now expired. Some had yet to be born. All of them, however, encircled the Pole Star, whose Incarna spirit—Vegarda, the Lady of the North—had taught the form to the sept long ago. If performed properly, Walking the Pole Star Path would expand the soul and provide a proper palace for the mind of enlightenment, the end goal for all Stargazers.

The practice also served as a very effective martial art, a variant style of Kailindo, the fighting art of shapeshifting and evasion.

Although the sun had barely set when his master had begun the lesson, Antonine did not stop to rest until well after the half moon had also set. The shadows were long and the air cold when a priest from the temple below came through the gate with a bowl of rice and a jug of water. He bowed to

Antonine and placed the food and drink on the ground. Antonine bowed back.

"Thank you," he said in Mandarin.

The man bowed once more and left. It had been a long walk up the mountain, but the trip down would be easier.

Antonine sat down by the food and began shoveling the rice into his mouth. He was hungrier than he had imagined; the bowl was empty in minutes. He then drank nearly half the jug of water before reminding himself that it wouldn't be good for him to drink so much so quickly.

He rested for a while more and then stood up again, walking back to the place where Master Chien had begun the form. He breathed deeply and once more resumed his practice.

As he shifted his weight to one leg and stepped out with the other, he was startled when he couldn't find the ground—his foot stepped into nothingness. His balance lost, he tumbled, falling through space, into the vastness of stars.

He fell into a massive spider web, its sticky threads catching him tight. He struggled to break free but could not move his limbs. He stared in fear at his surroundings and saw that the entire universe was caught in the giant web—each star formed the nexus of a grouping of threads, which stretched to catch other stars and still others, reaching throughout creation to ensnare everything.

Antonine remembered the Hua-Yin Buddhist concept of Indra's Net, the whole of creation seen as a vast, interconnected pattern. Nothing escaped its influence. But that vision was meant to instruct one about the reality of causal interconnectedness, how everything affected everything else. Behind the illusion of separateness, everything was One.

This web, however, was not a comforting unity but a sinister cage. Its strands served to impede vision and maintain the illusion of division and distinction, the loneliness of atoms separated by a meaningless void.

The Weaver, he thought. *Maya. The Web of Delusion that covers our eyes and weaves Form from Undivided Fullness. Here is where we mistake our dreams for reality. I must wake up.*

He stilled his struggling and tried to imagine himself waking up in the courtyard. When he opened his eyes, he was still trapped in the web. *I cannot will my way out of this trap! How can I dispel an illusion when I've never seen the Truth behind it? Oh, blessed Gaia, show me a glimpse of the True Gaia Realm. Help me to follow the Gaiadharma.*

Something moved nearby, causing the web to vibrate in the breeze it had created. A serpentine thing floated toward him. Its head was not that of snake, however, but a lion. It stared at him, daring him to plumb the depths of its infinite soul.

Antonine tried to bow before Chimera, his tribal totem spirit, the Lord of Enigmas and Master of Dreams, but the webs allowed him only a slight nod.

The totem's forepaw reached out and scattered the webs as if they were made of air. Antonine fell once more. He landed on a glowing path, lambent with moonlight. As he placed his hand upon it to steady himself and rise, he yanked it back and yelped in pain, staring at the burn mark on his palm. The pathway was made of silver.

A voice thrummed in his head: "Remember the Silver Thread, the Hidden Way into the Tapestry."

He shut his eyes, trying to withstand the pain, and then opened them to see a sun-brightened sky. It was morning in the courtyard. The sun's rays unraveled the mountain mists, sparkling in the pine dew. Something lightly tapped his face and he felt water on his brow.

Master Chien leaned over him, wringing a wet cloth over his head.

"Fool," he said. "When one is tired, rest."

Antonine sat up and looked around. He was in the practice courtyard at sunrise. "It was night... and there were spider webs everywhere. And Chimera..."

Master Chien frowned. "You saw the Weaver's webs? And the totem himself? Don't lie!"

"I do not lie, master," Antonine said. "I was practicing and suddenly fell into empty space and was caught in a web, one that reached everywhere and to everything. Chimera appeared and freed me. I then saw a silver path, like a moon path but made of silver. It burned me... ." He looked at his right hand and saw a faint mark there.

Master Chien grabbed the hand and looked at it. He grunted. "Moon burn. Luna's silver."

"Chimera called it the Silver Thread."

Master Chien sat back and thought, staring into the morning sky. "Chimera has shown you the Weaver, the cause of delusion in this world. Her webs keep us from seeing straight. But they are in the mind. Your bondage is not physical, it is only mental."

He stood up and paced about. "This silver… Hmph. I don't know what it means. An omen? We will watch and wait and see if it shows itself again. Until then…" he looked scornfully at Antonine. "You will practice only four hours at a time, until you learn not to exhaust yourself and pass out. This isn't karate or wrestling. Internal martial arts require relaxation and openness—a healthy, balanced body."

Antonine nodded. "Yes, master. I understand."

The older Stargazer helped the younger one to rise and placed his hand on his shoulder. He guided Antonine down the mountain and to the small temple where his sleeping mat was laid out in a corner. As the master left his pupil, he shook his head.

"Pay attention to your dreams. Never forget your dreams, for Chimera hides his wisdom there."

After his master had gone, Antonine looked at his hand. It did not hurt anymore, but he noticed that it glowed faintly in the darkness of the shuttered room, although its light was fading.

What the body remembers, it never forgets.

Chapter One

Finger Lakes Caern, New York State, now:

Antonine Teardrop waited outside the cabin by the lake. Sitting in lotus posture, he listened to the faint sounds from over the water, a light breeze stirring his white linen shirt and snowy, shoulder-length gray hair. Birds called to one another and a fish plopped over the surface. His eyes closed, Antonine could not see his shimmering reflection in the water, but he wondered: Could the beings below the water see it, and if so, what did they think of him? This middle-aged, human-shaped being in well-worn jeans and hiking boots who smelled like a wolf?

He was content. Even amidst the turmoil that had arisen of late, he serenely accepted what transpired in his world. Beyond the fractured illusions of diversity, suffering and sorrow, he knew there was unity, transcendence and love. Years of contemplative training had taught him to anchor himself in these thoughts, to take a stand there and weather what changes came for good or ill. Of late, however, he felt his legs very shaky and his grip loosening.

The door behind him creaked open, and a black woman, in healthy middle age like Antonine, came out of the single-room cabin and quietly closed the door behind her. Antonine sinuously slipped out of his stance and stood to regard her, no trace of anticipation on his face, although it was there nonetheless, hidden below the carefully controlled surface he presented to others.

The woman walked down the porch steps to stand beside him, shaking her head and looking at the ground. "A deep mystery lies on her, one I cannot fathom."

"How can I help?" Antonine said, his voice a deep and clear baritone.

"I have no idea," she said, meeting his eyes. "Years of traveling the Umbra and speaking to spirits high and low and I have no clues to her condition. The black-winged Bane is behind it, but this thing's nature—and its presence—eludes me. Something new, perhaps? Or very old?"

Antonine was silent.

"We will watch over her, Stargazer. She is one of ours. However, I pray your meditations yield some clues."

"So do I, Nadya. Thank you for your help."

"I will take the news to Alani Astarte." She began to walk toward the group of houses down the dirt lane behind the cabin but then stopped and stared at something down the path. "Antonine... the Silver Fang king comes. I will leave it for you to explain her condition to him."

Antonine looked down the road and saw Albrecht walking swiftly toward him, with Evan Heals-the-Past hurrying to follow. Since they were coming from the caern center, they had surely arrived by moon bridge and must have already consulted with the sept leaders. Nadya moved on, stepping to the side of the path so as not to hinder the king.

"Where is she?" Albrecht said as soon as he saw Antonine.

"Here, in the cabin," he said. "Everything that can be done has been done."

Albrecht slowed, his angry gaze replaced by a worried frown. "That doesn't sound good."

"Come," Antonine said. "You should see her."

He led them into the small cabin, into the single, dark room. The shutters were closed and a strange incense smell permeated the place. Lying on a bed was Mari Cabrah, Albrecht and Evan's packmate and sole survivor of the second pack chosen to deal with the newest Wyrm threat in Europe. Her breathing was so shallow she could be mistaken for dead.

Evan rushed to the bedside and leaned over her, his hand on her brow. "She's alive," he said with relief. Albrecht was silent, staring at her with a look of guilt.

"But in a deep trance," Antonine said. "Nadya Zenobia, the Black Furies' greatest Theurge in this sept, could not find a cure. When Mari was first brought in, she struggled against an unseen enemy. Those who saw her at the Anvil-Klaiven Caern report a black-winged Bane gripping her spirit. By the time she arrived here, it had disappeared. She has since either lost the strength to fight it or has gained some respite. Nadya fears it has hidden deeply in her spirit, and I cannot even find her Chimare—her personal dream realm. All paths to it are gone."

"I thought it was some sort of Wyrm storm in the Umbra that did this," Albrecht said, moving closer to the unconscious woman. "That's what I was told."

"A strange storm was involved, but none knows its true nature. It is like nothing anyone has seen before. The third pack encountered it in the local Penumbra, so it is not confined to Europe, but few have seen it directly since their departure for Serbia. All who have traveled the Umbra of late can sense it, however."

"Surely somebody's got to have seen something like it in the distant past—an ancestor or spirit?"

"If so, no one can summon them. Many have tried, here and in Europe. No one remembers such a storm."

Albrecht leaned over Mari. "C'mon, Mari. Snap out of it! You've been through worse than this. Don't get weak on me now."

Evan scowled at Albrecht, but the Silver Fang just stared intently at the unresponsive Black Fury. "No answer, huh? Cat got your tongue? Or are you too afraid to deal with it?"

"That's enough, Albrecht," Evan said. "I know what you're trying to do, but it's not right. Not now."

Albrecht frowned. "I know. I had to try, though. If anyone could get her riled, it's me."

Evan took Mari's hand. "Hey, you still here somewhere? If you can hear me, Mari, please wake up. We need you now. You've got to tell us what happened. Lots of lives depend on it. And we miss you. I'm not used to having you away for so long."

There was no response. Not a flicker of the eyes or even a change in breathing. Mari was elsewhere, if her soul still even lived.

"I don't think there's anything you can do for her here," Antonine said. "We should leave her to rest. She may be struggling on some level we can't witness, and need all the strength and concentration she can muster."

Albrecht placed a hand on Evan's shoulder. The young man nodded and stood. They left the cabin and walked together to the edge of the lake. A slender man stood nearby, leaning against a tree, watching them. Albrecht saw him and walked over.

"I recognize you from what Alani told me," he said. "Mephi Faster-than-Death, right?"

Mephi seemed startled to be noticed by the Silver Fang king. He stood up straighter and met the Silver Fang's eyes. "Yeah, that's me."

"Look, I want to thank you for bringing her back. It means a lot to me. If there's anything you need, at anytime, you let me know."

Mephi was speechless for a moment but then found his bearings. "Thank you, oh king. That's a most generous offer." He then smiled. "You know, *The Saga of the Silver Crown* is my most popular tale."

Albrecht could not suppress a grin. Evan, who was walking up behind the king, said: "I wish she could hear you say that." He clearly meant Mari.

"As do I," Mephi said. "She's a real hero." He paused for a moment, as if unsure how to continue. "Uh, there's something else you should know. The Screaming Trailblazers are no more. Ivar Hated-by-the-Wyrm, the last of them, fell with honor and glory among the first pack. It was they who discovered the mess that's going on now."

Albrecht's shoulders sank, and his size seemed diminished. "The Trailblazers were a good bunch. I owed them a lot. But they never came asking. How'd it happen? I mean, how'd the rest of them die?"

"That's a long story, one that deserves more than a summary. If you wish, I could tell it before your court sometime."

"I'd like that. Sometime when this is all over and Mari can hear it."

"Well, I'd better leave you to your business," Mephi said, picking up a cobra-headed walking staff. "I've got places to go." He turned and walked off around the lake, away from the caern center.

Antonine was sitting by the edge of the water, clearly waiting for Albrecht. Evan came over and dropped to the ground as if he had just walked ten miles without rest, but Albrecht paced about.

"There are other problems that beset you," Antonine said. "Tell me about them."

Albrecht scowled, his rage clearly close to the surface but still kept in check. "It's this whole Arkady thing. That bastard is at it again. I swear he lives just to piss me off. I should have never let Mari go to that moot in my place. Arkady is the thorn in *my* side, damn it! He's my problem to deal with, but I avoided it. And now look where it's gotten her…"

"You can't blame yourself for that," Antonine said. "She knew her mission was dangerous but took it for her own reasons. It had nothing to do with Arkady at that point."

"I know, I know. But if I'd gone, I could have cleaned up a lot of this mess in the first place. Arkady is a Silver Fang, and that means it's my business to kick him into line—or kill him like I should have."

"You know very well that it was Falcon's wish for you to spare him."

"Or so it seemed. He wasn't exactly clear about it."

"Yes he was. Don't doubt the past. Totem spirits know things we cannot. Falcon sensed some purpose left in Arkady, although I suspect even he didn't know exactly what it was."

"Regardless, it's my refusal to deal with his latest crap that's got everybody over in Europe kissing Konietzko's ass. He's the man of the hour now. I should be there. Things wouldn't be in the shit hole they are now."

"You have no evidence for that. The Margrave is up against tough odds."

"My gut says I could do better."

"Antonine?" Evan said. "Can I ask you about the third pack? The one you prophesied? I mean, what was that all about anyway?"

Antonine smiled. "I have many sources of wisdom to call on. All of them seemed to point toward a third pack to complement the two."

"But what are they supposed to accomplish?"

"That I am unsure of. Chimera himself may know, and he may have even shared this knowledge with Uktena, the third pack's totem, but he has yet to fully enlighten me on it."

"You mean you sent these guys off without knowing what they're supposed to do?"

"Yes," Antonine said, looking straight at Evan. "We cannot always know the future, no matter how many omens are delivered to us. We must sometimes trust the direction in which the winds blow even if we don't know to where they blow. Chimera's visions told of a third pack, and so I sought to introduce the idea to the conclave. Luckily, there is wisdom even among the Get of Fenris and Shadow Lords."

"I guess I wouldn't be so worried if John North Wind's Son wasn't part of it all. There are a lot of people in our tribe depending on him for other things."

"How can you know that this isn't part of his promised greatness? The cold North is not the only battlefield of merit."

"Speak of the devil," Albrecht said, pointing down the path toward the caern center from which he and Evan had previously come. "Isn't that them?"

Antonine and Evan looked down the path to see the third pack stumbling toward them, obviously exhausted and tired. Two of them wore the Glabro form and carried a third member between them, one with ramlike horns curling from the head of his unconscious Crinos form.

Antonine was up and moving more swiftly than even Albrecht had imagined him capable. Before he and Evan could even start toward the wounded pack, Antonine had covered half the distance—in Homid form, no less.

"What happened?" Antonine said as he approached the bedraggled pack. "Is everyone all right?"

"No," Storm-Eye growled from her Lupus form. "We failed."

"Cries Havoc is hurt," Julia Spencer said, motioning to the unconscious Garou she and North

Wind's Son carried. "Really badly. We don't know how to cure him."

"And that ain't the worst news," said Carlita. "Jo'cllath'mattric is free. We're fucked."

Antonine moved over to examine Cries Havoc, who was placed carefully on the ground by Julia and North Wind's Son. The young Child of Gaia—or Get of Fenris, depending on how one viewed the complicated situation of tribal allegiances at the recent European concolation—was in a trance not unlike Mari Cabrah's.

"I don't get it, Antonine," North Wind's Son said. "We were supposed to be the third pack! The ones who would succeed where the first two failed! But that didn't happen. We got our asses kicked."

"Hey," Julia Spencer said. "We did kill the corrupted river spirit. We did do that right."

"Yeah," Carlita said. "But it didn't mean shit to those Anvil-Klaiven bastards."

Antonine looked sharply at the young Bone Gnawer. "Careful. There's no cause for insult."

"No cause?!" Carlita cried. "The hell there isn't! Those shitheads refused to let us stay there after we'd barely got out of Serbia alive. Even the Jarlsdottir said she couldn't guarantee our safety if we stayed, after everything that's happened. That cold bitch!"

"Calm down," Antonine said. "It's clear that her tribe is taking failure badly. Morale is at its worst. She's probably having enough trouble defending her position as leader. Your presence there could have ruined what precarious balance she's managed to maintain. She did right to send you here."

"I don't buy it," Carlita said, growling, her rage rising. "What the hell did you set us up for, anyway? Some sorta hit? You surprised we're even alive?"

"Shut it, cub!" a loud voice growled from nearby, startling all the young pack members. Albrecht walked up to Carlita, towering over her. "Quit your whining. You've been through a lot, but so has every Garou ever born. You're heroes, damn it! Act like it. The worst thing you can do is get caught up in self pity."

He brushed past them and marched off to the caern center.

"I... I... didn't see him there..." said Julia. "That's King Albrecht!"

Carlita watched him go. Together, consternation and surprise outweighed her anger.

"Sorry about his manners," Evan said, coming up and clasping a hand on North Wind's Son's arm. "You're not the only ones who've suffered in this affair. Our packmate, Mari, lies in a coma in that cabin. But you're here, and alive. That means you did succeed, no matter what others may say."

North Wind's Son clasped Evan's shoulder in return, smiling for the first time in what seemed like days. He was relieved to see his former mentor and fellow tribe member.

Storm-Eye looked at the cabin and lowered her head. Her tail hung nearly to the ground, a sign of submission among wolves. She spoke in the Garou tongue, with short growling noises and postures to convey her meaning: "At least Mephi got her here. I was worried about him."

"He has already departed," Antonine said, standing up from his examination of Cries Havoc. There was no mark on the metis that could explain his current condition. "Albrecht's right. Now isn't the time to succumb to failure. We must heal wounds, but also plan the next move. This sept is already too crowded, and none here can help Mari. If Cries Havoc's wounds are similar, there is no reason for him to stay. I want you to accompany me back to my place. I can consult the stars there and hopefully find some answers to his illness."

North Wind's Son looked at Evan, who nodded and said, "It's a good idea. The Finger Lakes here are good for healing, but there's too much tension right now. Antonine's place would be best for you."

"Then I will go," North Wind's Son said.

His packmates nodded and shuffled their feet, ready for another journey, although they all knew this one would thankfully be shorter than the last.

"May the spirits bless your path," Evan said. He then turned to Antonine. "Could you walk with me a minute?"

"Wait here," Antonine told the pack. He followed Evan up the road.

"This news about Jo'cllath'mattric isn't good," Evan said. "I think Albrecht's resolved to go to Europe and lead the fight there himself. He's heading back to the North Country to gather whoever will follow him."

"I'm not sure this is wise," Antonine said. "Especially for you. This is a war party he's gathering; there's not much room for a Half Moon there."

"I know," Evan said. "I'm staying. Someone's got to watch over Mari. Besides, I know Albrecht wouldn't let me go. He can't stand the idea of Mari being sidelined; he's not going to let it happen to me. I'm beyond arguing with him when he's like this, especially since I think he's right. As much as I want to go put whatever did this to Mari in its place, I need to be here in case it tries to finish the job it did to her."

Antonine nodded. "I cannot advise Albrecht on this. I have seen no omens, and I'm a martial artist, not a warrior. Tell him for me, however, that I do not think he should confront the Margrave and oppose him. Instead, he should seek alliance and a joint command."

"Yeah, right," Evan said. "That'll happen."

Antonine sighed. "I know both tribes are stubborn on this issue, and they won't listen. But I've said it anyway. I've got to attend these cubs; they could be the key to winning this war. Go with Gaia, Evan. And the king, too."

"And you, Antonine. Thanks for everything."

Antonine left Evan to return to his wards. They shuffled around awkwardly, unsure what to do: lie down and rest or stretch their legs in preparation for further travel?

"I think we should step sideways," Antonine said. "Nadya assures me the local Penumbra is clear of the storm. I know a shortcut by moon path that will save us time."

"It's worth the risk," Julia said. "Anything to get me into a bed somewhere. I'm exhausted."

"Then look there," Antonine said, pointing to the lake. "Stare into its glimmering mirror and join me." As he spoke the last words, he faded from the material world and parted the Velvet Shadow.

Chapter Two

The Silver River Pack followed Antonine through the Catskills Protectorate's Penumbra. Fall was ablaze in its full glory here, igniting leaves into bonfires of yellow, red and green. Here in the spirit world, they even seemed to shimmer and gutter like flames, swaying in a breeze only they could feel. Animal Gafflings—rabbit, fox and mouse spirits—flitted in and out of bushes, curious about the wayfarers but unwilling to approach too closely.

It was a journey of sublime beauty and tranquility but for the ominous thundering in the far distance, and the darkness that seemed to hang on the horizon in all directions.

"It's that damn storm again," Julia said. "It's out there somewhere. Can't you hear it?"

"Yes," Storm-Eye said with disgust. "But it has not come near. It waits."

"For what?" North Wind's Son said.

No one answered. None knew what to say. Even Antonine was quiet.

The Stargazer traveled in Hispo form, alongside a similarly shaped Storm-Eye, both of them bearing Cries Havoc on their backs. North Wind's Son led the way, following the faint trail Antonine had set them on. Now and then, something sparkled on its edges, like minute shards of broken glass embedded in the dirt. Antonine told them it was the remnants of an old moon path; it still had some of that path's powers to guide them from place to place but could not protect them from enemies should they appear.

Behind Antonine and the Red Talon walked Julia, followed by Carlita, who every now and then turned to watch behind her, making sure they weren't being followed. Once, she thought she had heard something large in the bushes, something bigger than the Gafflings running about. But it refused to be seen and made no more noise, so she moved on.

There. She stopped and whispered to the others: "Something's out there."

They all stopped and looked around. Antonine gently lowered Cries Havoc to the ground, with Storm-Eye following his lead. He then sniffed the air with his keen wolf senses, circling the group. He stopped before a set of bushes to their left and raised his hackles, issuing a low growl as challenge.

The leaves parted and a sleek panther slid from the branches, its fur black as night but its eyes gleaming like twin, yellow suns.

Antonine shifted into human form, a smile on his face. "Shakar! My friend, what are you doing here?"

The panther metamorphosed its shape, becoming a dark-skinned man of medium height with jet-black hair, dressed in loose clothing more befitting a palace in India than the Catskill Mountains of New York State. A jewel-encrusted dagger was sheathed at his belt. He smiled at Antonine.

"Hunting, oh Stargazer," he said. "For the secret of the distant winds, for the source of the troubling scent and the home to the mysterious thunder."

Antonine nodded toward the dark horizon. "The storm?"

"Indeed. The storm. Or so we could call it, for it does resemble that. But it is no storm known to my kind, and it bedevils my curiosity."

"Don't go near it," Antonine said. "It's of the Wyrm and has already killed some and wounded the spirits of others, such that we can't awaken them." He motioned toward Cries Havoc.

Shakar took a step toward the unconscious Garou but froze when he realized that all the young cubs were watching him with looks of confusion and outright hostility.

"And who are your friends, Antonine?" he said. "Not Stargazers, I assume."

"The Silver River Pack," Antonine said, walking over to Cries Havoc. "And don't be hurt by their manners. They've had much to deal with of late. It makes sense that they would distrust even one I had named friend."

Julia flushed with embarrassment. "I… I didn't mean it. It's just that… well, you don't see too many cat-changers… uh, I mean Bastet, around these days."

"I apologize for my packmates and I," North Wind's Son said. "It was rude of all of us. We trust Antonine, and so his friends are our friends."

Shakar looked with bemusement at Storm-Eye and Carlita, who looked away nervously.

"What he said," Carlita mumbled.

Storm-Eye nodded but said nothing.

Shakar leaned over Cries Havoc and looked him over. He gently placed his hand on his face and pulled back his eyelid to examine the unseeing eye beneath. He shook his head and closed the metis's eye again. He then shapeshifted once more, returning to his panther form. He sniffed up and down Cries Havoc's body and then returned to his face, where he began to vigorously lick the cheeks and forehead as if Cries Havoc were a kitten who had stuck his face in soot.

When that proved to have no effect he paced away and shifted back into human form. "I see nothing wrong with him. And yet… some spirit far from our sight haunts him. Strange that we cannot see it here in the Umbra…."

"Thank you for trying anyway," Antonine said.

Shakar gave Antonine a strange look. "It troubles me that here is an enigma you cannot unravel, my friend. Many have been the nights where we traded riddles, and although months might pass without answer for some of them, you always solved them. Every one of them. I cannot believe this one is beyond your wisdom."

"I hope you are right, Shakar. I'm taking him home, where I can read the stars. All our fates are written there, although their glyphs are not easy to read."

"Good luck, my friend. I must return to my den, there to wait out this storm. I shall take your advice and for once ignore what has inflamed my curiosity. If it is the Wyrm at work, then who better to deal with it than Garou, eh?" He smirked as he spoke.

Antonine only nodded. "Your irony speaks truth, no matter the shame in it. You very well know my tribe greatly wishes yours were joined with ours in this."

"Ah, but it cannot be," Shakar said, heading back off the trail. "There are too few of us left, and we keep our secrets to ourselves."

He disappeared through the bushes, but his voice was still heard. "Farewell, Antonine Teardrop. I hope we may soon visit again and turn our minds to less Wyrm-ridden matters."

"Travel well, Shakar," Antonine said. He went back to Cries Havoc and waited for Storm-Eye to take her part of the burden before lifting him again.

The pack moved on.

After a while, Julia broke the silence. "All right. Enough's enough. You can't very well expect us to keep walking without explaining that. Who was that?"

"Shakar is, as you guessed, a Bastet. He is of the Bagheera, the werepanthers. Like Stargazers, they prefer thoughtful action over warfare. We have much in common."

"I'd say so," Julia said. "Especially since you aren't part of the Garou Nation any more."

"Untrue," Antonine said. "My tribe has elected to leave the nation, but I, an individual, remain."

"Yeah, but you're still a Stargazer. How can you be both in and out of the nation?"

"The Stargazers elected to sever their formal ties with the rest of the Garou, although many individuals still maintain what relations they had before then. I have spent too long trying to ally the tribes to forgo that task now."

"I don't get it," Carlita said. "Why'd you guys leave, anyway? All you've done is piss everybody off. What the hell did you gain from that?"

"If by everybody, you mean the Garou of Europe and America, then yes, we did anger them. But the world is larger than they reckon it. The heart of the Stargazers tribe has always been in the East. Unlike the other Garou and changing breeds of the East, we came West to spread wisdom. With mixed results."

"I thought most of the changing breeds—the Fera, right?"

"Yes, that's the accepted general term."

"Yeah, thought so. Anyway, I thought most of the Fera were gone."

"Most Garou don't know it, but the Fera are stronger in the East than here. They maintain the Beast Courts, whereby they strive for balance and harmony between all the breeds, not just Garou. Stargazers have been friends to those courts and have been for far longer than any Stargazer alliance in the West."

"Okay, I hear that. Old alliances die hard. But why cut out on us here? How does that help you there?"

Antonine was silent for a while but then spoke with a sense of defeat in his voice. "Do you know what it's like to lose a caern? It tears a hole in your soul. A place once vital, once deeply connected with your being, is now gone. Loss of place is one of the most spirit-draining tragedies of this whole war with the Wyrm. You can see it in humans who have no roots, no home. They're empty, forlorn.

Or they're manic, desperately trying to distract themselves from their rootlessness.

"The Stargazers lost their heart, the oldest caern dedicated to the tribe. The Shigalu Monastery in Tibet, one of the most ancient strongholds of knowledge and wisdom, finally fell to the Wyrm. It took a few years for the repercussions of that loss to set in, but when they did, the tribal elders had to reexamine our purpose.

"There are many paths to the same goal. The Get of Fenris seek to fight the Wyrm with claw and sinew. The Shadow Lords through guile and domination. Each tribe has its own method. The Stargazers have always sought to win through wisdom and enlightenment—to transcend the conflict itself and so diminish it by gaining a truer perspective on it. Like the other tribes, we have succeeded in some ways, failed in others. Our failures in the West far exceed our successes in the East."

"So that's it?" Julia said. "Because your tally sheet was in the red, you withdrew and gave up on the West?"

"No. It's more complicated than that. In some ways, the West gave up on us. We recognize the need for different measures in this conflict, and that means the contributions of the other Fera: the Bastet, the Corax raven-folk, Kitsune fox-folk, Gurahl bear-folk and others. Without them, we believe this war cannot be won. The West has completely alienated them, and still does." He looked pointedly at Julia, Carlita and Storm-Eye.

"For the Stargazers to successfully gain their full trust, we had to become a neutral party, outsiders to the Garou Nation."

"The Switzerland of tribes?" Julia said.

Antonine smiled. "Of sorts. If we stand outside of the nation, we can both criticize it and honor it without the taint of favoritism. In this way, we hope to better build ties with all other beings. Of course, we hoped the rest of the Garou would understand this. So far, few have."

"Well, you guys haven't exactly done a good job of explaining this to the others," Julia said. "You need a better public relations firm."

"Oh? I think we laid it all out pretty well to the elders. However, for some, the difference between understanding and appreciation is an abyss too large to bridge. They understood; they just didn't agree with us."

"Now, that I can understand," North Wind's Son said. "My tribe gets that all the time."

"Don't we all?" said Carlita.

The rest of the journey was spent in silence as each thought about what Antonine had said. Cries Havoc, his spirit far away in a place no one knew where, did not hear the discussion and so formed no opinions on the matter.

Chapter Three

The stars wheeled in the heavens. Antonine followed their dance, watching for meaning in their scattered, constellated arrays. He viewed the side-real menagerie through a telescope with lenses not of ground glass that refracted the physical world, but carefully grown crystals that revealed the firmament of spirit, the Aetherial Realm, home to the Celestines and Incarna whose souls fueled the fires of the stars humans saw with earthbound eyes.

The telescope was a fetish, its metal cylinder and crystals inhabited by star spirits, wisps of ether born in the spaces between the stars—spaces far from empty in the spirit world, suffused with life and consciousness. Although some of these spirits were bound to this earthly metal and crystal con-traption, their vision gazed homeward. Their incarnation in matter was no cage, but a willing vassalage to a servant of Gaia, their decades of bondage but a fleeting moment experienced from the perspective of celestial bodies.

Antonine sat back and ruminated over the im-agery. With a telescope as strong as his, he could see distant stars invisible to the naked eye, unseen even to those who stood within the Aetherial Realm it-self. These invisible stars formed constellations of their own when seen from the perspective of his lo-cation in the material world. The more obvious stars provided no easy clues for Cries Havoc's condition, so Antonine had to look deeper.

He could not help but notice the red star, of course. The baleful fire portending apocalypse had only recently shown itself within the sky, although it still remained invisible from most areas of the Umbra. It cast a crimson haze over his distant gleanings, obscuring vision. Did it likewise tug at the light of these stars? Did its gravity warp his vision and so warp any truth he could read in the stars' positioning? Or was that gravity itself somehow part of the secret grammar he must decipher?

Perhaps, and that in itself was an important factor in the matter at hand. Antonine did not know Cries Havoc's lunar birth signs. None of his packmates—joined too recently—knew the astrological happenings associated with his birth or First Change, only that it had occurred near the time of the appearance of the red star. Antonine had to rely on outside help.

Before settling into his chair at the eyepiece, he gathered his will in the manner the Chimerlings—spirits of dream—had taught him and yielded it to the cosmos. Once receptive to its influences, he opened his eyes and gazed at the stars. Far off, so dim as barely to be seen, three stars winked. Increasing the magnification, he examined them closer and saw the red haze. Calling upon the power of his telescope's spirits, he reversed the play of light on the lenses back to the time when Cries Havoc had been injured, and then played the stars' motions forward again, watching their dance intently. They spun counter to the earth, in spirals more complex than he thought possible for such a short time of examination.

And yet, it was not the stars that moved so dramatically, but their light, twisted and spiraled on its journey from molten flame to his eye, warped by the draw of the red star, Anthelios.

He called once more upon the wisdom of the spirits and requested a clue to the meaning behind these three unknown stars and their motions. Images occurred to his mind's eye, thoughts others might disregard as the residue of exhaustion or imagination. Antonine knew better. He paid close attention to these messages, the answer to his query, a question only highly ranked members of his tribe knew how to ask.

He saw Cries Havoc among his own kind, the Children of Gaia of the Sept of the Dawn. He hunted with his septmates, played with them and sang the old sagas with them. As the images flooded his mind, they seemed to get older, to seep into the past. Cries Havoc grew younger. Antonine watched moments of the metis's past played backward. But then they stopped, and only a void remained, emptier than a dark cave, for not even sound, warmth or cold existed here.

He opened his eyes, breathing heavily. He looked around for a moment, confused about his own surroundings, and then remembered where he was. He shook his head to rid it of the void and shivered. He now knew what it was like to lose one's past, to have a chunk of one's former being ripped from the soul. It was as if those memories no longer existed. Worse, it was almost as if the events themselves never happened—not that they were replaced by an alternate memory, but that they had been yanked from time itself, leaving an absence, an open wound, behind.

The Garou were not simply beings of flesh and blood. Their bodies were composed of spirit, and that spirit consisted of songs, stories, sagas. You could not reduce a Garou to mechanistic, random chance, for his very being was composed of a mythic tale of birth, destiny, struggle and heroism even in the grip of defeat. You could destroy the flesh, even bind the spirit, but you could not alter the essence of who a Garou was and what he was meant to be.

Or so I once believed, Antonine thought.

* * *

Carlita paced around the living room of the spacious cabin, bored and still too keyed up to sleep. Like the others, she had collapsed as soon as they got to Antonine's, but unlike her packmates, she woke up again barely two hours later. The rest still slept, Julia in the guest bedroom, North Wind's Son on a foldout cot in the living room and Storm-Eye on the floor, curled in her wolf form. Cries Havoc lay in his coma in the master bedroom. Carlita had slept on the easy chair, Antonine's reading chair. It was comfortable enough; that wasn't the problem. It was the uncertainty, the looming unknowable that now stood before them: Where to go? What to do?

She wandered into the kitchen and browsed the cupboard. Lots of rice, soup cans, tea packets. Bread on the counter. In the fridge, she found some ground beef. *And I thought Stargazers were vegetarians,* she thought. *Ain't that supposed to be the way with spiri-*

tual types? Maybe for humans, but I guess it ain't easy for a wolf not to eat meat.

Pulling a frying pan from its hook over the counter, she dug a spatula out from a drawer. She opened the beef packet and pulled out a handful of meat, then slapped it into a circular patty that she threw into the pan, setting the burner for medium-high heat. She knew she could eat it raw with no problem, especially if she shifted into wolf form, but she preferred cooked and seasoned meat, a delicacy Bone Gnawers didn't always have the option to choose, living on the streets and eating from garbage cans like all to many of them did.

She found a black-pepper grinder and scattered prodigious amounts of the spice onto the frying burger. While it cooked, she snatched two pieces of bread from their package and dropped them into the toaster. In the refrigerator, she found mustard and ketchup but no mayonnaise.

The sizzling smell wafted about the room, eliciting a smile. She felt better already. Food was one of the best cures known to human or wolf.

She flipped the burger a couple of times to get it evenly cooked on both sides, but still pink in the center, and dropped it onto her toasted, mustard-and-ketchup-splattered bread, and then bit into the delicious morsel. *Holy shit, I needed this!*

Munching on the hot burger, she wandered back into the living room to find Storm-Eye sitting up and sniffing. The wolf gave her a look of disgust.

"Why do you ruin your food by burning it?" she growled.

Carlita just smiled and plopped herself back down into the easy chair. "Calm down; there's still some raw meat on the counter for you."

Storm-Eye got to all fours and sauntered into the kitchen.

Carlita watched North Wind's Son, still sleeping on the cot. *How can he sleep so silently? Not even a heavy breath, let alone a snore. Do they teach him that sort of stuff in his tribe?*

The door to the observatory opened and Antonine came down the stairs. He looked tired, as if he had gone too long without sleep. He seemed deep in thought, barely cognizant of the others in the room.

Carlita held up her burger—almost gone, two bites left. "Sorry. I got hungry. Hope it's okay."

"Of course," Antonine said, smiling at her, although it seemed more like an afterthought than a genuine gesture. "I would have offered food before, but you all needed sleep."

"Find out anything?"

"Yes. A clue. To proceed further, I need Julia's help."

"What's up? You need to consult the stock market or something?"

"Summon spirits."

"Yeah, right," Carlita said, quickly hiding a smile. "I knew that. Just joking. Want me to wake her up?"

"No, let's let her sleep for now. I need her to be rested."

"Okay. So what now?"

"I need to meditate, to prepare myself. For that, I'm going outside. If you need me, I'll be by the stream, but please don't interrupt unless it's important."

"Got it."

Antonine walked out the front door and closed it quietly behind him. Storm-Eye padded from the kitchen, smacking her jaws, licking loose bits of raw meat from her teeth.

"You didn't eat it all, did you?" Carlita said. "The others are going to be hungry, too, y'know."

Storm-Eye hung her tail guiltily.

"Oh, girl! You're supposed to be our leader!"

Storm-Eye raised her head defiantly. "I shall hunt." She moved toward the cabin door and pushed it open, disappearing into the early dawn mist.

"Great. Raw roadkill. Just what we need." Carlita, her stomach full and satisfied, curled up again into the easy chair and soon fell back into sleep.

* * *

The smell of roasting venison wafted in through the open cabin door, waking her again. She groggily got up and stretched and looked out the window. By the way the light slanted in, she figured it was sometime in the afternoon. North Wind's Son was no longer on the cot. She heard voices speaking outside, from some distance away.

She figured the others were having a cookout with Storm-Eye's kill. Before joining them, she made a quick pit stop and then checked on Cries Havoc. He breathed normally but had not changed position since they had laid him down on the bed last night. She sighed and quietly closed the door behind her.

The door to the guest room was open and there was no sign of Julia. *She must be outside with the rest of them.*

Carlita sauntered out the front door, down the steps and around the wooded bend, following the scent of cooking flesh.

The others were sitting around an open fire pit, where a skinned deer carcass roasted above a large flame. Portions of its haunches lay on the ground nearby, slowly being gnawed on by Storm-Eye. Its splattered blood stained the grass a dark brown color.

John North Wind's Son slowly turned the spit and nodded at her as she walked into the clearing. Julia, sitting on a wooden bench nearby, clacking away on a keyboard fixed to her PDA, waved but did not turn to look at her.

"So what's up?" Carlita said. "Any word from Antonine?"

"He's meditating," North Wind's Son said. "That way, over by the stream."

"Hey, Julia," Carlita said. "Did he tell you he needs your help to summon a spirit later?"

Julia looked up from her typing. "No, he didn't. We haven't talked to him yet. Did he say what kind of spirit he was looking for?"

"Nope. I guess he figured he needs a Theurge to help out."

Julia nodded and went back to her tiny screen. "There's no news. Nothing on the net at all. Nobody knows anything else about Jo'cllath'mattric." She turned off the device and plucked it from its keyboard cradle. She then folded the keyboard like an accordion and snapped it together, like shutting a book.

"I don't expect whatever happens to be broadcast," North Wind's Son said.

"It's not broadcast media," Julia said. "It's Glass Walker internet. Requires a fetish—" she hefted her PDA "—to access it. There's always a good rumor mill going on. Our fiasco in Serbia is being bandied about—I corrected some factual errors in the accounts—but there's no other news from Europe."

"It does not matter," Storm-Eye said, growling in the Garou tongue. "We can't do anything for them now. We must look after Cries Havoc. What harms him will soon harm others. If it can be cured here, the cure will work there."

"We need Antonine for that," North Wind's Son said.

"If hearing us yapping away here doesn't draw him out of his meditation soon," Carlita said, "then the smell of this deer will."

They sat down to watch the deer cook. Nobody knew what else to say. Soon enough, Antonine Teardrop appeared in the clearing (Storm-Eye was startled at how silently he came) and sat down at the wooden bench.

"Is that deer ready yet?" he said.

"Yes," North Wind's Son said. "What part do you want?"

"Since I see the hunter has already chosen her earned portion," Antonine said, nodding toward the bones lying before Storm-Eye, "I won't worry about precedence. Just slice off a piece of the side for me, and thank its spirit while doing so."

"I never eat the flesh of another without first honoring it. It is the way of my people."

"It should be the way of others also. That's a good slice. Thank you." Antonine took a steaming red slice of flesh and muscle from the Wendigo chef and silently said a prayer to the spirit that once nurtured it. He then sharpened his teeth into wolf canines and tore into it, thankful for the sustenance.

North Wind's Son served the others and they all ate, after each paused to thank the deer spirit in his or her own way. Julia felt awkward; she had never really done this before, had never really even thought about it. Meat was meat. But it did come from someone—someone who once lived. After all, if *she* were one day consumed, she'd expect the bastard to at least mutter a word of thanks for the trouble. She felt a bit guilty about never having considered it before and then thanked the deer for everything it had given her—or was about to give her. She took a bite.

After meticulously chewing and swallowing, she looked at Antonine. "Carlita said you wanted me to help you summon a spirit."

"That's right," Antonine said. "I could use a Theurge to aid me. I've done it before, many times, but it's not really my forte."

"So what kind of spirit?"

"A sun spirit. A Jaggling who serves Helios."

Julia's perplexity showed on her face. "That's… uh, odd. What do you hope to gain from that?"

"A story. A tale. Some snippet of Cries Havoc's past, some event mighty enough to have been told to all members of his sept."

"Okay. But I still don't get the sun spirit bit. What does that have to do with Cries Havoc's sept?"

"The Sept of the Dawn? Think about it. Its leader is the legendary Sergiy Dawntreader, a Child of Gaia renowned for his love of sunrise. None of you knows anything about Cries Havoc's past, at least nothing old enough to be of use to him now. But it's just possible that, when Cries Havoc was a young cub, he performed a great deed that the Dawntreader sang of to the dawn. This might have been heard by any number of spirits attending the rise of the sun. They might remember the song and tell it to us."

North Wind's Son spoke: "How can you know to summon the right spirit? There must be hundreds of them!"

Julia raised her hand, waving it as if urging them to hold their horses. "No, it can be done. It's a real long shot—the odds are pretty astronomical, no pun intended—but there is a chance we can call upon a spirit who could have heard the Dawntreader tell such a tale. The real question is why? What good will it do?"

Antonine stood up. "Cries Havoc is physically healthy. He has no wounds beyond healing. But he is missing a part of his past, and hence a part of his soul. The soul is wounded and still bleeds. We must patch it. He cannot know who he is without regaining it."

"So this spirit can heal him by restoring a memory from his past?"

"No, but it may revive him enough for him to regain consciousness. Whatever story this spirit can tell—should we be blessed enough to accomplish its summoning—would be small, not nearly so much as to patch the wound in his soul. But it would be a start. It might be enough to awaken him."

He began to walk toward the cabin. "Julia, I would like you to join me by Cries Havoc's bedside at noon. I'll have everything ready."

"All right," Julia said. "I'll be there. But I have to warn you: I'm only good with tech-spirits. Sun spirits may be out of my league."

"Don't worry. They're well within mine."

"What about us?" Carlita said. "What do we do?"

Antonine looked back over his shoulder at them as he turned the corner of the bend. "Guard the cabin. Be prepared to ward off anything that might answer our summons without an invitation."

"Like what?"

"Anything without a sunny disposition," Antonine said, smiling, as he disappeared around the bend.

"Sorry I asked."

"Forgiven," Antonine said, his voice carrying through the trees. "Let's get started."

Storm-Eye shrank back to her Lupus form, looking ready for action. North Wind's Son lowered his head and seemed to pray. The wind stirred lightly, blowing hair into Carlita's face. She brushed it aside and tore off another hunk of meat from the spit.

"Great," she said. "Guard duty."

Chapter Four

The room reeked of spice and pine scent. Incense smoke wafted from ceiling to floor. Julia scrunched up her nose as she stood in the doorway to the bedroom, where Cries Havoc lay unconscious on the bed in his Crinos form. As a metis, it was his natural form, one of the many reasons Garou such as he were not usually allowed to live outside of caerns—the risk of sparking the Delirium, an overwhelming fear in humans facing the Crinos war-form, was too great.

"Close the door," Antonine said. "Don't dilute the incense."

Julia slipped into the room and shut the door behind her. "What kind is it? I've never smelled anything like it."

"It's a special mixture developed by the Purest Resolve Sept in China, designed to aid communication with star spirits."

"I thought we wanted a sun spirit," Julia said, placing her PDA at the foot of the bed. "I know the sun is just another type of star, from a scientific perspective, but they really are different from an Umbral perspective: stars are distant and weird; the sun is close and regal."

"True. But this is the best I have. They are related, in that they share the same realm, although they reside in different quarters of the sky. Nonetheless, it will help you sympathize with the Aetherial Realm in your summoning and aid the spirit in passing through the Gauntlet."

"Uh… Gauntlet? It's really a lot easier to summon spirits from the Umbra. Aren't we going to step sideways first?"

"I don't recommend it. That storm is still out there, looming in the distance. It may not bother us now, but something from within it may be attracted by a summoning, even if it is uninvited."

"Gotcha. No sun in the sky during stormy weather. Makes perfect sense. I should have thought of it." Julia looked around the room and saw that, in addition to numerous cones and sticks of burning incense, candles guttered along the shelves and windowsill. "Okay, how are we going to do this thing? I'm summoning, I assume, but what are you going to do?"

"Once you get the spirit here, I'll converse with it and hopefully coax it to tell us a story."

"Then let's do it."

Antonine held out a bronze bell carved with odd sigils. "Use this to call it. It's from the Shigalu Monastery. It rings throughout the Aetherial Realm. Normally, it's used to send messages to a Stargazer monastery there, but I've attuned it so spirits will hear."

Julia took the heavy bell and shook it. A low, deep clang resonated throughout the room. "Interesting…."

She took her PDA and turned it on, then used her stylus to touch activate an application. The screen displayed a list of icons. She tapped the stylus on a spider image and the screen went blank but for a slowly pulsing glow.

Julia sat silently for a while, her eyes closed and mind centering itself for the task. She then touched the PDA screen. Instead of tapping the clear plastic, however, her finger sank into it, as if it were a still pool of water. Ripples of force circled outward from the point of contact, washing over the entire room and outside the walls, misting away into the spirit realm.

"This is Julia Spencer, Glass Walker of the Old City Sept. I'm trying to reach the brood of Helios. Is there anyone out there, near the sun, basking in its light, who can tell me about Cries Havoc, metis Garou of the Children of Gaia tribe, former member of the Sept of the Dawn?"

Antonine whispered: "Try the bell."

Julia shook the bell vigorously, and its reverberations seemed to join the ripple spreading from her finger. She could hear it echoing off into the cosmos, and it seemed to rumble distantly overhead like a brewing thunderstorm.

"It has reached the Aetherial Realm," Antonine said.

Julia waited and repeated her question. After another pause, she repeated it once more.

The ripples changed, bouncing back into the room as if another series of ripples were counteracting them. New ripples became visible, spiraling in and around Julia's finger. When they formed a vortex around it, she slowly withdrew her finger from the screen, drawing the congealing ectoplasm with it. As it streamed out of the screen, its glow became fiercely bright, so much so that both Antonine and Julia had to squint their eyes. The room became suddenly brighter.

The spirit rose up toward the ceiling, forming an orb that radiated shimmering heat and light, a miniature sun floating above their heads.

"Greetings, servant of the sun," Antonine said.

"Greetings to you, Gazer upon Stars," the spirit said in a deep, rumbling voice, the voice of an old man long in years and wisdom. "And to you, Walker upon Glass. I heard the bell and then listened to your query. I know of this Cries Havoc, a young pup reared in the ways of the wolfchangers by Sergiy Dawntreader, favored of our lord Helios."

"I am glad to hear it. Would you tell us what you know of him, oh bright sun, so that he might also hear it? For his body lies in this room but his spirit resides elsewhere. If he hears a tale of himself, he could perhaps be coaxed back into flesh."

"I will do so, for Cries Havoc is beloved by the Dawntreader. But it is not the Dawntreader who asks this task of me, but you, a stranger, although one known to my cousins, the stars. There is a price for my wisdom."

"Ask it."

"If the cub's spirit is roused by my lore, he must deliver respect to Helios in the manner of his own elder. At dawn he will greet the sun with open arms and song, as does the Dawntreader. He will do so at least once a moon—as wolfchangers reckon time—but will gain favor if he chooses to honor Helios in such a manner every day."

Antonine looked at Julia. "I am hesitant to promise anything in his name. You are his packmate, however. The decision must be yours."

"Hardly a choice here. Coma or morning prayer for the rest of your life? I'll take morning prayer for five hundred, Alex."

Antonine addressed the spirit above. "Agreed. Cries Havoc's packmates will ensure he keeps to this promise."

"Then know this," the spirit said, "as it was told to the rising sun by the Dawntreader…"

A new voice resonated throughout the room, a deep, hearty voice with a hint of laughter, full of joy: the voice of Sergiy Dawntreader, as it sounded years ago.

* * *

Ho, oh spirit of warmth and wisdom! Heed this account, a tale of my own fostern, Cries Havoc, hero to the Sept of the Dawn, on this, the first day of his Garouhood, upon completion of his Rite of Passage.

It was but a week ago when his small pack left the caern, pups all, new to their shapeshifting skins, to seek the source of corruption we all knew to exist in a village to our west. Humans were murdered, one by one, their bodies left in the woods. It was an ethnic dispute, for the victims were immigrants from the east. That such hate and bitterness should exist among humans is nothing of note, but that it should be accompanied by Banes to chew on the souls of those murdered—that is unconscionable beyond measure.

Once arrived, the young pack members, unproven as yet, scoured the town by night for the scent of evil. They found no trace of it. Undaunted, they walked as humans, pretending to be tourists to the district, asking questions that would wisely draw out the evil. Though their behavior was rude by human standards, they did indeed attract those who hated with murderous intent.

Three nights after their arrival, they split up to search the night again for sign of corruption. Cries Havoc, alone on the empty streets, was cornered by a mob of hateful humans seeking to kill once more the object of their hate—this time, friends to the foreigners who they believed stole their livelihoods and threatened their sense of self-sufficiency. This, too, was not unusual, for it is seen many places in Europe.

But their ringleader was exceptional. Tall and imposing, he was an experienced hate monger, a skinhead of old and now rabble-rouser for the latest fashion in hatred. In his strong, athletic body writhed a Bane, rotting in his soul, choking all inkling of compassion or pity. He was no longer human, but fomor. The others followed him not through supernatural coercion, but simply because he gave them a focus for their fears.

Wielding rocks and clubs, they set upon the young cub. As the rain of blows fell on him, he did something most unusual for a young Garou: he remained in his human form and suffered the blows, even though they harmed him greatly and might well have killed him. He raised no fist against them, but only collapsed under their assault.

Weak? Is this what some think? No. Wise.

Cries Havoc waited, feigning unconsciousness, for the leader to approach him. Once near, he lashed out, shifting forms instantly, and gutted the Fomor from front to end. In the Umbra, the Bane wailed, unmoored from its body. There, Grey Mountain, fellow cub of the pack, heard it and finished its existence.

With the ringleader slain, the mob dispersed. Some ran in fear, unable to remember the source of their fear, clouded by the sight of Cries Havoc's battle form, wreathed in the Delirium. Others drifted away in confusion. Ever after, their hatred of foreigners will evoke fear, not anger. Whenever they summon murderous intent, they will shudder and sweat for no cause they can discern and then think other thoughts, fleeing as far as they can from the night Cries Havoc spared their lives.

Honor him, oh sun! Honor one who knows compassion, who knows whom to strike and whom to spare. A true Child of Gaia this one, he who is called Cries Havoc!

* * *

The voice fell into silence. The smoldering spirit faded, leaving only the sudden darkness of candlelight. Antonine and Julia stared in anticipation at Cries Havoc. Had his breathing changed? Was his hand in a different position than it had been earlier? Neither of them could be sure.

Minutes passed, with no change. Julia shut off her PDA and placed it in her pocket. She drew in a breath, about to speak, when Antonine raised his hand, bidding her to remain silent. He had not looked away from Cries Havoc the whole time, and now seemed to see something she could not.

She realized he was peering into the Umbra to view the metis from the perspective of the spirit realm. That made no sense to her. They had searched the Penumbra around Cries Havoc before and could find no sign of activity near his soul. Since he was presently in the material world, Antonine shouldn't be able to see him on the other side.

Nonetheless, Julia called upon her own spirit endowment and likewise peered past the Velvet Shadow. There, in a room that looked remarkably similar to its physical counterpart—unusual for the Umbra, which usually reflected entirely different realities—a dark cloud was slowly coalescing over the space occupied by Cries Havoc in the physical world.

She stared at it, trying to figure out what it was. It was definitely related to the storm—in fact, it looked like part of the dark thunderclouds of that strange phenomenon. But as she watched it, it didn't grow larger or darker, but instead seemed to unravel, to thin out and float away across the Umbra in multiple directions, dragged by the airts.

Someone coughed. She looked around but didn't see anyone. The room was empty. She then realized that she was still staring into the Penumbra and that the cough had taken place in the physical world. Withdrawing her sight from the spirit world, she looked at Cries Havoc.

He coughed again and rolled his head back and forth as if fighting a nightmare. Antonine was now standing over him. He placed a hand on his brow and Cries Havoc's eyes flew open. The metis convulsed in surprise but then calmed when he recognized the Stargazer. He let out a groan of confusion and worry.

"Cries Havoc!" Julia said. "It's me, Julia. You're okay now. It's all right. There are no Wyrm creatures here."

Cries Havoc looked at her, staring at her as if he thought her dead and now suddenly returned to life. He then looked back at Antonine, who stood smiling. "What...? Where...?"

"You're at my place," Antonine said. "Back in the Catskills. Far from Europe."

Cries Havoc shuddered and let out a long sigh. He rubbed his eyes and cradled his head. "I... don't remember... what happened?"

"Hold on," Julia said. "Don't rush this thing. We'll tell you in due time. For now, you need to shake it off, whatever it was that had you in its grip."

"I agree," Antonine said. "Stand up, move about. Let's get you some air." He walked over to the windows and extinguished the candles on the sill with his fingers, then opened the shutters, letting in the late afternoon light and air.

Cries Havoc stared at the trees outside as if he were witnessing an oasis after a long journey in the desert. He smiled. "It's beautiful. It's alive. I didn't think I'd ever see it again."

He stood up and almost fell before recovering his balance and strength. He smiled at Julia, who had jumped up to catch him. "I'm okay. Where are the others?"

"Waiting outside," Julia said. "C'mon, this way." She opened the door and led him out by the hand.

As they left the cabin and walked down the wooded path to the fire pit, where the others were still gathered, Cries Havoc stared at everything around him like a cancer patient who's just been given a new chance to live. He was still in his Crinos form, towering over Julia's human shape. He didn't seem to realize it.

"Holy Mother of Gaia," Carlita cried upon seeing him. "It's a miracle. You're awake!" The Bone Gnawer ran up to him, grabbing his shoulders and shaking him as if to see if he was real and not an apparition. Cries Havoc's toothy grin widened and he couldn't suppress a laugh.

Storm-Eye pranced over to him and circled around him, howling. North Wind's Son also took to his wolf form, adding to the howl. Carlita and Julia followed suit. Four wolves circled around the grinning Crinos Garou, howling to the heavens. From the cabin porch, another howl joined theirs: Antonine's.

Cries Havoc slipped into his wolf form and joined the dance, howling with joy and companionship. He could remember very little about what had happened to him, but for now, he was glad he couldn't. The ecstasy of the moment was all that mattered. That, and the presence of his packmates, greeting him as wolves—no hidden agendas, just the bond of togetherness.

A memory he hoped he would never forget.

Chapter Five

Rain spattered across the rocks and turned the river surface into a quivering, sloshing pane of glass, shattered with every raindrop and instantly mended again by the onrushing, overflowing, ever-replenishing wetness. Cries Havoc stepped carefully over the slick stones, careful to place his feet on wet moss wherever possible. The moss was slick, but not as frictionless as the smooth stone. He wore his human form but considered taking the wolf for the extra legs.

Reaching the bend in the river, he leaned around a large boulder restricting his view downstream and finally saw Antonine standing on the rocks in the middle of the rushing torrent. Cries Havoc shook his head in astonishment, envying the Stargazer's sense of balance. Antonine stood on one leg, half submerged in the rain-swollen river. The force of the water's flow would surely knock down a normal human; Antonine had obviously practiced this before and seemed completely undisturbed by the tugging froth.

His eyes were closed and his hands placed one atop the other before his belly, both palms facing up. The forefinger and thumb of the top hand (the left) formed a circle. He looked calm and at peace. Cries Havoc couldn't help thinking that the hand formation resembled an "A-okay" sign.

The young Garou rounded the bend and began to cautiously move into the river, approaching the Stargazer slowly but loudly enough so as not to surprise him. Antonine showed no sign of noticing him.

As Cries Havoc came closer, the Stargazer suddenly shifted forms into Glabro, then Crinos, then Hispo, the prehistoric dire wolf form. As he assumed the quadrupedal shape, his four paws shifted perfectly onto the rock, with no scrambling for position or balance. Then into wolf form, where his body was almost submerged—but still unmoved, eyes remaining closed. Slowly, he shifted forms back again, one-by-one, into human shape, and then opened his eyes.

Cries Havoc smiled in amazement. "That's, uh, that's amazing balance you have."

"Anyone can learn it," Antonine said, lowering his other leg.

"I'm sure it takes a while, though. Lots of training."

"It takes patience and commitment, like any endeavor."

Antonine walked back to the shore, showing no signs of the struggle Cries Havoc waged against the strong current. He walked onto the thin bank and climbed onto a large rock, where he sat facing Cries Havoc, who also began working his way to the shore.

"You didn't come down here in the pouring rain, standing in the middle of a raging river, to talk about balance," Antonine said.

"No," Cries Havoc said, pulling himself onto the shore. "I guess I've got a lot of questions is all. We've hardly talked since I woke up a few days ago."

"You needed time with your packmates. They were with you at your wounding. You needed to hear them tell you about it."

"Yeah, but I know it now. I accept that the Bane—or whatever it was—took some of my memories. I still can't remember a lot of things from a few years ago. The whole Anvil-Klaiven affair is still here," he tapped his head, "but not much about my early years. I can't even remember my First Change."

"Some Garou would consider that a blessing."

"Maybe. But it's not just that the memory is gone. It's something else. Every time I try to remember it, I feel awful, like staring into an abyss that's going to suck me in."

"Then don't think about it. At least, not yet." Antonine climbed down from the rock onto a trail on the other side. Cries Havoc couldn't see him, but he still heard him over the falling rain. "Don't pick at scabs until they're healed. I suppose it's time we talked. Let's walk a while."

Cries Havoc's shoulders drooped. He had hoped they could go someplace dry. He shrugged off his disappointment and clambered over the rock onto the thin deer trail Antonine now walked, away from the cabin and into the deeper woods.

After a while, the Stargazer spoke again. "Your wound is unique. It's not simply spiritual. I've seen soul damage before—traumas and tragedies written on the soul, forcing their victims to enact cycles of abuse throughout generations. Your affliction is different. It's not so much a wound as an absence of spirit. What was once part of you is gone, and your spirit cannot replenish the lost parts to fill the gaps or close the wound."

"I... I don't know what to do," Cries Havoc said. "How can I heal from this? How do I even live with it?"

"You have to restore what has been taken. It cannot be replaced by something else. Your original essence must be regained."

"How do I do that? The Bane ate it! Am I supposed to go to Malfeas to get it back?"

"No!" Antonine stopped in the path and turned to glare at Cries Havoc. "Don't even start talking like that. You are not beyond repair. You can't even give up hope of it for a minute. The closest thing I've ever seen to this affliction is Harano. You're dangerously close to falling into a depression you can't get out of. But this isn't Harano. Nothing is inevitable here."

Cries Havoc nodded and walked past Antonine, picking out his way on the trail himself. Antonine walked behind him. "Okay. I get that. I'll try to keep up the positive thinking and all that. But what do I actually do? I don't think I can think my way out of this. There hasn't been a therapy session invented to handle this."

"No, you're right. You've got to do something, to take action, to integrate your mind, body and spirit again. The answer to this lies in the nature of what you are."

"A Garou? A wolf shapeshifter?"

"Partly. You are not simply a physical being. Your essence is spirit, but that spirit is formed and shaped not by genes but myths. This is especially true for you, a Galliard. Your fate is tied up with these stories more than most. In many ways, you are a caretaker of our very beings, not simply our culture. The answer lies in recovering those myths, reinforcing them. The source of our being is constantly replenished. Our physical regenerative capabilities are just crude examples of this, and our spiritual energy that empowers the spirit teachings—the Gifts—is but a more subtle version of the same thing. But there is an even more subtle truth behind these phenomena—the endless, infinite True Gaia Realm."

"Is this Stargazer theology? I've never heard anything like this—at least, I don't remember hearing it."

"Sort of. It's mostly my conjectures concerning your problem." He stopped speaking as they reached the top of a rise. The trees cleared and they looked down into a valley, bright even in the rain with fall's flaming colors.

"Well," Cries Havoc said. "What's the verdict, then?"

"You tell me. What is the most important treasure of the Garou?"

Cries Havoc thought for a minute. "Uh… our shapeshifting? Our spirit Gifts?"

"I don't mean our capabilities. I mean something outside of ourselves."

"A fetish?"

"You're getting warmer."

"Oh, come on. Why play games? Just tell me."

"Riddling is an important step to recovering memory. You need to practice wracking your mind in pursuit of a goal, which is not the same as your aimless attempts to remember what isn't there. I think this would be easier for you if you had all your memories, but I'll give you another clue, oh Galliard: it crosses generations and spans the world, from the Dawn Times until now."

Cries Havoc wrinkled his brow in puzzlement. "The Litany? No, wait—the Silver Record!"

Antonine nodded. "The greatest tales are preserved there. Everything that we are about is wrapped up in the Silver Record."

"I still don't get it. I'm not in the Silver Record. No way have I done anything to merit that."

"Not yet, maybe. But that's not the point. The point is that there is someone who keeps the record, one who understands the importance of stories more than most. I think you need to seek him out and ask him everything you've asked me."

"The Record Keeper…" Cries Havoc looked out into the valley, as if searching it for someone. "He's said to be very wise, but also unpredictable."

"I'm out of answers, Cries Havoc. I urged the necessity of a third pack—your pack—based on dreams given to me by Chimera. I asked the stars for clues to your affliction and sought a sun spirit who had heard of you by way of your sept elder. Others may believe my wisdom to be infinite, but my well has run dry here. I can't solve this enigma on my own. I'm not a Galliard, but a Philodox. As such, it's my job to point you in the right direction. In this case, it's to the Record Keeper. I've done all I can."

"Don't think for a second that I don't appreciate everything you've done, Antonine. That goes for the whole Silver River Pack. We all know you've done your best. Hell, I can't imagine anyone who's done as well in this whole affair. At least you haven't screwed anything up like we have. Yeah, I know—" he said, holding up his hands to stop Antonine from interrupting, "—don't talk about defeat. I'm just being realistic here. I think the Record Keeper is a great idea. If anyone can figure out how to restore the lost 'saga of myself,' it's him."

"Then there's no more reason to delay. You're as physically healed as you can be. Your pack is rested, and getting rather bored, actually. You need to discuss this option with them and figure out how to accomplish it."

"That's the hard part. I have no idea how to even begin finding him! The Silver Record is the most precious resource of all the tribes—the Record Keeper is intentionally hard to find, for enemies as well as friends."

"Well, as a Garou elder, I think I've earned his respect. I can help you with that, should your pack choose to go."

"Well, we better break the news to them, then. Besides, I'm soaked through. I'd really like to be dry now."

Antonine shifted into wolf form and howled in the Garou tongue. "Then follow!"

Cries Havoc's shape also melted into a wolf's and chased after the quickly moving, gray-furred Stargazer.

* * *

"The Silver Record, huh?" Carlita said. "I guess that figures. So we gotta find this Record Keeper guy, then? Where do we start?"

"Hold on," Julia said. She, like the others, sat in Antonine's living room, sipping tea as they debated their future course. Cries Havoc and Antonine sat nearby, drying off from their extended walk in the pouring rain. "Let's discuss this first. This search could take a while. I don't know if we have that kind of time. We should be figuring out how we can help stop Jo'cllath'mattric."

"No," North Wind's Son said. "We put the needs of our packmate first. We've done all we can in Europe."

"Why choose sides?" Storm-Eye said in the Garou tongue, which couldn't convey as much nuance as English. "Helping Cries Havoc helps heal damage in Europe. Think: Cries Havoc suffered first, but others will follow. We must know what took his spirit and how to restore it. That will defeat the Wyrm."

The rest of the pack nodded in agreement. Storm-Eye was right. Finding the Record Keeper and restoring Cries Havoc was the best thing they could do for their packmate and the effort in Europe.

Storm-Eye turned to address Antonine. "The stolen memory... is it the same that attacks Mari Cabrah?"

"No," Antonine said. "She suffers something darker. Something I believe is closer to the power of Jo'cllath'mattric itself. I think Cries Havoc's problem is caused by something else. Whatever Banes attacked him, they're related to the overall problem, but they're different than the black-winged thing coiled about Mari."

"Can you do nothing for her?"

"Nothing new, no. The answer to her problem still lies in Europe. While you were bringing Cries Havoc up to date over the last few days, I contacted Evan and told him the situation. He's hoping King Albrecht can find something more when he arrives in Europe."

"The king of the American Silver Fangs is going to Europe?" Julia said. "Oh, I don't know if that's wise."

"I second that opinion, but I also cannot offer an alternative. Albrecht is very capable. I saw how he handled the Seventh Generation problem here. I don't doubt his ability to aid the fight over there. The problem will come when he and Margrave Konietzko differ over tactics and leadership."

"Part of me wants to see that," Julia said. "But the other part wants no part of it. I'd prefer the Silver Record option. That keeps us here, right?"

"Maybe. I don't know. The Record Keeper travels all over. For all I know, he could be in Europe now. That's where the big story is. Of course, he might wait for the story to come to an end before recording it. He could well be here in the States."

"So how do we find him?"

"He provides certain Garou with a means to contact him. He gave me such a method after the Seventh Generation affair, which he recorded in the Record."

"Whoah," Carlita said. "I forgot that you're in the Record! That's twice at least, for the Silver Crown saga and this Seventh Generation thing you mentioned. What was that about?"

"Ask him," Antonine said, standing and walking to the stairs to his observatory. "If you do find him, don't be so shy as to let the chance to read the Record pass you by. I'll be right back." He walked up the stairs and into the observatory.

"If we find him," North Wind's Son said. "What then?"

"I guess we explain my situation," Cries Havoc said. "And hope he's got some clue for resolving it. We're in his hands now."

Everyone was silent for a while, each thinking about the coming quest. Julia stood up and stretched.

"Well," she said, "I guess it'll be good to hit the road again. As much as I'd like to get home to London, I'd also like to see more of the world, wherever this search for the Record Keeper takes us. The thing is: do we walk or ride?"

"How do we ride?" Cries Havoc said. "None of us owns a car."

"We don't need to own one. We just need to rent one. I've got a healthy balance on my credit card, so that's no problem. What I don't have is a United States driver's license. Which one of you does?"

"I've got one," North Wind's Son said. "I've never really used it, though."

"That's okay. We'll set you up as the driver. They don't normally allow that, but I think I can talk our way around that, with some help from the spirits."

"I'm not sure I like this option," Storm-Eye said, a frown on her face. "Why can't we just walk?"

"I guess it really depends on where this guy is and how far we have to travel. Let's wait until we know more to decide anything. All right?"

Storm-Eye nodded assent but still didn't look happy.

Antonine came down the stairs holding a metal compass with a leather thong. He handed it to Cries Havoc.

"This will guide you to him. It's a talen, so be careful how you use it. Once it gets you to him, it won't work anymore, so don't do anything to cause him to leave. You won't find him again. When you activate it, he'll know. So, as you travel to him, he may also be traveling to you, depending on his own whims. Obviously, it's not a real compass—it doesn't point north, but instead points at the Record Keeper, telling you the direction you need to go."

"This is better than I expected," Cries Havoc said. "We're sure to find him with this!"

"Maybe. I should warn you that he'll be expecting me, not you. When you get close, he may check you out. If you're not who he wants to see, he may move on without you even knowing he was there. At least until the compass stops working. Then you've missed your chance."

"I guess it's the best we can hope for," Cries Havoc said.

"You can always have him call me for confirmation, if he lets you get so far as an interview. He knows my number—by phone or spirit messenger."

"Then when do we leave?" Carlita said.

"Tomorrow," Storm-Eye said. "After sleep. We may get no other sleep soon." She padded across the living room to the front door, which she nudged open with her shoulder. Before going out the door, she turned and growled: "Get sleep now. No more talk."

"I'll see you off tomorrow morning," Antonine said. "I'll prepare some provisions in case you can't get to a store anytime soon."

"Thanks," Julia said, heading down the hall to the guest room she slept in.

The others mumbled their own thanks and stretched out on their beds—or chairs, in Carlita's case. Cries Havoc still slept in the main bedroom. Antonine disappeared into his observatory, shutting the door behind him.

* * *

The sun had barely peeked over the tree line when the cabin burst into activity. Each pack member got up and gathered his or her belongings and prepared to hit the road. Antonine was outside on the porch, tying the straps on a backpack full of hiking provisions: jerky, trail mix and water bottles. He stood to greet them as they came out, ready for walking.

"Good luck to you all," Antonine said. "I don't know how long your journey will take, but make sure you let me know the outcome."

"Don't worry," Cries Havoc said, taking the backpack and shouldering it. "You'll be the first we tell, if we get a chance. Thanks again for everything you've done for us. It's a lot more than the other tribes have offered us."

"Yeah," Carlita said. "I don't care if you Stargazers aren't official members of the nation no more; you're okay by me."

"We really wouldn't have known what to do without you," Julia said. "If you ever need anything, email me here." She handed him a slip of paper. "I can read my mail on the road. I'll try to update you when I can."

"That's very helpful," Antonine said. "Garou usually spurn such methods."

"You're telling me!" Julia said.

Storm-Eye, already waiting on the lawn, let loose a howl of farewell. The others joined in, their human-throated warbling not as authentic as Storm-Eye's but nonetheless a better imitation than most humans could muster.

Antonine bowed to them as they gathered on the lawn. They waved and turned down the path, following Storm-Eye's lead. In moments, they were gone, although Antonine's sharp ears could hear the sounds of their crunching shoes and boots for a while longer.

When he could hear them no more, he went into the cabin and closed the door.

Chapter Six

The still of the night was undisturbed by the sounds of guests, Garou or otherwise. Normally, Antonine cherished these moments of stillness and solitude, time in which to meditate or plan future actions against the Wyrm. Now, however, it seemed too quiet. The lack of sound wasn't merely silence but absence. The lack of others.

Antonine left the cabin and walked down the slim trail to the small clearing that hosted the fire pit and bench. He sat looking up at the stars, wondering what these bothersome thoughts meant. It wasn't like him to get annoyed at a lack of social activity. He had more than enough functions to attend to among the local tribes: diplomatic endeavors, attempts to unite the fractious elders across tribal boundaries. Such work was more difficult now that his own tribe had defected, but he continued it nonetheless.

These moments where no social service or quest impinged upon him were the best times for self-transformation, the internal quest to better reach peace with his own spirit, to center himself against whatever threatened to push or pull him from his deepest convictions—and there were many people or events that had done that before. It was all too easy to compromise one's goals or values in the service of a short-term victory or to avoid uncomfortable conflict.

That's why he should now be beginning meditation or honing his Kailindo skills. Things best done alone, with no bothersome Garou to intrude.

But he couldn't still his mind enough to settle down for the practice. He was too charged with... what? What was it that bothered him and disturbed his normally serene resolve?

Was it the quest of the Silver River Pack? Did he worry too much about them? No, that wasn't it. He had sent many younger packs off on even more dangerous quests before. *But perhaps none so important for all our futures*, he thought. Still, he knew that their fate wasn't what now troubled him. He trusted in their abilities and the grace of Gaia to get them through whatever waited ahead.

No, it all came back to Cries Havoc's problem. The loss of self. It disturbed Antonine deeper than he had been willing to admit to himself. Mari's affliction was bad enough, but even that was explainable by the actions of a Bane, albeit a strange, new kind none had seen before. But this loss of memory and very spirit that Cries Havoc now suffered... this was different. More dangerous. More dangerous to Antonine personally.

Nothing was more valuable to him than his sense of self, his hard-won, disciplined and unified consciousness, forged over years of hardship, toil, loss, tragedy and triumph. Everything that made him what he was, that allowed him to effectively bring others together and guide them to collective solutions, was tied up with his skills, his practice, his undiluted connection to his inner being. And what was one's inner being if not a precious strand of past selves, each a lesson in what one could become, if one was willful enough to keep transcending them, to grow into something more encompassing?

Without knowledge of the past, how can we forge a future?

Much of his Stargazer training taught him to forgo such reliance on an existential self—on any self at all, in fact. To dissolve one's past, present and future—*and we all make our futures in the here and now, even if they haven't been enacted yet*—into an undivided, unified now. The ever-present, timeless truth of the True Gaia Realm.

Unlike his eastern tribemates, however, Antonine believed there was purpose for his—and others'—existence in the world of duality. There was a reason they had not yet attained full consciousness of the Gaiadharma. His teachers would say this is, like all other thoughts, an illusion based on ignorance, the delusion of the Weaver's web, wrought to make us blindly strive for what we already have— peace, Oneness.

Antonine didn't buy that. Yes, on the highest level of being and consciousness, he knew this to be true and hoped to one day attain it such as to transcend the world of conflict. But here and now, duality impinged and caused suffering, and there had to be a reason behind it besides the accident of an insane Triat mismanaging existence.

And to continue to combat it, I need to cling to my sense of what I am, what I have become and what I can be. I cannot risk losing that.

He stood up and wandered about the clearing. How to deal with this threat? What could one do to prepare against succumbing to it, should it reach us here, so far from Europe where it began?

He walked back to the cabin and—without missing a stride—leapt onto the roof and then climbed over the dome of his observatory. He came to rest on the top and settled with perfect balance at the apex of the dome.

It had been a long time since he had considered his distant past, his early days as a Garou. He knew he had to reclaim them now, to sink into them, relive them as best he could from this distant vantage point. He slowed his breathing and performed the rituals taught him by the tribe, those for entering a deep meditative state wherein lucid dreaming could take place—to sleep while awake.

As the outside world—the slight breeze of the chill autumn night, the hoot of an owl in the distance—grew more distant in his perception, he cast his thoughts back to his youth, to that day 42 years ago when everything in his world changed irrevocably....

* * *

Saugerties, New York, 1959:

Antonine was fourteen years old when he left home for the open road, a rucksack on his back and a copy of Jack Kerouac's *Dharma Bums* in his back pocket.

The first place he went was the Adirondacks, to lose himself in the immensity of nature for a while, before hitching his way to California.

His father didn't notice he was gone until three days after he left.

The old man spent his veteran's checks on draught beer at the local watering hole and bandages to wrap up the cuts and bruises from his constant brawling. Losing his wife during childbirth had not been easy on him. Neither had the war. He left both his dead wife and his left arm in Hong Kong after World War II, returning to his childhood home, a small farm in Saugerties, New York, with his infant son.

He hadn't intended on becoming an inveterate drunk. But then, no one really does. He wanted to start over, to build something new. But the depression ran too deep. Over the years, he cared less and less about his mechanical work and growing son and became more concerned with the arguments to be had with his friends over mugs of beer at the bar.

The young lad's surrogate father was his grandfather, a distant man obsessed with his books and scholarly research into classical history. Nonetheless, he took time out to tutor the boy—his namesake, actually: Robert Antonine Erikson—and managed to instill in him a deep love of knowledge and learning. Young Robert became as much of a bookworm as his grandfather.

He read anything he could find, not just the histories and mythologies of ancient Greece and Rome beloved by his tutor, but philosophy, science fiction and even comic books. On a day trip to New York City with his grandfather, he wandered the paperback section of a bookstore and found a book with a title that spoke to all his yearning desires to leave the safety of home and travel the wide world: Kerouac's *On the Road*. He bought it with his own money, hiding it in his pocket so his grandfather couldn't see him "wasting his time with that mass-market trash." Once home, he lit out into the woods and settled in beneath his favorite tree, where he began reading.

From that moment, it was only one more year before he was gone.

Things didn't go as well as he'd hoped. Roughing it all by himself in the woods at fourteen wasn't as easy as he thought it'd be. He didn't have much money, and without a gun it was impossible to hunt game. He knew how to skin a deer if he caught one—his dad taught him that much—but catching it was the tough part. Once his jerky and canned goods ran out, he was forced to limp into the nearest town and ask for work sweeping floors and stocking shelves. He didn't need much, just enough to get more provisions to survive on his way to California. It helped that he looked older than his years, due mainly to his overly mature demeanor.

Hitching went well until he reached the plains states, where rides would dry up for days on end. He eventually found a train and hopped the rails to the Rockies, sharing cars with other hobos, huddled around Sterno fires against the worsening cold as autumn died and winter came on.

His hardtack days ended rather abruptly. He was rudely awakened one morning in a train depot near Denver, rousted out of the train car by rail workers with clubs. They loosed a dog on him and laughed as he ran screaming, praying he'd reach the fence before the barking Doberman could tear a hunk of flesh from his legs.

He had no such luck. As he vaulted to grab the top of the chain-link fence, its barbed tops cutting into his desperate, grasping hands, the dog leaped and sank its teeth into his left calf. The pain was incredible, even with the adrenaline pumping through his veins. He cried out and fell, but the dog refused to let go, thrashing itself from left to right to gnaw away a chunk of muscle.

A wolfen howl of rage and pain broke across the rail yard. The dog whimpered and ran like the devil was on its tail. The rail workers—staring in awe and fear at the misshapen thing that now stood where the boy had been only moments before—screamed and ran, hot brown stains running down their legs. But the boy-thing chased them, running on all fours, and tore into the straggler of the herd, tearing its own share of flesh from the dog's owner.

When the hot blood flooded into the boy's mouth, he suddenly stopped, startled at the sensation. The man lay on the ground, trying to crawl, crying like a baby, his eyes shut tight, desperately hoping that whatever attacked him would just disappear like a bad dream.

When he didn't feel any further gnawing, the rail worker slowly opened his eyes and peered around. The thing was gone. No sign of it. He shuddered as a final wave of fear shot through his body. He then stood on his shaky feet and wondered what had just happened. Was that a bear that they chased out of the car? Must have been. Never heard of such a thing, but that was the only reasonable explanation. He limped off to call an ambulance and warn the police about the runaway bear.

Robert Antonine Erikson didn't stop running until he was well into the woods and out of sight of anyone, the now-torn and twisted chain-link fence well behind him. He then collapsed onto the pine needle–strewn ground and gulped for air. He wasn't hairy anymore and didn't have claws or sharp teeth like he'd had moments ago. In fact, he was naked. His clothes had torn off him when he suddenly changed into that… that wolf.

He could barely believe what had happened. He had turned into a monster. No doubt about it. He looked for his wound and couldn't find it. The place where the dog had bitten him was completely healed. Did he imagine the whole thing?

No, the taste of blood was still in his mouth. He tried desperately to think, to remember if he had been bitten by any animal within the last few months, but no memory came. That couldn't be the answer. But if not, what the hell had happened to him?

He looked up into the sky, at the morning sun, and shook his head. It was daytime. Monsters were supposed to come out only at night.

He picked himself up off the ground and snuck back to peer at the rail yard. He waited for a while until he was sure there were no men about, and then crept over to snatch his rucksack with its change of jeans and shirt. His boots were beyond repair, however. He would have to find some way to get new ones without people wondering why he was walking around barefoot in the freezing cold.

In the end, he resorted to stealing. He crept around Denver at night until he found an unlit shoe store. After carefully figuring its layout from the window, he broke the glass, jumped in, and snatched a pair of boots and socks in his size. He then ran like hell for the shadows. He waited for the cold to numb his pounding heart and fear before next robbing a coat store. His travel gear restored, he hightailed it out of the city limits and hitchhiked the rest of the way to California.

Over the next few weeks, the wolf incident became like a dream. He wasn't even sure it had actually happened. He had seen a small newspaper article about a bear that ran loose in the train yard, savaging a rail man. The date was the same as his wolf incident. He began to convince himself that it had been a bear, and this his fear played tricks on his mind, making him think otherwise. Sure, the bear was a fine excuse: it explained the torn clothes. But it didn't explain the taste of blood.

He finally reached California, the San Francisco Bay area, home to the beats—the poets and rebels who had so inspired Kerouac and thus Antonine. He found a job stocking groceries at a city market and spent the nights browsing bookstores—City Lights!—and coffeehouses. He went to poetry readings by Allen Ginsberg, Gary Snyder and other members of the poetry renaissance birthed here in the city.

He found himself falling in love with Chinatown and its street markets, offering all manner of food, from fish to octopus and other things he'd never heard of. He ate lunch one day in a small park near Chinatown Square and there witnessed his first glimpse of Tai Chi. An old man led a group of Chinese immigrants—both elderly and young—through the strange, flowing, earthy yet airy formations.

After they had completed their practice, Antonine followed the elderly leader and politely asked him if he could learn with the rest of them. The old man frowned and spoke back in Chinese. He clearly did not understand English. Antonine tried to imitate the Tai Chi and then pointed from the teacher to himself and made a prayer gesture—something he hoped communicated a universal "please." The old man shook his head and walked away, ignoring the Westerner.

Antonine shuffled his way back toward the market where he worked when he noticed a Chinese man standing in a doorway across the street watching him. He was maybe in his thirties, dressed in khakis and a white tee-shirt. He nodded to Antonine and motioned him over.

"You can't win his respect so quickly," the man said in perfect English. "It takes time to get the old masters to pay you attention."

"Oh?" Antonine said. "So should I just keep coming and hope he'll let me follow along some day?"

"Yeah, if you really want to learn, that might work. But it'll take a long while. You want to learn martial arts?"

"I don't know. I've never really been interested until I saw Tai Chi. It looks… peaceful but useful."

The man smiled. "Tai Chi *is* a martial art. You're just watching it in one form. It's really a fighting style."

Antonine remembered his run-in with the rail hands. "I guess I do want to know self-defense. I've run into trouble before."

"Then I'll teach you! I don't do Tai Chi so much as Bagua. But I can show you Tai Chi also."

"Bag-what?"

"Bagua—Eight Trigram Boxing. It's sort of based off the I Ching. You know what that is?"

"Oh, yeah! I've thrown coins before. I got into it after reading Carl Jung's opinions on the oracle."

"Who?"

"Carl Jung, he's a famous psychologist."

"Huh. Okay. But I don't teach psychology, I teach fighting."

Antonine smiled. "Fine by me. When can I start?"

"How about tonight? Come by here and we'll start in my place upstairs. You'll be my first student."

"First? Why me?"

"Because you're interesting—an American who wants to learn internal arts. Besides, I just got here, and I have to start somewhere."

"Just got here? From where? Your English is too good for China."

"Ha! Shows how much you know! They speak quite good Queen's English in Hong Kong, I'll have you know."

"You don't sound British," Antonine said, smirking slightly, eyebrows raised.

"I used to. Then I moved to Chinatown in New York for a year. I was almost sounding like an Italian when I got out of there!"

Antonine laughed. "Okay, I buy it. I've got to get back to work, though. I'll be back tonight. What'll I call you anyway?"

"Laughing Crane."

Antonine laughed again. "Any first name?"

"Just Laughing Crane. I'll see you tonight, Antonine."

Antonine shook his hand and headed back to work. It wasn't until he was slapping price stickers on canned peas that he realized he'd never given Laughing Crane his name.

Chapter Seven

Laughing Crane was a revelation. At their second meeting, Antonine's first training class, he performed a series of martial maneuvers. After each lesson, he turned to Antonine and said, "Now you do the same."

Antonine diligently tried to imitate him, with only fair results. Laughing Crane, shaking his head with a mix of approval and disappointment, transformed into a giant, wolfen creature and stared at Antonine with his piercing yellow eyes. They spoke of infinite depths and dimensions beyond the material.

He then said, in a deep voice with a rumbling growl: "Now you do the same."

Antonine stared aghast, trembling. But before fear could start his quivering legs to running, something in Laughing Crane's demeanor calmed his nerves and heart. Instead of fear, he was overcome by relief, freedom from the confused pain and doubt of his rail yard experience. It had indeed been real.

Antonine's Garou training began in earnest. For the next two years, he trained with Laughing Crane not only in the ways of the internal martial arts—Bagua, Tai Chi and Hsing-I—but in the ways of the Stargazers, werewolves devoted to Eastern ways of knowing.

He learned that being a werewolf did not consign him to hunt humans under a full moon, fated to be shot dead one day by a silver bullet. The knowledge that his rage and his shapeshifting powers could be controlled through a disciplined mind was the happiest discovery yet of Antonine's young life.

Antonine later learned that Laughing Crane had been watching him in secret since he arrived in the city. The Theurge's spirits had told him of his coming, and he had soon realized that Antonine did not yet know who or what he was. He believed Antonine had a powerful Kin-Fetch—a spirit dedicated to him at birth by a Garou rite—looking out for him. After questioning Antonine carefully on the circumstances of his birth, he concluded that his mother was Kin-folk and that her Stargazer relatives had bonded the Kin-Fetch to Antonine soon after he was born. This Kin-Fetch had made sure Antonine would one day find a fellow tribe member who could train him. Laughing Crane was that one.

More than his discovery of being Garou, Antonine was most overwhelmed by his first step into the Umbra, the spirit world that lay beyond the Gauntlet erected around the material world by humankind's unwitting acceptance of the Weaver. When Laughing Crane took his young pupil to the Aetherial Realm for the first time, to meet the Stargazers there and witness the vast firmament, Antonine saw his calling in the stars, spelled out for him as if the constellations were pages in a book. He saw a Half Moon destiny of service to Gaia, an attempt to bring accord between divided parties, to create unity amid diversity. He prayed then to the spirit of the central star in his vision—Vegarda, the Pole Star of the North, axis of the heavens—for the will to take up this task and the wisdom to achieve it.

Over the course of the year, two more cubs joined Laughing Crane's school. Like Antonine, they had been discovered by Laughing Crane or his spirits.

One of them was Catrina Scarborough, daughter of a wealthy British tea magnate based in New Delhi. She had been sent to boarding school in California at a young age and barely knew her family. It turned out that her grandfather had been a Stargazer; the heritage skipped a generation.

The other was Wen Chou, son of Chinese immigrants to Chinatown. His family members were longtime friends with Laughing Crane's human Kinfolk, and he was the reason Laughing Crane had come to San Francisco: to train Wen Chou upon his First Change. This took place five months after Antonine had taken up tutelage, upon Wen Chou's fifteenth birthday. Thus, he and Antonine were almost the same age. Catrina was older; she had not experienced her First Change until she was seventeen.

They all became fast friends. After two years had passed, Laughing Crane announced that it was time for them to journey to the heartland of Stargazer power: Nepal and Tibet. He would not accompany them, for they had learned all they could from him at this time in their training. They needed to now find septs in the East to take them in and complete their passage from beginners to seasoned Garou.

Antonine took the others on backpacking trips across California to teach them how to travel light through various types of terrain. Of course, he was still learning himself, but these journeys were much easier now that he had Garou abilities to call upon— he no longer needed a gun to hunt deer, for instance. Tracking game was a breeze with wolfen senses. The same for long-term endurance; their different forms provided different degrees of strength and staying power. After a few months of such extended trips, they figured they were ready for any hardship Asia could throw at them.

They left by merchant marine ship, with stop-overs in Tokyo, Hong Kong and Singapore before landing in Ceylon. They walked across the island to Talaimanar and there took a ferry to India.

Laughing Crane had urged them to avoid the Indian Penumbra, for it was populated by strange beings with unreadable agendas, some hostile, some merely selfish. It was best for them to wait until they contacted one of the Stargazers he told them of before attempting an Umbral journey there. A guide to its different ways would be necessary.

They backpacked across India, by foot, bus and train, visiting various human shrines—dedicated to Hindu gods and the Buddha—meeting with holy men and women in various ashrams they stayed at along the way. Their knowledge of human religion and philosophy deepened, but they remembered Laughing Crane's dictum that human spiritual truths were different than Garou truths. Humans had their own role to play in Gaia's realm, separate but often similar to that of the Garou.

Eventually they reached Kathmandu in Nepal and there met with Stargazers of the Sept of the High Caves, whom they had been told about and who were expecting them. They had arrived at a very auspicious time, for the next week, in the afternoon of February 3 and for three days thereafter, a great conjunction of the planets, sun and moon was to occur.

Many of the local humans were afraid that it portended the end of the world, but the Stargazers saw in it a great opportunity to awaken a new generation around the world to Eastern wisdom. Antonine and his fellow pupils were perfect symbols in flesh of what the Stargazers hoped the stars promised: a new wave of Eastern wisdom brought to the West.

The cubs were led to a hidden monastery in the high mountains, a system of caves that, on the outside, appeared to be the retreats of Buddhist monks or Hindu ascetics but led inside to a warren of caverns where the tribe held its rites and nourished a caern—a place of spiritual power where the Gauntlet between the worlds of spirit and flesh was thin.

From here, the monks opened a moon bridge to the Aetherial Realm, where they would join Stargazers from around the world for a great rite commemorating the planetary conjunction. Here also one of the three new students would be allowed to declare his or her commitment to the ways of the sept and remain afterward for years of study. Only one of the three cubs would be allowed to so commit; the other two would have to seek admittance elsewhere.

Meeting together that night, the three discussed who would stay. It was soon clear that Catrina best loved what she saw here, and so Antonine and Wen agreed to allow her the honor. After the great rite, they would move on, seeking another sept for themselves. It was a night of bittersweet parting but joyful exultation, celebrating Catrina's newfound place for herself in the Stargazer world.

The great conjunction rite was confusing to Antonine. Although he had studied star lore with Laughing Crane, the powerful goings-on amongst the gathered Stargazers of revered rank were beyond his ken. After a time of frustration, he gave up trying to understand it all and just soaked in as much as he could, hoping to one day remember enough to piece together what was happening.

As the conjunction began, Antonine froze in awe and wonder at his first sight of his tribal totem, Chimera. The lion-headed dragon had appeared before his tribe to bless the event. As the dragon whirled over their heads, Antonine thought he saw the great spirit looking at him. Later, Wen admitted the same. Perhaps the totem had examined all the newcomers.

When it was over three days later, Antonine and Wen shouldered their backpacks and said their farewells to Catrina and the sept leaders. They had been given directions to the Shigalu Monastery over the mountains in Tibet, and so set off that way, joining a group of pilgrims—some of them Stargazer Kinfolk—in evading the border authorities who tried to prevent anyone from entering Chinese-occupied Tibet.

After a long, hard journey—again, avoiding the Umbra—they arrived at the secluded monastery and were greeted by the Sept of the Snow Leopard as valued guests. Shigalu was the oldest Stargazer caern and held the tribe's greatest treasures, although young Garou like Antonine and Wen were not allowed access to them. Maybe after years of service to the tribe, they would be allowed to view them. But not yet.

They spent three idyllic months there, learning to meditate as Stargazers, encountering spirits valued by the tribe and gleaning secrets from them—the famed Gifts that allowed Stargazers their uncanny sense of balance. They also learned about the darker matters threatening the tribe and the world, about the Wyrm and its devouring maw and corrupted minions. But most of all, they learned about the Weaver, who had caused the Wyrm to become a force of pure corruption. It was the Weaver that the Stargazers had to be wary of. The other tribes paid her little heed, figuring her to be too distant to affect their fates so deeply.

"It is like a finger pointing to the moon," a venerable Shigalu monk said. "The Weaver is the moon, but the other tribes worry about the finger."

His words carried wisdom beyond their mere meaning, for he demonstrated to Antonine and Wen the power of sound, how its very vibrations could unlock thoughts in the mind, awakening one to instincts long buried in most humans. He instructed them in the chants that could reveal the Elemental Mind, the primal mind unhampered by the duality of logic and forms, a mind that flowed like water, rose like fire, spread like air and rooted itself like earth in the True Gaia Realm beyond the Weaver's webs of falsehood.

He taught them the Five Mantras of Primal Creation, each a chant to summon in the listener's mind the elements that made up the world, including spirit. Proper vocalization of these mantras could ground one in the True Gaia Realm and strip away delusions haunting the mind and body. Their pronunciation was well beyond the skill of the two cubs, but they swore to practice them over the years to come, to one day master their sounds.

Finally, however, the idyll came to an end. It was announced that only one of them could stay to join the sept and help guard the caern. Such was the Stargazer way; only one student would be accepted.

Antonine and Wen both wanted to stay. They could not agree on which one would leave and soon fell to fighting, calling one another names, their rage rising, threatening to burst forth into bloodshed.

The monks pulled them apart. The lama declared that they would indeed fight to see who had the right to stay, since it was the form they had chosen. But they were Stargazers, and so must fight as Stargazers. The duel was to be fought with Kailindo, the tribe's special martial art that involved subduing an opponent rather than clawing him to pieces. What's more, whichever cub succumbed to rage would be automatically declared the loser and forced to leave the caern.

Antonine and Wen were separated for a week as monks taught them each the basics of Kailindo. It came easy to them, for they were already adept in Laughing Crane's human style martial arts. As the day of the duel approached, Antonine grew morose. He had never intended this journey to result in the loss of a friend. He remembered the destiny given him in the stars at the conjunction rite. As a Half Moon, it was his duty to bring others together, not tear them apart with bickering. But he also desperately wanted to stay. The Shigalu Monastery was the most important caern. To become one of its caretakers meant unrivaled access to lore in the years to come. How could he forego that? Surely Wen would understand this if Antonine won the contest, and not hold it against him.

On the night of the duel, Antonine noticed clutches of unknown Stargazers at the caern. Apparently, others had come from nearby septs to witness the duel. Antonine felt a wave of shame. If he had not fallen to fighting with Wen in the first place, this could have been resolved with a riddle contest or through other intellectual means, such as a duel of knowledge or lore. It was his own anger that had brought on a fight.

A sparse circle of smooth rock had been prepared as the fight zone. Wen waited on the opposite side, looking just as nervous and apprehensive as Antonine. The chief lama rang a bell and all the other monks stepped away to watch from the shadows of the surrounding rocks.

Antonine and Wen carefully approached one another, each sizing the other up, looking for a weak spot. They had sparred many times before and knew each other's weaknesses. But in so knowing, they had helped one another to overcome them. Now, each was unsure where to seek an opening in the other's defense.

Wen threw the first blow, quickly shifting into Crinos form and leaping at Antonine, whose human form reflexes were not so sharp. Nonetheless, Antonine managed to barely sidestep the huge wolfman form and launch a quick kick at Wen as he passed by. The blow did little more than cause him to catch his balance.

Antonine shifted into wolf form and ran beneath Wen, and then shifted to the larger dire wolf, hoping to uproot him with the sudden increase in mass. Wen seemed to have expected this, however, and leaped up and kicked Antonine in the head in midchange. Antonine went sprawling, stunned by the force of the blow.

Before he could recover, Wen was on top of him, locking his arms under and around Antonine's forelegs, gripping him in a painful hold. Antonine shifted back to wolf form and used the split-second in which Wen had to adjust for the loss of mass to slip away, leaping forward, slapping his tail into Wen's face.

He shifted into Crinos form and spun around, ready to face whatever Wen attempted. Instead of charging him, though, Wen sat fuming, his anger obviously rising. His eyes grew more unreasoning, and Antonine realized that he was struggling desperately to control his rage—and losing the attempt.

If he succumbed, Wen would lose and Antonine would be the victor—if he survived Wen's frenzy.

Antonine had no fear of that, however, for the vastly superior monks gathered all around them would step in to stop any true bloodshed.

Realizing that he was about to win at the cost of shaming his friend, Antonine knew it was a price too great to pay. Before Wen could lose complete control, Antonine let down his own barriers to the roiling anger that always existed deep within a Garou, coaxed to rise like heat from a flame by action, made even hotter by the Crinos battle form. His resolve laid aside, all fetters to his anger broken, Antonine went berserk, charging forward at Wen like a freight train, all reason abandoned in his mind.

He remembered nothing of it. He came to in the iron grip of Lama Radhika Snowpeak, his Kailindo instructor, his rage spent, his intellect returned. Wen was being led away by a group of Shigalu monks, but he looked back over his shoulder at Antonine, a look of worry and concern on his face. Apparently, only a minute or two had passed.

Most of the monks walked away without glancing at Antonine, but some could not hide their disappointment at his loss of control. Antonine hung his head in shame. Had he done the right thing? He could no longer suppress his sorrow and sobbed. A single tear ran down his cheek.

An unknown voice spoke from nearby: "Do you shed a tear for yourself or for fear that your friendship is at an end? Cry not, young Teardrop, for you have done well. He who can master his rage enough to evoke it when truly needed shows wisdom."

Antonine looked up at a Chinese man sitting nearby. He wore the black robes and hat of a Taoist priest. He wrapped his fists together in front of his chest and extended them toward Antonine, a traditional sign of respect in the martial arts world.

Lama Snowpeak released Antonine and placed a hand on his shoulder. "I most deeply regret that you cannot stay here, especially after your supreme expression of self-denial, so rare in a cub." She bowed to Antonine and walked away to join the others monks at the caern, where they welcomed Wen.

The Chinese man stood up and walked over. "So, where do you go next?"

Antonine shook his head. "I don't know. I have no idea where to go."

The man raised his eyebrows in mock surprise. "Untrue. Surely not so. Then you must come with me and accept my hospitality."

"Thank you. I greatly appreciate the offer. Could I ask your name and where you live?"

"Ha, ha! Of course you may! I am Master Chien Mountaintop and I come from the Purest Resolve Sept. I would be honored to have one such as you as my pupil!"

Antonine could scarcely believe what he heard. "But I lost this duel. How does this make me worthy?"

"You lost for reasons you chose. Honorable reasons. You don't belong here, anyway," he said, opening his arms wide to indicate the snowy mountains. "It's cold and barren. You're a man of the forest, I can tell."

"Oh? And how do you know this?"

"Vegarda told me," he said, winking.

Antonine could not hide his astonishment. "How…? How did you know I was connected with the Pole Star?"

Chien frowned. "I told you: she told me! If she can write you messages in the sky, she can write them for me, too! The Purest Resolve Sept is dedicated to her, and so she teaches us special rites for the furthering of her goals. She has chosen you, and so it only makes sense for you to come to a caern dedicated to her."

Antonine couldn't help smiling. It all seemed to make perfect sense now. He had known deep down all along that he didn't belong here, that there was another place for him. He had simply become starstruck with the caern, and that blinded him to his true place. He was relieved now that Wen had won, no matter that some of the other monks thought less of him for his supposed loss of control. Master Chien and Lama Snowpeak knew better, and that was enough. He needn't wear it as a badge. And he certainly couldn't let Wen know; his friend deserved to believe he had won on his own.

"Come," Master Chien said, walking back to the sept center. "I'm hungry. We've got a long journey back to China, so eat up now!"

Antonine Teardrop followed behind his new master, pleased to finally find his place in the world.

Antonine spent the next five years training under Master Chien at the Purest Resolve Caern on a mountain in western China. He learned the sept's secret Kailindo style and special rites associated with Vegarda, the caern's totem spirit. He studied reams of Stargazer and human lore and practiced the riddling games that helped the tribe to transcend paradox and solve the numerous enigmas that challenged the mind in its Umbral journeys. Unlike the other tribes, the Stargazers dared to travel the Ephiphs and Chimares, realms of pure thought and chaotic dream, from which they brought back wisdom jewels—or perished in the attempt.

Even though he was rather isolated in the Purest Resolve Caern, he heard tidings from the West and became intrigued at the cultural revolution going on in America and elsewhere. He remembered the dream of freedom and limitless possibilities that the writings of the beat poets and authors had instilled in him, and he was glad to see them finally taking form in mass consciousness.

The urge to see it firsthand, and to help it along by getting into the thick of it, grew within him. Although it rarely hampered his studies, he knew that his time in the monastery was coming to an end. He had work within the world to accomplish.

Master Chien sensed this and began to teach him important Gifts and lore he might otherwise have held back. Once he believed Antonine had learned all he could, Master

Chien acceded to his pupil's desire to leave the caern and return home.

Excited at the prospects for the future, yet sad to leave the caern he had come to deeply love, Antonine shouldered his backpack and embraced his master by the shimmering light of the moon bridge the Gatekeeper had opened for him. With no further farewell, he walked into the silvery light and onward to the bridge's exit in America.

He sank roots once more in the Catskills and strove to fulfill his duty as Philodox and Stargazer. Perhaps in no other place in America were the strands of intertribal community so frayed as in New York State, as Get of Fenris fought Wendigo, and Shadow Lord sought dominance over Uktena and Silver Fang. Here, there was real work to be done in the uniting of the Garou Nation.

Over the coming decades, Antonine slowly earned the grudging respect of most of the tribes, although many tried to write him off as some back-woods, hippie crackpot who refused to give up the '60s. Of course, the Children of Gaia at the Finger Lakes Caern found common cause with him, but it was a struggle of many years before the others recognized the usefulness of his wisdom.

All his victories, however, were ultimately tempered by the tragedy of Shigalu Monastery's fall to the Wyrm. Most of its defenders were killed—including his old friend Wen—and its treasures sacked. Only a few survivors escaped to tell the tale.

This dire event initiated the Stargazer's withdrawal from the Western Garou Nation. A concolation was called at the High Cave Caern in

Nepal, and all Stargazer elders were expected to attend. Antonine went hoping to convince the tribe not to secede, but knew soon after his arrival that the weight of opinion was against him.

The divisions within the tribe were now openly displayed. Where before they were hidden under a guise of reasoned discourse, arguments now broke out among all quarters and camps. Those who had always envied the prominence of the Snow Leopard Sept used the moment to condemn the arrogance that had done it in. The Snow Leopard's defenders, however, still in the majority, criticized what they called the sway of anger and jealousy that the Wyrm's victory had delivered to their once united tribe.

What was supposed to be a calm, solemn gathering descended into a series of physical duels between enlightened masters, each trying to win sway for his or her ideas by physically besting the opposition—relying on the ancient instincts of wolfen alpha dominance over reasoned argument. This, however, was not unknown within the tribe, which ever walked a quivering tightrope over a gulf of wild instinct. Unlike modern humans, whose reverence for reason was accompanied by a fear of instinct, most Stargazers knew that both factors formed an indivisible continuum, a constantly changing interplay of yin and yang, heaven and earth. It was the height of Stargazer wisdom to honor contradictory positions, to embrace paradox and respect all cosmologies.

Antonine sat outside the caern on the chilly rocks that evening with his old friend Catrina, now called Catrina Cateyes, and an elder of the caern.

"You know this is wrong," he said to her. "Retreating is not the best way to resolve our differences."

"And you know that there are times to retreat as well as advance," she replied. "The cycle of yin and yang calls for withdrawal as well as involvement, each to its time. The time has come for withdrawal."

Antonine sighed. "If viewed from a cosmological perspective, I agree that the times can be interpreted as such. I can't help but think, however, that this particular interpretation is wrong. Retreat from assault, yes, but not from alliances."

"Those of us who are more skilled at reading the stars than you think otherwise. I do not mean to belittle your own talents, merely to remind you that there are Stargazers here older and wiser than you or I."

"Yes, true indeed. I know the reasons are sound. The Beast Courts will surely play a more important role even in the West in the coming years. We need their trust. It's just that… we should be allied with everyone, not just one side or the other."

"Politics. Ain't it a bitch?"

Antonine laughed at his friend's reversal to her old way of talking, from when they had learned under Laughing Crane. He turned to her and smiled. "You've grown into quite a noble monk. So different from your younger, impetuous self."

"And you have grown into a man deeply sure of himself. So different from your younger, doubting self."

"We've both grown. And changed." He paused before continuing, looking out at the distant but immense mountains that stretched across the entire horizon from his vantage point. "I can't leave my work, you know. No matter what they finally decide, I can't give up on the others. I've tried for too many years to bring them together. I can't abandon that now."

"No one will ask you to. The elders cannot tell an individual what path to follow, as much as they might want to. They know better. That's what makes us different from the other tribes."

They watched the night together for a while and then Antonine stood up. "I have to go. There's no reason for me to wait for the resolution to their meeting. I've said all I can to them and I'll hear the results one way or another."

Catrina stood and took his hands, looking into his eyes. "Farewell, Antonine Teardrop. Do not ever veer from your path, no matter if all the tribe goes another way."

He nodded and they touched their foreheads together. He then turned and made his way back up the mountain to the caves and the Gatekeeper, to the moon bridge that would take him home.

* * *

Antonine's palm itched. Its discomfort had grown throughout the night and refused to go away, finally distracting Antonine from his memory meditation. It felt as if a painful rash had broken out. Still perched cross-legged atop the cabin observatory, he opened his eyes to look out over the night woods. It was perhaps 3 a.m.

He examined his hand, expecting to see a patch of red marks, but was startled by the throbbing glow of moonlight. A thirty-eight-year-old burn mark now glowed anew on his hand, reminding him for the first time in years of the event that had caused it— his vision of Chimera and the glowing pathway whose touch burned his skin like silver.

Why had it ignited again now, after all these years? Was there something in his memory meditation that had awakened it? Or was it somehow related to the present, to the events that transpired in Europe?

He slipped carefully down from the observatory and onto the wooden roof, and from there jumped to the ground. He looked about the clearing and saw nothing unusual that could be related to the renewed glow, and so stared instead at a mirrored wind chime dangling from the porch nearby. Holding his glowing palm up to catch its brilliant reflection in the chrome, he pierced the Gauntlet with his vision and stepped sideways, following the path made by the advancing light.

The Penumbra was still. Not unusually still, though, for he could hear faint crackling noises from the deep woods as small spirit Gafflings foraged through the crisp autumn leaves carpeting the loam.

His hand glowed even fiercer now, and he held it out before him. In the distance he saw an answering gleam, the slight shimmer of a faint moon path reflecting back the lunar light.

He stepped quickly into his cabin and grabbed a satchel there, one he kept in the Umbra just in case he needed to make a quick journey. He exited the cabin and followed the glow to the far moon path, withdrawing his klaive from the satchel and hooking its sheath through his belt.

He didn't know where the path would take him, but he suspected he was years late in walking it.

Chapter Nine

The moon path wound into the Deep Umbra, leading Antonine away from the Penumbra around his cabin and the Catskills. He followed it for the rest of the night until it began to slowly fade with the setting of the moon and the coming of true night in the Umbra. Along the way, various side paths split away, leading to small realms, mostly glades—miniature woodlands or other swaths of wilderness, whole worlds unto themselves.

As the path grew faint, he searched for one of these glades to pass the night in and chose one that seemed to promise a waterfall, judging by the faint roaring sound that could be heard even on the moon path. He entered its borders, stepping off the path, and stood in a small, sunlit meadow before a gorge. Stepping carefully to the edge, he looked into it and saw white water rushing far below. The roaring sound was especially loud to his left, around a bend in the rock. He suspected the waterfall, source of the river far below, was off that way somewhere.

He turned back to the meadow and walked its periphery. Wildflowers grew between the rocks that hemmed the green grass plain, and a few trees rose from the soil. In the distance, forested mountains could be seen. He began to wonder if he weren't in a glade so much as a Penumbral pocket of the southern Appalachians.

It mattered little to him, however, and he unrolled his blanket and lay down upon the ground. He was soon asleep, although even in sleep's deepest stage, his senses were still honed to awaken him at the first signal of danger.

He woke hours later. The unseen sun was already behind the mountains, and mists arose to wrap the Precambrian giants in gray cloaks. He sat up and listened for any sign of spirits. In the distance, birds twittered. Otherwise, it was silent.

He opened his pack and pulled out an empty metal water bottle. It was marked with glyphs and sealed with an old leather wrap. He held it in both hands and seemed to pray before it, focusing his will to awaken the spirit within the bottle. The tiny being unfurled itself within, becoming a whirlpool within the confines of the bottle, growing to fill the container to the brim with fresh, pure water. Antonine thanked it and drank from the fetish. The spirit became quiescent again but the water remained.

He sealed the bottle with the leather wrap and placed it back in the pack. He then pulled out a bag of jerky and chewed a few pieces, watching the flowers sway in the faint breeze coming up from the gorge. When he had his full, he rolled the bag up and shoved it back in his pack. He then stood up and did the same with his blanket, tying it to the leather straps at the bottom of the pack.

It was now dark. Hefting the pack to his shoulders, he stepped back into the shadow of the rock through which he had come, and so left the glade and stepped once more onto the moon path.

He looked at his hand. It no longer glowed. He would have to rely on the path now and on his Umbral travel experience. He had no idea where the path led, but he was sure it was someplace important to Chimera's vision. In light of recent events, he had no choice but to follow it. It was his only lead.

He marched until High Moon before stopping on the path to munch more jerky and gulp down more water. If necessary, he could go for days without nourishment. A mountain spirit had taught him the trick of forgoing such bodily needs and subsisting on pure resolve for a time. However, it would not work forever; he would eventually need more food. He was reluctant to call on such lore until his supplies were gone and all hope of replenishing them was diminished.

He continued on.

The region he now walked became sparser, with fewer sub-realms branching off the path. The spaces between seemed gloomy, uninhabited by even Gafflings or Jagglings. He wasn't sure where he was. Nothing was familiar; he'd never heard of such a place. He figured it to be some forlorn, untraveled part of the Deep Umbra, abandoned some time ago by its spirit residents. But why? What had caused them to leave?

After a while, he began to notice old dried and cracked strands of spider web in the distance. Weaver minions. This place had once been owned or inhabited by Weaver spirits, but the webs were so frail and crumbling that it must have been a very long time ago.

Antonine stopped in the path and shifted into the bulkier Glabro form. He sniffed the air. No scent of Wyrm taint was present. The place was truly empty and abandoned, and it wasn't Wyrm creatures that had chased the residents out.

The mystery of the place both thrilled and troubled Antonine. He was no Theurge, and although he had spent much time learning about the Umbra and spirits from others, it had not been the focus of his training over the years. He did not know enough Umbral geography to identify the site or its possible appearance in any legends.

With no other clues to go on, Antonine kept going, searching for the end of the path.

The moon was again close to setting, the path dimming, when the trail ended at the edge of a realm. This was no glade, however, for no sign or scent of nature leaked from within. If anything, it resembled something like a cyclopean cliff built from evenly carved blocks, each carefully fit to another to form the immense wall, its rim reaching far out of Antonine's sight. Peering carefully in the gloom, he could see carvings and hieroglyphics but could not make out their shapes or meanings. With the light quickly fading and the path almost invisible, he had no choice but to step into the unknown realm.

Everything within gave off a feeling of immense antiquity. Antonine stood within a huge cavern built from the same blocks. Here, however, rounded pillars lined up in two rows stretched onward into the infinity of space before him. He could see the carvings now, worked into spirals from the bottom of the pillars to the top, telling linear narratives in pictures.

He carefully approached the closest pillar and began to examine it. The art style resembled something like a cross between Mayan and Chinese—the flat, rounded and iconographic figures of Mayan carvings, but with landscapes hinting at mists and water, similar to Chinese landscape painting. It gave the appearance of primal, abstract beings walking in finely detailed but distant landscapes.

A quiet, low voice whispered near his ear: "Ah, yes, the tale of Chief Killingspear and the winning of his griffin steed…."

Antonine spun around, instantly assuming a defensive posture. The slim, robed woman with dark hair tied in ringlets made no move toward or away from him. She looked at him with a blank expression, although Antonine thought he could detect a hint of whimsy in it.

"Who are you?" he asked, dropping his stance but still standing such that he could assume any number of defensive or offensive postures in an instant.

"I am the Librarian of Dreams," she replied, seemingly confused now that he had to ask her identity. "And this is one of the oldest archive rooms. Why have you come if you did not know this?"

Antonine looked around the "room," looking for any sign of walls besides the one near the entrance he had come in. He saw none. If this were but one room, he feared to see the others. Could a single mind comprehend such a sight of infinity?

"I was led here," he said. "By a moon path."

She gave him a quizzical look and widened her eyes, seemingly urging him to continue.

"A trail laid by Luna, the Moon."

Her left eyebrow raised. "Oh? Then why are you in the Archives of Civilization? I'm sure you want either the Celestial Histories or Animal Courts."

Antonine was curious now, for both suggestions seemed to promise forgotten lore, but he had been led here for a reason. "No. I believe I am in the right place. You see, I am a child of Chimera."

"Yes, but of course you are. You couldn't be here otherwise. Now, why Civilization? Is there a particular topic you wish to research?"

"Yes," Antonine said. "A silver moon path. A spirit pathway made of moon silver."

"Hmm," the librarian said, seeming to think for a moment. "I don't recall anything like that. Although… wait a moment. Ah, yes, there is a cross-reference. I can take you there." She walked off into the immense chamber, not even looking at Antonine, seemingly sure he would follow her.

He did. Walking a short distance behind, he followed her past more pillars, each depicting different characters and scenery. The old room became even older, as dust piled on the floor and within the nooks and crannies of the pillars.

"Here we are," she said, stopping before a pillar. She wiped away what appeared to be old cobwebs with her hand. "I haven't seen this one for quite some time. In fact, I don't think anyone's ever come to read it. Well, you'll be the first." She smiled at Antonine, nodded and then walked back the way she had come, her steps echoing and receding through the vast space.

When she was out of sight, Antonine got down on his knees to examine the base of the pillar. The iconography was full of spiders and animals, primal landscapes and, above it all, the moon. As he ran his fingers over the carvings and tried to follow them from the bottom toward the top, moving around the pillar to follow the spiral story, he felt his eyes grow heavy. He felt sleep come upon him but could not shake it off. Before he could do anything to prevent it, he was dreaming….

* * *

Grandmother Spider obsessively wrung her eight hands together in distress. She didn't know what to do. Every web she wove, every carefully constructed pattern she wrought, was soon destroyed by the rushing whirlwind of the Wyld. It heeded no plea and ignored all compassion, ripping through her works in a frenzy of destruction, leaving her art in tatters.

She was going mad. How could she keep building things only to see them destroyed? She begged the Wyrm, the great world serpent, to devour the Wyld and stay its swath of destruction. The Wyrm heeded her not.

Or so she believed—in truth, beyond her harried sight, it worked to constrict the whirlwind and direct its path away from the Weaver's works, according to the rise and fall of the seasons. When the webs had grown too tight or too old, it would unleash the Wyld and hinder no more its chaotic path—until once more the seasons changed and the work of creation was once more underway.

But the Spider did not understand this. All she could see was destruction, never the creation that the Wyld left in its wake, the new forms that could now grow to new potentials once the excessive patterns and laws woven by the Weaver were broken.

She hatched a plot to contain the Wyld, to turn the power of the Wyrm against it in all seasons. Unreasoning, caring only for her poor, torn crafts, she began to weave a mighty web around the Wyrm, snaring it in her sticky tangles, leashing the serpent to her will.

The Wyrm was no slave. It thrashed and howled and hissed in its confinement and tried to slink from the cords that bound it. Its sinuous movements only drew the web tighter. Desperate, it shed its skin, hoping to slide through the silk threads while its old skin held back the tightening gauntlet. To no avail.

The Wyld did not heed its howls of rage and pain, for the Wyld heeds no one.

The Celestial Spider wove a cocoon about the struggling Snake. So busy was she in her task that she blocked out the world around her, heeding only the web and the complex work of patterning it just right, so as to catch the Wyrm utterly.

She did not see the ray of moonlight enter the cave where she had bearded the serpent in its den. The ray of light became a thread of silver that worked its way—yes, like a snake—into the black webbing the Spider spun from her orifice. The silver thread mixed into the black, silken yarn and followed its convoluted path around the Wyrm, unnoticed by the Spider.

Now entering the cave came legions of spirits, answering the bellows of the Wyrm of Balance, the serpent whose embrace held together the world. They sought to untangle the thread but only made its maze worse, trapping themselves, becoming Banes. Nothing could reach to the Wyrm through the labyrinth of thread without going mad, for the Spider's own madness was worked into the pattern of that cocoon, a trap no reasoning mind could escape without shedding its logic.

Finally, Garou arrived, howling as they leapt into the fray, tearing at the web with their teeth and claws. But they, too, became snared, trapped in its twists and turns, their eyes losing all light of reason as they descended into gibbering madness.

They had, however, managed one final, mighty feat. Through the black, undecipherable pattern they had carved a single path. It wound in curves and spirals throughout space and time beyond the ken of sentient mind, but it worked its way into the heart of the cocoon, to the screaming maw of the howling, mad Wyrm itself. And yet, because of its proximity to the other threads, and its maddening twists and turns through multiple, paradoxical dimensions, none could walk it without losing his purpose. Even the greatest of Garou who dared it at best reached the final, spiraling circle only to forget duty and become power mad in a delusion of godhood.

Hidden behind and near it, unnoticed and unremarked by the maddened wolves, was the silver thread formed by moonlight. Untrodden, forgotten. A secret, occult weave obscured from the Spider's own sight.

As Antonine, an insubstantial observer, witnessed this, his hand began to burn once more, its throbbing in sync with the faint, pulsing light of the silver thread that wound its way to the mouth of the Wyrm.

* * *

He awoke on the moon path. No sign of the archive realm in any direction. His hand had once more returned to normal, with no sign of the mark upon it.

Antonine knew now that the silver path he had once touched in his vision was none other than the Silver Thread, the mirror of the Black Spiral Labyrinth, which was itself nothing less than a path carved through the Weaver's web, the strands woven to bind the Wyrm into service. But it would not serve.

He could scarcely believe what he had seen. If true, it implied that the Black Spiral Dancers, rather than being merely corrupt and evil creatures, were once the heroic, would-be saviors of the Wyrm when it was still the force of Balance, before it became the Lord of Defilement. They had succumbed to the madness of the Weaver, and their minds were trapped in the endless labyrinth she had crafted around her prisoner. They now shared in the captive serpent's corruption.

Antonine was no fool. Corruption was corruption, the epitome of evil, dangerous not only for its complete lack of balance and morals, but because it was contagious. Regardless of the original reasons for the Black Spiral Dancers' madness and corruption, they were now mere pawns of a force festering in its own infected wounds.

Why had he been shown this? What good was such knowledge except to evoke pity to accompany the traditional disgust that a Black Spiral Dancer deserved? The important message lay in the Silver Thread. Why had no one seen it before? Surely this path, unlike the Black Spiral Labyrinth, held a promise of hope for any who walked it, forged as it was by Luna? But why risk such a walk?

Antonine knew the answer: to reach the center of the Weaver's Pattern Web cocoon, the heart of her illusion factory, beyond all false forms, images or thoughts. To free the Wyrm trapped there and restore the Balance.

Was it possible? Could it be done?

Antonine remembered the immense pain of his burn and knew that he could never walk this path without dying of its touch. Moon silver required purity. Only one truly pure in intent and lineage could touch it without burning.

Like the Silver Crown.

And the only one who wore that relic was King Albrecht. Antonine became excited. He had to get back to New York to catch Albrecht before he left. He was sure that the Silver Fang king's destiny was tied to this vision, not a battlefield in Europe.

As he ran down the moon path, retracing his steps, he furiously reviewed the situation, looking for any clues that could help Albrecht.

It seemed to him that Luna could not warn others about the thread for fear that the Weaver would discover it and unweave it from her twisted tapestry. Yet, Chimera had dared to warn him about it, risking the Spider's notice. Or did he? Chimera always wove his visions in deep metaphors and puzzling images. His dream sendings taxed even the minds of the wisest Stargazers, often leading them in wrong directions. Cubs complained that such obfuscatory enigmas only hid the truth rather than reveal it, as the elders claimed. But Antonine was sure now that, like members of a secret society who had to hide their knowledge from others for fear of political persecution, Chimera and his minions spoke in riddles to throw off the Enemy, and so reward only the wise with their messages.

His excited thoughts almost distracted him from noticing the landscape around him. It was no longer the barren area he had come through. He was somewhere else. The path had led him in a new direction.

A direction away from home.

Chapter Ten

Antonine's heart raced. If he didn't get back soon, he would miss Albrecht. The path, however, had previously led him to a lost tale of the past. Perhaps it now led him to yet another link in the chain of remembering.

He traveled the gloaming trail, calming himself with a mantra, a low, deep-throated "om" sound drawn out to vibrate through the air. It slowed his heart and settled his nerves. He accepted that the path was in the lead, not him. His task for now was merely to follow.

At one point, the path branched in three different directions. He carefully peered down each one, looking for any clue as to which fork to follow. On the middle path, barely visible but for the slight darker indentations they made on the luminous dirt, he could make out tracks of some kind. Boot prints?

It was the only sign in an otherwise barren landscape. Antonine stepped forward onto the middle fork and followed the tracks, which became clearer at times and more obscure at others. They were definitely boot prints, however, although of a manufacture unknown to him. None of the standard hiking boot treads he knew.

In the dim distance, a silver glimmering spiraled in the air above the path. A Lune.

As he approached the enigmatic spirit, its slow spinning in place increased in speed. It seemed agitated, as if warning him away. He refused to halt and kept moving. Lunes often challenged those who attempted to pierce moon secrets or traverse areas of the Umbra they had been set to guard. Antonine had all along expected to face a challenge at some point along the way. He was lucky he had come as far as he had without one.

The Lune suddenly spun forward at Antonine, but the Stargazer lithely stepped aside at the last minute, sending the animate slice of moonbeam off the path and into the gloom beyond. Before it recovered, he took off running down the path, trying to cover as much ground as he could.

The Lune swished back onto the path and gained speed, rushing after Antonine.

Antonine shifted into wolf form and put on more speed, his extra legs more than doubling his distance. But the Lune seemed to gain momentum with every moment and drew closer and closer. As it came close to his heels, Antonine shifted into Crinos form and drew his klaive. He spun in a circle as he ran, slashing behind him with the silver blade.

It sliced through the Lune and separated the wisps of its being into two. Each part halted its chase and drifted apart, wafted on invisible winds, slowly unraveling and dissipating into nothingness.

Antonine sheathed his klaive and rested, catching his breath. He looked around him and saw that the path ahead bent around a hill of some sort. What's more, the boot prints were more obvious here. But also visible were other prints—wolf prints. Judging by their impressions on top of the boot prints, he knew they had followed behind the booted person. But how far behind? Were they companions or hunter and prey?

Beyond the bend he could see light of some sort, not the dim glow of the moon path, but the flickering of fires. It appeared to be a realm of sorts.

As he resumed his pace, he halted and listened. The faint sound of growling came from up ahead, its source unseen around the bend. More growls accompanied it, the sounds of wolves marking dominance. They were cut off by more guttural sounds, deep, wolfen laughing with a screeching tone that sent a chill up Antonine's spine. There were Garou ahead for sure, but the hint of a bat screech in their howls meant they weren't members of the Thirteen Tribes. They were the lost tribe of Black Spiral Dancers.

He shifted back into wolf form to present a lower profile and more silent step and cautiously moved forward on the path to the point in the bend where he could glimpse around the corner.

The path slowly ended, becoming an ancient paved road of stones that had once been well cut but were now worn to uneven boulders. It looked like an old Roman road. It led along a winding path through what appeared to be moors, judging by the scattered, sickly heather and thick mists, ending at a low hill. In the side of the hill was a dark cave mouth, a circular entrance into the earth covered with moss.

Along the side of the road, Black Spiral Dancers sat in small groups around small campfires, chortling or growling at one another. There were nine of them—that many within sight, at least. Antonine suspected there might be more nearby, scouting or hiding. Skirting them would be a feat.

He drew back from the bend and looked around the area. If he slunk across the moon path to the other side, he could slip through the moors and attempt to flank them. Once he came near the cave, he could quickly bolt for it before any of them could reach him. But what then?

He was sure that the cave was an entrance into a realm of some sort. Something old and powerful, strong enough to bleed part of its reality into the nearby Umbra, a phenomenon usually seen only near the material world and its Penumbra.

He couldn't be sure that entering the realm would provide him safety from the Black Spiral Dancers, but he suspected their presence here meant they could not or would not enter the realm for some reason. He couldn't begin to conjecture whether a rival Wyrm creature resided there or Gaia-allied beings waited within. He had to rely on faith that Chimera and Luna wouldn't lead him here just to deliver up his doom.

He padded forward, keeping down low, moving excruciatingly slow, stopping every few paces to lie prone and listen and look carefully all around him. He called upon the lore of the wind spirits and opened his senses to the area, his perception now keener than any wolf's, honed by the wisdom of the wind.

He heard breathing ahead and to his right. A sentry, hiding out like him in wolf form.

Antonine crept backward and slunk down a low gully he had passed. It wound to the right and around again. It might take him behind and past the guard. Resuming his slow, stop and go pace, he crept past the unsuspecting Black Spiral Dancer.

He was so concerned with the tainted Garou that he failed to notice the Bane descending from the dark sky. The ragged, pus- and tumor-wracked crow swooped over him and let out a terrible cawing, sounding more like a tortured scream than a warning cry.

The Black Spiral Dancer guard was up in an instant, leaping toward Antonine, now obvious thanks to the Bane crow. The misshapen Garou howled as he swiped at Antonine's back legs with his claws.

Antonine spun around, shifting instantly into Crinos and bowing low under the leaping Garou, then rising up to catch him in the stomach with his shoulder, knocking the wind out of him. Spinning again to channel the leaper's momentum, he bent over at the same time he grasped the Garou's wrist, flinging him forward into a throw. The Dancer's body sailed through the air and thudded into the hard ground.

Before the sentry could rise up, Antonine followed through with a running claw slash across his throat as he passed by, bolting now directly for the cave. Blood sprayed into the air. The Dancer grasped his throat, trying to stem the tidal flow of lifeblood, but could only cough and wheeze as he quickly lost strength.

The others were now roused and rushing from all directions. Five converged ahead of him, attempting to block him before he reached the cave. He whipped out his klaive and called upon its spirit, slashing it through the air ahead of him. A glimmer of stars appeared before and to the side of him, and the five Black Spiral Dancers altered course to intercept its lights, ignoring his true location. The Distraction spirit bound into his klaive had done its job.

He veered somewhat to the left to avoid the gang jumping onto the illusion they all saw but which was invisible to others, and increased his speed.

There were no other Black Spiral Dancers before him. They were all behind, howling as they sought to catch up to him. If he could maintain his pace, he would reach the cave before them.

He was suddenly knocked sideways by an invisible force, as if a wall had been thrown at him. He collapsed to the ground, dizzy, trying to get his bearings and rise before whatever hit him leapt in to finish the job.

Nothing came. He shook off the pain and started toward the cave again, but something tripped his foot, slamming his face into the dirt. This time he was ready for the pain and spun in place, kicking out. His foot connected with something and he heard a yelp.

Staggering away from him was a brown-furred Garou in Crinos form wearing tattered Tibetan monk's robes. He had remained unseen by moving at incredible speed, keeping to Antonine's blind spot. But he was now revealed.

Antonine leapt to his feet and into a defensive martial arts stance. His opponent, whoever he was, was clearly a master martial artist himself.

Instead of attacking again, however, the Garou regained a steady stance and smiled. He shifted into human form, and Antonine's heart felt empty and void, drained of strength.

Wen Chou, his former packmate, laughed at him.

The chuckle had the same screeching, fingernails-on-blackboard pitch of a Black Spiral Dancer laugh. Beneath the tattered robes formerly worn by members of the Shigalu Monastery, Antonine could see a spiral glyph tattoo on Wen's chest, glowing slightly with a sickly green haze. The sign of one who had been branded by the Black Spiral Labyrinth.

"I did not recognize you at first," Wen said. "I should have known. I have tried hard to forget my past, but I cannot forget an old packmate. Greetings, Antonine." He made a slight bow.

Antonine remained in his ready stance, watching the encroaching horde of Black Spiral Dancers out of the corner of his eyes while focused on any move Wen might make. "Wen. I had thought you dead."

"If enlightenment is a form of death, then yes, I am dead. But only to my past. I have been reborn to true wisdom, not the lies peddled by Stargazers."

The other Black Spiral Dancers came nearer, growling. Some of them stared at Wen as if he were mad—or worse, sane. "Finish him!" one yelled.

Wen snarled at the speaker. "No! I claim him for the Wyrm!"

The others seemed impressed with this and backed away slightly, grinning and hooting, anxious to see what would happen next.

Wen turned back to face Antonine. "I knew it would not be long before someone followed his trail. I didn't think it would be you. I never figured you for a fool. You're too late, of course. He'll be ours soon, out of your grip."

Antonine knew Wen referred to the mysterious tracks he'd seen earlier, but still had no idea who had left them. He knew he had to play as if he did. "I beg to differ."

"Ever the optimist. Your kind has spurned him one too many times. We've always been here for him."

"We? You're a Stargazer."

"Was. I have you to thank for my enlightenment. If I had not been at Shigalu Monastery, I would never have learned the truth about the Wyrm. I would have still believed the lies about the Weaver and been blinded to the dragon's majesty. It was your selfless sacrifice—oh, yes, I knew you faked your rage to lose that fight—that gained me admittance there and so readied me for this, my true destiny."

Antonine felt a wave of guilt rise up. If he had not purposefully lost the fight, maybe he would have instead been at Shigalu when it fell, saving Wen the horror of his present corruption. "I did not intend things to be as they are."

"No? I can return the favor. Let me enlighten you, Antonine. I can show you wisdom undreamed of in even the puerile and limited dreams of that totem you still serve, the misbegotten Chimera, always embarrassing us with enigmas we can't possibly decipher. Well, I've discovered a way to solve them all: render them meaningless. In madness lies the answer to all conundrums. Take away the ground rules, and everything is permitted."

"How can you be so sure? Is this what the Wyrm told you? You know better than to trust untested wisdom."

"I knew of my own accord, from inside my deepest being, as everyone I had ever love perished around me. I don't need to question it."

"No? Years of training in debate, the constant examination and deconstruction of reality, have cured you of the need to prove your propositions?"

Wen looked nervous, unsure. "I have indeed overcome the need for intellectual answers. The truths of the Wyrm need no such assurances."

"But *you* do."

Wen snarled. "I admit it. I am still weak. I have doubts. The lies the Stargazers shoved into my mind at Shigalu still haunt me."

"Then let's put them to rest. If they are as weak as you say—lies, even—then surely they can't survive the test of Witscraft."

Wen smiled a wicked grin and began chuckling. "Oh, wise, Antonine. Very wise. But your own wisdom shall be your own undoing. I accept the challenge. When I win, I shall claim you for the Wyrm. You shall join my tribe and use that sharp intellect against the dragon's enemies."

"And if I win? Will you let me pass untouched?"

"If? You can't win. However, I'll play that game. If your failed perspective can unhinge me, then I shall order all here to let you pass."

"If I do unhinge you, you will be in no shape to issue that order."

"Then I shall do it now!" Wen growled. He turned to face his army, staring the Dancers in the eye. "If I lose this bout, he is to be let free to go where he will! Do you hear me?"

The Black Spiral Dancers growled and looked at one another, unsure how to answer. One among them edged forward. "Who are you to tell us what to do? We were born to the Wyrm—you are only a latecomer."

Wen frowned. "I have come late to enlightenment, yes, but I was great before I ever saw the Wyrm's truth. Do you wish to test me?"

A hideous howl was Wen's answer, as the Dancer leapt at him in full battle form. The other Dancers lost little time and broke toward

Antonine, foam slavering from their mouths in anticipation of the coming kill.

Antonine could afford Wen no attention. The eight Dancers came at him from all directions. He chose one direction and charged two Dancers, hoping to unbalance them and increase his distance from the others. They were indeed startled at his sudden offensive and backed up to avoid the slashing arcs of his blade. He deliberately swung to the left and right in a hypnotic rhythm as he approached, giving the Dancers a false sense of expectation, and then changed the direction of his swing at the last minute, cutting the snout off the rightmost Dancer. It roared in pain and retreated, its resolve broken.

The other Dancer clamped his teeth onto Antonine's arm, but the Stargazer shifted into Glabro form and slipped out of the grip in the scant second before the jaws could adjust for the shift in mass. This was what mastery of Kailindo was all about—the judicious use of shapeshifting to confound one's foes. Before the Dancer could adjust its attack strategy, Antonine drove his klaive through its belly, killing it instantly.

Its whelp of pain stopped the others short. They paused, pacing to and fro as they sought an opening. Just as one of them began to edge forward again, a brown blur of motion shot past it, snatching it by the neck and throwing it across the road. It thudded onto the hard ground with a resounding snap of its spine and a pained whimper.

The rest of the Dancers backed away from Wen, who glared at them, blood dripping from his hands, waiting for another challenge. They looked over at the one who had challenged him and saw only an unmoving mass of fur and steaming entrails. They each bowed head and tail to the formidable newcomer.

Wen turned to face Antonine as if nothing had happened and motioned to the craggy rocks of the old road at their feet. "Sit. No reason to stand for this. It could take a while. Your stubborn belief in Stargazer indoctrination is strong and may take time to wear down."

"I will sit," Antonine said. "But I shall not be sitting for long. It will take but a few words to convince you of the errors you have committed."

Wen smiled but did not respond. He sat in a lotus posture and closed his eyes, calming himself after the heated battle, sharpening his intellectual reflexes. Antonine noticed, however, that he could not suppress a twitch in his eye.

Antonine sheathed his klaive and also sat. He knew his enemies could turn on him at any moment and that he would not survive the assault. With nothing to lose, he also closed his eyes and meditated, transforming his rage into iron will. When he opened them, Wen was smirking at him.

"How arrogant. Typical Garou. Typical Stargazer. You assume that your paltry communion with Gaia is enough. Your tribe's problem is that you can never admit error. Failure is only seen as a misstep in interpretation. How idiotic."

"Is this what they taught you at Shigalu?"

Wen smiled. "No. Their problem was that they did not know this. And now they're dead."

"But you live? How? Did you betray them?"

Wen frowned and he growled low before answering. "They failed me. I stood ground until the last. As they fled or fell, I stood and kept the worst of the enemy at bay. Finally, alone, I chose to listen when they spoke. They sought to fool me with words, and I sought the same against them, sure that I was the better in such games.

"How wrong I was. I tried to use logic, little realizing then how illusory it was. How completely and utterly without foundation. Only the Wyrm is real."

"You must be kidding me," Antonine said. "Loss of faith in logic is one of the first lessons we learn. The universe isn't a mathematical equation, it's a puzzle, an enigma. If you put your faith there, no wonder you failed."

"Failed? Who said I failed? I won. My reward was the chance to learn from the great serpent himself, to walk the Black Spiral Labyrinth that guards the way to his lair."

Antonine froze, trying not to hide the chill he felt when he heard those words. Did Wen know what he was seeking? "And how far did you get on that path?"

"Far enough. I danced enough steps to know the true from the false. To forget my past failures and forge on anew, slick with the sweet afterbirth of my new life."

Antonine again struggled to maintain a neutral composure. Here again seemed to be another clue— a great forgetting. Could it be the same as Cries Havoc's? "You chose to forget your past? Or was it taken from you?"

"I chose to have it taken. I yielded it up to the Wyrm and it gladly devoured it. Enough of the past! You seek to stall, to eke out more heartbeats than you deserve. It is time we engaged in our contest. Please,

Antonine, begin. How can you possibly convince me that the Stargazer way is greater than the Wyrm's?"

Antonine stilled himself, forcing himself to put aside for now the clues Wen had given him—knowingly or not—about his quest. He took a moment to gain a deep breath and then responded not with words, but with a sound, vibrating deep from his diaphragm. It was the Elemental Mantra of Earth.

Wen stared aghast, sweat breaking over his body. He tried to raise his hands to cover his ears, but they felt like stone, too heavy to lift. He snarled and tried to respond with a sound of his own, but it was drowned out by Antonine's next sound, the Elemental Mantra of Water.

Antonine knew the sounds had no real power over others. They were mainly mnemonics used to remind a Stargazer of his true purpose, a meditation tool to remove clutter from the mind. To a Stargazer trained in sounding them, they were triggers that opened up areas of the mind normally difficult to access through the haze of rage and worry that often harried Garou.

To Wen, who had been a Stargazer far longer than he had been a Black Spiral Dancer, they were like keys turning the locks he had placed on his consciousness, those suppressing his former life. As Antonine chanted the well-known mantras, the barriers burst one by one, flooding Wen's memories with visions of his previous life from before the horrors that had overcome him. He remembered.

If he had not trained for so many years in the Five Elemental Mantras—a special lore of the Shigalu sept—he would not have succumbed so easily. To any other Stargazer or Garou, the sounds might temporarily enchant but they would not cloud the mind or intent of the listener. Wen had not only studied the sounds, he had perfected them. When Wen heard them again for the first time since the destruction of his sept and his terrible transformation, they were like potent smells, summoning unbidden forgotten moments from the storehouse of memory. Only a few living Stargazers still knew the mantras, for so few had survived the fall of Shigalu.

As Wen writhed in place, trying to hold back the intensity of his memories, Antonine proceeded to vocalize the rest of the sounds: Air, Fire and Spirit. Once they were all sounded, their humming throb hung in the air, buzzing around Wen like invisible wasps, stinging at his consciousness.

The Black Spiral Dancers shuffled nervously, unsure what was happening. They whined and looked at one another, seeking one among them with initiative.

Wen stopped struggling and slowly met Antonine's gaze. A single tear ran down his cheek as he remembered everything he had once been but could be no more. Thoughts he had believed gone, devoured by his new master, had only been hidden. This was the great lie of the Wyrm: that it could not destroy, only suppress and corrupt. Wen's corruption was too deep. A crack had opened in his spirit, allowing a semblance of his old self to emerge, but it could not remain for long. Its appearance was but a final elegy for a fallen master of wisdom.

Antonine stood up and walked away from him, heading for the cave. The horde of Black Spiral Dancers looked at one another, questioning what to do. A few of them moved to block Antonine's path.

He looked back at Wen, and his old packmate bowed to him. Among humans, this was a sign of respect. Among wolves, however, it was a sign of submission. A sign of weakness. The Dancers' instincts took over and they howled, charging the object of their hatred, the one who had betrayed them to play mind games with their prey. All but one leapt at Wen, who fell before the horde, his amazing reflexes forgotten in the confusion of identities he now fought.

The one remaining Dancer went for Antonine's leg. As his jaws snapped forth, Antonine jumped into the air and snapped his foot forward. The heel connected full with the Dancer's ear, knocking him to the ground. He reeled, stunned, trying to get his bearings, but Antonine was already running past him and toward the cave mouth.

As he reached the entrance, he stole a glance back at his old friend. Wen was now standing, tearing at the maddened pack with his claws, the light of reason that had briefly shone in his eyes now gone. He had even forgotten Antonine in his frenzied fight for survival against his new allies. His Wyrm allies.

Antonine looked away and into the tunnel. He shifted into wolf form and bounded into the hole, following the tracks that suggested a possible ally against the enemies gathered behind him.

Chapter Eleven

The tunnel was pitch dark and rank, the stench of animal rot all around. Antonine shut out the scents as much as he could, focusing only on running through the slick, muddy dirt as the passageway curved left then right, its grade going up then down like a roller coaster. Hundreds of insects swarmed across the floor in wide rivers, broken only by the banks of mud he sloshed through between them. He heard the crack of carapaces shattering under his tread and the squishy wet pop of soft millipedes, centipedes and a dozen unidentifiable worms being crushed as he ran.

No sound of pursuit followed him. His suspicion that the Dancers feared to enter the tunnel seemed correct. He hoped he could survive whatever kept them at bay.

Finally, ahead in the gloom, light filtered through tangled vines. He increased his speed and barreled out of the cave mouth and into a dimly lit, scraggly weeded moor. The moon shone from behind a bank of clouds, its gibbous phase ready to wax to full.

He stopped and listened, peering cautiously in all directions around him. He heard and saw no signs of animate life. The boot treads, however, resumed, heading over the far rise.

He shifted from his wolf form into Glabro form and drew his klaive and began to quietly follow the trail.

As he approached the rise, he heard the clang of metal on stone and a guttural curse in a language he couldn't identify. He slowed even more and carefully raised his head above the rise, peering down into the cove.

The moon stood below, shining in full splendor, brighter than the one hidden by the clouds in the sky.

Antonine paused, unsure of what he saw, and focused his vision more carefully. The glowing moon was a Crinos-shaped Garou, its pelt of the purest white snow. The Garou cursed again and raised his klaive high, bringing it down hard onto what looked like a flat rock blocking the entrance to an ancient burial caern. The rock was carved with weather-worn Celtic spirals and knot work.

The silver sword rebounded from the unyielding stone, giving off sparks. The Garou tossed it away and paced in a circle, anger emanating from him like a magnetic field.

Antonine saw his wolfen face and recognized him. He had the sudden realization that he had been wrong all along, that fate had played a very different hand than he thought had been dealt. But it made perfect sense. No, more than that, it completed a circle, returning him to the beginning of the matter.

He stood up and spoke loudly to the Garou below: "Arkady!"

Arkady looked up, assuming a threatening posture. His eyes squinted as he examined the one who had called his name. "I know you... I have seen you before...."

Antonine began to walk down the rise, toward the Silver Fang lord. "I am Antonine Teardrop. Yes, we've seen each other before, at the court of King Jacob Morningkill."

Arkady nodded, still wary. "Yes... yes, I remember. You tried to convince the king about a hidden

Wyrm conspiracy." His lips drew back, revealing his sharp rows of teeth. "And I also know that you aided Albrecht against me."

"I did. And you know the reasons why. Do you not repent of them? Or are you a traitor to Gaia as they say?"

Arkady's fur bristled and his eyes became smoldering fires. "Lies! I should tear your tongue out and feed it to you!"

Antonine stopped, standing in an unobtrusive stance, but one in which he could initiate a number of martial maneuvers at an instant's notice. "And yet you do not act on your threat."

"You are more trouble than my effort is worth. The nagging of gnats, at best."

"Or is it that you suspect I would not fall so easily?"

"Do not test me, Stargazer. I know of your prowess, but I am Arkady of House Crescent Moon, purest of the Silver Fangs. I have slain more Wyrm creatures than you can catalog in your library! Don't taunt me unless you wish to join their ranks in the pits of the dead."

Antonine motioned with a flick of his head to the rise he had come down. "Are you aware that a band of Black Spiral Dancers is following you?"

Arkady growled and glanced at the rise. He backed up and snatched his klaive from the ground. "They have dogged my trail for days, fearing to come near." He looked at Antonine again, warily, suspiciously. "Why are you here? How did you get past them?"

"An old… packmate led them off. They did not follow me into the cave. I suspect you know why…."

"They fear this place. They cannot go where I intend to go. But you have not answered me: Why are you here?"

Antonine sheathed his klaive. He felt that his posturing had successfully established equality in the alpha dominance game. Arkady may have been a Silver Fang lord, but Antonine was a Stargazer elder; he did not give sway to anyone without good reason for it.

"I followed your trail, although I did not know it was yours."

Arkady bent his head quizzically. "Then who did you expect to see?"

"I didn't hazard a guess. Why are *you* here?"

Arkady was silent for a moment, seemingly judging whether he could trust the Stargazer. "I seek the Silver Spiral, the mirror of the Black."

Antonine could not hide the shiver of excitement that swept through him. A Silver Spiral? Could it be the same as the silver path? "What do you mean?"

A slight smirk grew on Arkady's face. "I think it is your turn now. Why have you come?"

"I seek the Silver Thread."

Arkady's eyes grew wide. "What is that? Speak!"

"I think you know. I've never heard of the Silver Spiral but I suspect it's the same thing I'm looking for. Tell me what it is and how you learned of it."

Arkady scowled and seemed to measure for a moment whether to attempt force against Antonine or concede to his request. He eventually decided that giving Antonine his due would best get him what he wanted.

"Have you ever heard of the Silver Spirals?" When Antonine did not react, he continued. "They are our tribe's greatest shame: those who become lost and fall to the madness of the Black Spiral Labyrinth."

He walked over to the large stone he had been assaulting and leaned against it. "There are legends among our kind—and among the Black Spirals—about these Fangs. Most of these stories are misinterpreted. Many ancestors of our tribe have fallen for petty reasons, but some sacrificed themselves in attempts to win a great prize for all our kind.

"I have studied these attempts and discovered the key to their fall. I, however, will not fall, for unlike them, I am destined to do this task. There has not been one of purer blood than me in generations, and all that has brought me here has been orchestrated by fate to ensure that nothing now holds me back."

"From what? What is this task you speak of?"

"To walk the Silver Spiral—the mirror opposite of the Black—and reach the heart of the Wyrm. To slay it in its lair, where it waits unprotected, its belly waiting to receive my klaive."

Antonine winced. "Is this what you believe? That your task is to slay one of the Triat, the three primordial forces of creation? That's not what the Silver Thread—or Silver Spiral, as you called it—is for. The Silver Thread is a hidden pathway into the Weaver's web and the cocoon that binds the Wyrm. It is woven behind and besides the Black Spiral Labyrinth, to hide it from the eyes of the Weaver. It leads not to destruction but liberation. The Wyrm must be freed from its bondage, not killed."

Arkady looked at Antonine like he was mad. "The Wyrm freed? So that it can wreak unlimited destruction on of all of Gaia? What sort of mad Stargazer lore is this?"

Antonine wistfully shook his head. "It is clear that you and I, of different tribes and auspices, see matters very differently. I tell you this, though: My tribe has long sought to see through all illusions to achieve a clear vision of reality. We have been welcomed as councilors by even the most bloodthirsty of Garou, for even to an Ahroun, our wisdom has proven true even if it called for a cease to conflict. I ask you now, Arkady, will you take my council or rely only on your own? I have been delivered here not through the study of legends but by the prophecies of Chimera and Luna. I am not wrong on this."

Arkady seemed to look anew at Antonine, sizing him up once more. "And do you also give council to Albrecht? He who wears the crown in my place?"

"He knows enough to heed my wisdom. It helped him gain that crown. Frankly, I had thought to seek out him for this quest. I did not expect you to be the one called."

Arkady smirked. "But it was not he who risked the ire of the entire Garou Nation to win this secret, was it? It was not he who fought numberless Wyrm creatures to get this far, to the very portal of the path. I grant that your wisdom must be good to have allowed Albrecht to find the crown. But you must swear to me that your words are true and not some trick to once more reward Albrecht with my destiny."

"I didn't steal destiny from you, Arkady. If you are here now, seeking the Silver Thread, then the crown was not yours to wear. I realized before I got here that only the purest of Silver Fang could walk the path. I thought it would be Albrecht, but it appears that the Thread is your fate."

Arkady nodded, as if he knew this were true but had wanted to hear it from another. "Then help me remove this rock from the entrance. Inside lies the first step on the Silver Spiral. I searched long for this, only to now find an unmovable barrier."

Antonine looked around. "First, tell me where and what this place is. A realm of some sort?"

"A pocket in the Penumbra of Scotland, hidden from view by ancient wards. It can be approached only from the Deep Umbra, although it can be exited by simply stepping sideways into the material world."

Antonine frowned. He squinted his eyes and attempted to peer past the Gauntlet into the material world, testing if what Arkady said was true. His vision saw into a darkened moor.

"What you say seems true. Where in Scotland are we?"

Arkady sneered. "Near the Wyrm pit where the White Howlers lost their souls."

Antonine's hair rose up on the back of his neck. He barely suppressed the unreasoning wave of fear that passed over him. That pit was one of the most fearsome Black Spiral Dancer hives, for it was the site of their original spawning. It was rumored to open into Malfeas itself, onto the Black Spiral Labyrinth. Antonine put aside the worries that now arose concerning his own escape from this place, and he turned back to Arkady.

"You keep calling this a mirror. What do you mean by that?"

"Exactly what it says: a mirror companion to the Black Spiral, but one that is white in contrast to its black." He pulled a crumpled sheet of notepad paper from his pocket and handed it to Antonine. It displayed a pencil sketch of a spiral, drawn with a single black line, with arrows emphasizing the white areas that delineated the black line.

"I think I understand. But a two-dimensional metaphor is no guarantee of a three-dimensional reality. Nonetheless, this seems to accord with my own vision of the Silver Thread." He told Arkady about the dream legend he had witnessed, wherein the Luna wove a silver thread into the black spider silk that composed the Weaver's web.

"So you see, since the Black Spiral Labyrinth *is* the Weaver's corrupted web, nothing sane can traverse its convoluted pattern, for it is the very substance of delusion itself. The Silver Thread that is woven near and behind it, hidden to the eyes of the mad, holds a hope of sanity to those who walk it. But even here, we can't possibly know if it remains uncorrupted by its twisted route. Remember, even Luna is mad at times, although her madness often hides a paradoxical wisdom that points beyond duality."

Arkady sighed. "Words, words, words. You speak in metaphors and abstracts. Your vision spoke truer: images and actions. I will hold to these, not conjectures."

"Even judging by my vision—which, like dreams, was veiled in forceful imagery—you can't possibly know where the thread leads. Just because Luna introduced it doesn't mean it travels to the same place as the Black Spiral. It was still woven by the Weaver, even if she seemed unaware of it, and none can trace such threads through thought alone; they must be walked."

"Then walk it I shall."

"Even if it means madness and corruption?"

"Like my ancestors before me, this is the risk I bear. I bear it alone, for this is the only way left to me. The other tribes have exiled me in their mock court, daring to judge me without my own testimony. Fools! Expecting me to come, so sure their moot was more important than my own task!"

He stood up full and stared at the moon. Antonine could not help but feel somewhat awed by the sheer regality of his poise, so unconsciously perfect. He wore his prowess like skin, close and unnoticed to himself but so obvious to others.

"None will ally with me now. I have no army to heed my commands. I take this task alone and undaunted, no matter the consequence to myself. But ever after, my name will be sung in all the caerns and spirit realms. No cub shall be Firsted without hearing my tale. No glory shall outshine mine. The Silver Record will be but an addendum to my deed, its stories told only to show how much greater is my own."

Antonine shook his head in wonder at the bald-faced egotism Arkady displayed. "You are bold, Arkady, I'll give you that. I only hope your excessive self-confidence helps you rather than hinders. I will help you however I can, short of following you on the path, for it has already shown its scorn for my touch." He looked at his palm, but there was no sign of the burn mark there.

"Then help me move this rock! It is the final barrier to my task."

Antonine walked up to the rock and examined it. It looked like an old Celtic caern stone, not dissimilar to those seen in Ireland, such as at Newgrange. The knot work, however, while superficially resembling Celtic art, was far more convoluted than it first appeared. As his eyes followed it, they began to swim and lose focus. He stepped back and reeled, barely regaining his balance.

"What?" Arkady said. "What is it?"

"There's more than simple knot work there. It's some sort of multidimensional image. The more I looked at it, the more spacious it became. I couldn't follow the knot."

"What is it here for? Who would put up such a defense?"

"Weaver minions. Somehow, they suspect what waits within. Rather than destroying the Thread, they've blocked the way to its outermost strand. Perhaps they don't even know what they're blocking."

"How do we destroy it?"

"We can't. I've got to decipher it. I have to follow the knot through to the end. That should unlock the web here that blocks the way."

"But you could hardly view it without falling!"

"I'm prepared for it now. I can do this. Why else was I sent here? I have spent years studying the webs that occlude our sight from the truth underlying all reality. I can walk this one."

Arkady looked skeptical but said nothing.

Antonine approached the stone again and ran his fingers along the carvings, focusing his concentration and latching his eyes onto one strand, and then following it through its spirals around, behind and before other knots. Once again, the horizon stretched out and his peripheral vision lost any sense of the sky around him and even the stone before him. All he could see was the knot. He bent all his will toward staying on the path, following the thread through the maze.

He began to feel restricted and felt his arms tighten to his sides. He refused to look away. His legs drew together against his will, and he felt ropes wrapping about him, climbing up his torso. Again, he refused to withdraw his vision and continued to follow the single thread he had chosen.

Arkady watched as the knot-work carvings unpeeled themselves from the stone and wrapped themselves around Antonine, building a cocoon about him from his feet, up his body and toward his head.

This didn't look right to him at all.

The Stargazer didn't seem to notice and stared intently at the knot work, which now seemed to double up and grow in size, increasing the space Antonine had to unravel. Arkady growled. In another matter of seconds, the knots would swallow up the Stargazer. Regardless of what he had said, Arkady was convinced this wasn't a feat to win over but a trap to become lost in.

Without any further hesitation, he stepped forward and sliced his klaive cleanly through the knots growing from the stone that stretched to entrap the Stargazer. The threads exploded outward as their tension was released. They fell to the ground, now mere shards of clattering stones.

Antonine sucked in a deep breath, only now realizing how constricted his breathing had become. Another few minutes of that and he would have suffocated. The thread he had so laboriously followed with his mind now lay in pieces in the ground. A thrill of anger rose up in his belly as he realized that the impatient Silver Fang had rendered his hard work useless.

Before he could act on his anger, however, the large stone before the entrance—now bereft of its carvings—began to crack and splinter. It collapsed into a mist of dust, which quickly settled to the ground as a pile of loose gravel.

The way into the caern was unobstructed.

Arkady let out a grunt of satisfaction, looking at Antonine with a superior expression.

"Thank you for drawing out the webs. They could not be cut when on the stone, but were all too vulnerable when wrapped about you."

"A trap," Antonine said, rubbing his limbs to get the blood flowing again, his anger abated at the sign of victory. "Even with all the warnings I'd seen—the visions of Garou and spirits drawn into the web—I still fell for it."

"But you were not alone. Let that be a lesson for your tribe, Stargazer. If you gaze too long within, you miss what's going on without."

Arkady stepped forward and peered into the gloom. A distant glow within could be seen.

Antonine's palm began to itch. He held it before his eyes and saw his moon burn glow. He held it out to face the cavern before him and saw an answering gleam deep within.

"It's there. The Silver Thread—or Spiral, if you prefer."

"Then I shall wait no longer." Arkady bent down and walked into the cave. Antonine followed.

The interior was agleam with blue light. Mica deposits in the walls caught the glow and sent out sparkles in all directions, giving the cave a shimmering, electric atmosphere. Ahead of them, in the center of a widening cavern, was a pond of water, collected from the tiny, trickling streams coming through cracks in the ceiling. In the frenzied light, the scattered rain looked like permanent columns of lightning stabbing into the waters from the heavens.

The water was less than waist deep. Glowing clearly beneath it was the source of the light—the silver moon path. Its origin seemed to bubble up from the deep, as if it were formed from swirling whirlpools. Antonine thought of old legends about the moon submerging itself into the sea when it set, traveling under the ocean to the other side of the world before it rose on the following night in some secret lagoon. This seemed like that place.

Across the cavern, on the other side of the pool, the path rose clear of the water and spiraled around rocks, rising and falling, before disappearing into a tunnel. Its light still glowed down the passage, but its destination could not be seen. The smell emanating from it, however, evoked not the wet moors of Scotland, but dry deserts.

"I think the path leads back to the material world," Antonine said. "That smell is too earthy to be a spirit realm. The path may wind in and out of the Penumbra and the material world. I doubt you'll be able to anticipate its track. Tread carefully."

Arkady stood silently staring in awe at the path. He seemed to have barely heard Antonine, but a slight nod of his head showed that he understood, or at least pretended to.

He stepped forward, his feet splashing into the pool. "I will start at its beginning. Tell them that, Stargazer. I did not join this halfway, but took the full road."

"I will tell them. Perhaps the others will reconsider your status and aid you where they can."

"It matters not. They will regret their foolishness at the end of this. Only then will I choose whether to be gracious or hold grudges."

He placed a foot on the first portion of the silver that was visible. He did not hesitate for a second, anticipating no pain, so great was his confidence in his right to walk it. His slowness was due only to the ceremonial manner he adopted for the occasion— the first steps of a hero into greatness.

He followed that step with another, and then another, and quickly increased his pace, striding from the water to the shore, following the path's curve over a mound and around a rock. He did not look back at Antonine, knowing full well that the Stargazer would not be able to withdraw his gaze from such a momentous beginning. His march onward was unhampered by any sign of doubt or regret.

He passed into the tunnel, his shadow casting a dim shape on the wall behind him. It soon disappeared, leaving Antonine alone in the cavern.

Antonine sat there for a few hours, waiting in case Arkady howled for aid or returned seeking further council. He did not.

Long after the moon had set and he was sure the sun was shining in the material world, he stepped sideways onto the moor. Heavy cloud cover obscured the sky, but the sun was there, although it provided only a gray, forlorn light.

He crept about the chill hills in wolf form, seeking any sign of civilization or fellow Garou—allied Garou, not Black Spiral Dancers. The region was desolate, seemingly barren of animal life. Occasionally, the sound of crows could be heard in the distance, but the wind would soon turn and take the sounds with it.

As he paced along, creeping from hill to hill, taking what cover he could behind scraggly bushes, he occasionally felt an unnatural shiver, as if something had brushed across his neck. He considered peering into the Umbra, suspecting that some Bane lurked there, trying to reach at him through the Gauntlet, but knew that to do so would only give it a form of passage into the world. He steeled himself against its incursions and moved on.

As the sun drew toward the horizon, he heard voices ahead. As they approached, he flattened himself against the ground and tried to make out what they were saying. It sounded like singing. As the song grew in volume with their approach, he could hear at least three voices raised as one. He listened to the lyrics and was surprised to hear a drinking song.

Three figures could now be seen. As the mists began to rise from the hills around them, they halted their march and their song.

"We'll not get further tonight," one of them said, his Scottish accent thick. He was tall and broad, with long red hair and beard.

"Na, we'd best turn back," another said, also with heavy accent. He was thinner and dark haired. "It's only trouble out here now. If'n your friend's here of his own will, he deserves his fate."

"Arkady can't go it alone," the third one said, peering out onto the moors as if looking for someone. This one's accent was not Scottish. It sounded more like southern American. "He ditched me before out of pride, but he'll fail without someone beside him."

Antonine smiled at the mention of Arkady. If these were his friends, it was doubtful they were Black Spiral Dancers.

"Oh, aye, we're pack animals at that," the red-bearded one said. "But not him. He's alpha all the way. I'm sorry for him, but we're not risking our necks anymore. We're too close as it is, at the wrong time, too. We got's to go back."

"All right," the American said. "I'm tired of this, too. I guess my story will have to go unfinished for now."

The three turned and began to head back the way they'd come. Antonine, exhausted after his long trek, had no more patience for stalking alone through hostile territory. He barked out a wolf greeting.

The three men spun around and spread out, ready for anything. The American returned the wolf greeting. Antonine knew for sure they were Garou, or at least Kinfolk. He stood up, shifting into human form, and moved cautiously toward them.

"I am Antonine Teardrop of the Stargazers," he said.

"Holy shit," the American said. "I saw you at the moot! What the hell are you doing here?"

Antonine stopped and looked at the group. They were obviously Fianna—the torques and tattoos were a dead giveaway. "Finishing a long quest. And you are?"

"Stuart Stalks-the-Truth," the American said, stepping forward and offering his hand. "And these two are Colum Treehefter and the Grim Smiler." The red-bearded one waved a greeting while the dark, thin one smiled a threatening smile.

Antonine took Stuart's outstretched hand and gave it a hearty shake. "I must admit, I'm rather relieved to find allies out in this no man's land."

"And we're pretty suspicious finding you here," the Grim Smiler said, still smiling. "Stuart, who is this fella?"

"A Stargazer elder. He's the one who planted the idea of the third pack at the Anvil-Klaiven moot. I told you the story."

"This one? Here? What in blazes is he doing walking these cursed moors?"

"It's a long story," Antonine said. "I'd be happy to tell it in safer—and warmer—environs."

"Ah, to the pub then," Colum said. "I'll buy the first!"

"And I'll get the next," Antonine said, as the group began walking again, back from where they had come.

"Please tell me you've seen Arkady," Stuart said. "The odds of two elders roving around this Gaia-forsaken moor without bumping into one another are pretty slim."

"Yes, I saw him. He's beyond our help now."

"The Silver Spiral? Did he find it?"

Antonine stopped and looked at Stuart. "How do you know about it? How many people discovered this, anyway?"

"Just me," Stuart said, smiling proudly. "I figured it out, after watching Arkady pace about for a while."

"Well that solves a certain riddle. I wondered how he'd deciphered it. It didn't seem to be his style."

"Ah, don't sell him short. He's a determined one, more so than most of us. If anyone can make something good of this, it's him."

"I sincerely hope so. For his sake and ours."

"So then, you can tell me all about your role in this. I mean, how'd you find out about the Spiral and all? I have to have something I can use to wrap up this tale and start telling it. Stalking the truth, you know."

"When you know the ending, let me know. I fear it will be a long time coming."

The other two, obviously believing their companions were far too serious, broke into a new drinking song, one that required each person there to finish a refrain. No one would escape full participation under their watch.

"It keeps the beasties away," Colum said, gesturing at the air. "If you know what I mean."

Antonine did indeed feel the oppressive feeling lift from his shoulders. Something about the song—or the singers—did not please the Bane that had haunted him. He smiled. Tired though he was, he summoned enough wit to rhyme a few hastily created lines in the ever-evolving song as the four of them marched across the darkening moor to the promise of ale and warmth ahead, leaving old horrors behind.

About the Author

Bill Bridges was the original developer for White Wolf's **Werewolf: The Apocalypse** storytelling game line. He has numerous writing credits on most of White Wolf's World of Darkness line, including the Werewolf novel **The Silver Crown**, which first introduced the conflict between King Albrecht and Lord Arkady. He is presently developer and cocreator of *Fading Suns* for Holistic Design Inc. His current projects can be seen at www.fadingsuns.com.

Tribe Novels 5: Children of Gaia & Uktena

THE RAGE CONTINUES...

The Garou, the bestial werewolves who fight to save the natural world, have their backs to the wall.

In Tribe Novel: Children of Gaia, the storyteller Cries Havoc, robbed of his memories by the Wyrm, fights to become whole again.

In Tribe Novel: Uktena, another songkeeper named Amy Hundred-Voices comes face to face with Lord Arkady, the Silver Fang accused of conspiring with the Wyrm. Can she turn him from his destructive path?

March 2002

WEREWOLF THE APOCALYPSE